Mistaken Ecstasy

Cassie struggled to escape. But the more she strove to free herself, the more tightly Ned pulled her to him. Dimly she was aware of her surprise at the strength in his arms and the hardness of his chest. As his lips became gentler and more persuasive, a wave of warmth and languor swept over her. The rigidity seeped out of her body and she found it molding itself to his, her lips opening under his insistent pressure.

But just as her senses threatened to be overwhelmed by these new and disturbing sensations, the voice of reason asserted itself once again. *Whatever are you doing, Cassie Cresswell? It's Arabella he wants. . . .*

After studying eighteenth-century literature in college, EVELYN RICHARDSON decided that she would prefer to have lived between 1775 and 1830. She wrote this novel at her home in a seacoast village south of Boston, where she lives with her husband and her cat, Sam.

SIGNET REGENCY ROMANCE
COMING IN NOVEMBER 1990

Irene Saunders
Lady Lucinda's Locket

Vanessa Gray
Best-Laid Plans

Leigh Haskell
The Vengeful Viscount

Miss Cresswell's London Triumph

Evelyn Richardson

A SIGNET BOOK

SIGNET
Published by the Penguin Group
Penguin Books USA Inc., 375 Hudson Street,
New York, New York, 10014, U.S.A.
Penguin Books Ltd, 27 Wrights Lane, London W8 5TZ, England
Penguin Books Australia Ltd, Ringwood, Victoria, Australia
Penguin Books Canada Ltd, 2801 John Street,
Markham, Ontario, Canada L3R 1B4
Penguin Books (N.Z.) Ltd, 182-190 Wairau Road,
Auckland 10, New Zealand

Penguin Books Ltd, Registered Offices:
Harmondsworth, Middlesex, England

First published by Signet, an imprint of New American Library, a division of
Penguin Books USA Inc.

First Printing, October, 1990

10 9 8 7 6 5 4 3 2 1

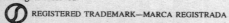

To Anson and Sam

CHAPTER 1

"Aunt Cathie, Aunt Cathie, letters from India!" Theodore shouted, rushing into the library as fast as his short five-year-old legs could carry him and waving two stained envelopes in his pudgy hands. "They're from Uncle Freddie and Ned," he added unnecessarily.

Cassandra looked up from her reading and smiled at the bundle of energy which had interrupted a morning spent rereading select passages of Homer. The small white terrier at her feet cocked his head expectantly at all the commotion. Fond as he was of Cassie, he had found life sadly flat since the departure of her rambunctious twin Freddie two years ago, but Theodore's eruption into the library promised some interest. Theodore was still too young to provide Wellington with as much excitement as the twins' adventures had brought the little dog, but he did appear to be cast in the same mold as the twins and therefore had a great deal of potential, which, if encouraged, was sure to bring activity again to a household that had become, in Wellington's opinion, far too orderly and serene.

"What do they say? Read them to me, pleathe, pleathe," begged Theodore, his eyes shining with anticipation as he plopped himself at her feet. Cassie opened the envelope that was nearly totally covered with her twin's disorderly scrawl. Knowing her nephew's bloodthirsty nature, she felt sure he would prefer the catalog of tiger hunts, elephant rides, and narrow escapes from murderous thugs certain to be in Freddie's letter to the probable discussion of the Hindu religion and its effect on British/Indian relations in Ned's.

7

His letters, filled with descriptions of temple architecture, Hindu customs, sculpture and painting had piqued her curiosity, stimulated her thoughts, and relieved much of the boredom she had suffered in the absence of her best friends and most constant companions.

"Does he say anything about any more tiger hunts? I wath hoping he would get a tiger at the next one tho we could have itth head here over the fireplace," Teddy announced, indicating the spot now graced by the portrait of a venerable ancestor which would be much improved by such a replacement.

Cassie looked down into his earnest chubby face whose missing front teeth only added to its endearing expression. "I'm sorry, Teddy, my wits were wandering. Let's see what is the latest news." She picked up Freddie's letter and began to read.

If Freddie were to be believed, India existed solely to challenge the skill and daring of adventurous young Englishmen. His wild scrawl related one colorful episode after another, the most important of these apparently having to do with a signal service rendered to the Nabob of Bhopaul, whose gratitude had been effusive and rewarding beyond their wildest dreams. Having amassed a vast sum and, as an aside, having accomplished what they had set out to do, he and Ned were heading home hoping to see everyone at Cresswell and Camberly in the not-too-distant future. At this last piece of news, Theodore let out a whoop and went running in search of his mother. "Mama, Mama, Uncle Freddie and Ned are coming home. Mama, Mama . . ."

Cassie listened to his voice echoing down the hall, remembering the day several years ago when Freddie's voice had echoed much the same way, "Cassie, Cassie, we're going to India!" How she had missed them! Her thoughts strayed back to the other letter and its writer. If she had missed Freddie's *joie de vivre* and his penchant for tumbling them into one mad scrape after another, she missed even more Ned's insatiable thirst for knowledge, and the smile that lurked at the back of his eyes as he teased her and challenged her to think and question as well. If Freddie had been exuberant at the thought of high adventure in the fabulous Indian subcontinent, Ned had been subdued over their departure—subdued and determined to overcome his unhappy memories and to change that part of his personality that had occasioned them in the first place.

Poor Ned. Cassie's image of her dejected friend remained as clear as it had been the day his misery began. She had been sitting reading, much as she was now, when he strode in, his blue eyes dark and hurt in a white, set face. "She won't have me, Cassie," he had groaned, throwing himself into the nearest chair.

Knowing full well who "she" was, Cassie had heaved a mental sigh of relief before urging him to pour out his tale of woe. Privately, she thought Ned well rid of the vain and spoiled Arabella Taylor, who had, in Cassie's opinion, remained as selfish and obstinate as she had been when she had insisted on tagging along after them as children and then refused to play any games that had not been proposed by her. But Cassie knew that she was the only person in the entire neighborhood who continued to retain these unkind thoughts in the face of Arabella's flashing dark eyes, riotous dusky curls, bewitching dimple, and lilting, childlike voice that only added to the enchantment of a mouth too often compared to a rosebud. Everyone, even the studious Ned, had been overcome when Arabella reappeared on the local scene, polished to perfection by an exclusive seminary for young ladies of gentle birth and high expectations. Even Freddie, inclined to dismiss all women except his sisters as useless and helpless creatures, seemed to have forgotten completely the whining, crying child who had always insisted on being the center of attention. She was no different now, Cassie reflected, just more practiced and charming at claiming that attention. But Cassie loved Ned nearly as much as she loved Freddie, and she felt his pain intensely, so it was with real sympathy that she heard him out.

"She wouldn't even listen to me, Cassie! When I"—he paused and gulped for air—"when I told her how much I admired her, she laughed me off. But when she saw that I was serious and wouldn't be fobbed off, she told me straight out that she was looking forward to a brilliant Season and was not going to be deprived of it by someone she had known this age. And then''—his fists clenched at his sides as he continued—''and then she said that we should never suit anyway because she had to have gaiety and parties and that everyone knew I was''—he drew a deep breath—''a prosy old bore.''

And that, thought Cassie, is the only intelligent observation Arabella Taylor has ever made. Empty frivolity is all that she understands and someone of Ned's intellectual capacities would be bored silly within a fortnight. However, she concealed her true feelings about her childhood playmate, generously defending her instead. ''She's young, Ned, and very pretty. Of course she wants to go to parties and be the reigning beauty. For her, the idea of settling down and giving all that up would make her reject even the most dazzling of Corinthians.''

He brightened somewhat, ''Do you really think so?''

''I am certain that it is more the loss of a brilliant Season than a distaste for your company that turned her against the notion,'' she reassured him.

''But she called me a prosy old bore. Am I a prosy old bore, Cassie?'' he asked anxiously.

Cassie smiled and stretched out her hand. ''No. You are our own dear friend who enlivens the dullest conversation at assemblies and parties and keeps them from being a complete waste of time.''

He stared fixedly out the window until what seemed hours later, when in a hard voice devoid of all emotion, he announced, ''No. She's right. I am a prosy old bore, but I shall change that. If Freddie can go to India, so can I! And when I return, I shall immerse myself in so many *ton* parties that no one will recognize me.''

Cassie could happily have killed Arabella for causing his brave smile to go awry. She was overwhelmed by a great rage at Arabella in particular and the type of women in

general who seemed to have nothing better to do than dress
for one social occasion after another so they could chatter
empty-headed nothings and enslave as many luckless swains
as possible. It was true that most of these victims were equally
busy with their tailors and valets preparing to do exactly the
same thing in return, so why couldn't it have been one of
these fops dying for love of the toast of their Hampshire
society that Arabella had rejected instead of poor Ned, who
had so much greater a heart to lose than the squire's son and
his would-be Corinthian cronies? Cassie knew there was very
little comfort she could offer. In time he would bless Arabella
for having been so blind to his good qualities, but for the
moment it was best to put her out of his life and his mind.

"It would relieve me no end to have you with Freddie in
India. He's a dear and he means well, but sometimes his
enthusiasm gets the best of him and he doesn't think," Cassie
remarked. This was a patently obvious observation, as the
impetus for Freddie's departure had been an ill-judged prank
at university. The master of Balliol had not found it amusing
to return to a sow and six piglets rooting around his rooms
and lapping up his best sherry, spilled from what had been
a precariously placed decanter. So Freddie had been sent
down. He wasn't repining, school never having been his
strong point. When his attention was engaged, he was as good
a student as the next man, but Oxford had offered too many
distractions for a young man possessed of an abundance of
high spirits and conviviality.

Rustication soon palled on someone as active as Freddie,
and he began to toy with the idea of purchasing a cornetcy,
having made up his mind he wasn't cut out to be a student,
nor was he interested in taking up politics or any of the other
occupations people took up. Before he could take more
drastic measures to occupy himself, his brother-in-law hit
upon a plan that offered an exciting alternative. Many years
ago Lord Julian Mainwaring had inherited the fortune and
far-flung concerns of a childless uncle who had been one of
the Empire's first nabobs. For a long time Lord Mainwaring
had looked after these interests himself, but his brother's

untimely death, which had brought the burden of running several estates and the guardianship of his children, coupled with his subsequent marriage to the twins' sister, Lady Frances Cresswell, and his involvement in politics had left him with little time to do more than glance at the reports submitted by the agents appointed to administer these establishments for him. Julian Mainwaring liked Freddie and knew him for a decent and intelligent, if rash, young man. He seemed the perfect representative to send to remind the agents of Lord Mainwaring's continuing interest in their effectiveness in discharging their duties. Such a task would provide an outlet for the restlessness natural to an active young man, who had, since the beginning of their acquaintance, evinced a singular knack for tumbling from one scrape to another. As he had also demonstrated an equally strong propensity to overcome every mishap and emerge unscathed, Julian felt confident that Freddie would acquit himself admirably when challenged by truly adventurous situations.

So it had been decided that Freddie was to spend a year in India, or however long it took to visit and oversee Lord Mainwaring's operations. He had been preparing for an imminent departure to that mecca of every young man bent on winning his fortune when Ned had suffered his unhappy setback.

Ned, unlike Freddie, was a student—a scholar in fact—if enthusiastic masters were to be believed. Raised in a quiet household which, after his parents' death and before Lord Julian had taken over his guardianship, had been dominated by women, he had withdrawn to his grandfather's abundant library for companionship. He loved his effervescent sister Kitty dearly, but she had always turned to Lady Frances Cresswell for friendship, and the twins had been a little wary of one so quiet, well mannered, and clean as Ned. It wasn't until he'd accompanied Kitty to London for her come-out that he had really become acquainted with Cassandra and Frederick Cresswell, though there was little more than two miles between the gatekeeper's lodge of Camberly and the drive to Cresswell.

In London, deprived of their normal pursuits, the neighbors had been thrown together more often while Lady Frances accompanied Kitty and lent her moral support at social functions. The exuberant twins had taken to riding in the park as one of the few permissible ways of working off excess energy. It was during one of these rides that Ned had caught their interest. Oddly enough for one who was naturally quiet and reserved, he was a bruising rider and disported himself with ease on a mount that the twins admitted would have been too challenging for them.

When they had returned to the country, they had remained riding companions and friendship had blossomed. Freddie discovered Ned to be a far more expert judge of horseflesh than his louder, more boisterous acquaintances. Ned also possessed a seemingly inexhaustible knowledge of history, which was, at least the military and exploratory part, one of Freddie's true interests. Cassie liked him better than anyone else Freddie spent time with because he accepted it as natural that she should do everything her brother did—sometimes, as in the case of climbing trees, with much greater skill and daring. To her, their five-year difference in age made him practically an adult and she was flattered that he shared his thoughts with her as though she had been grown up. On his part, Ned had found Cassie to have a mind that exhibited all the curiosity and adventurousness of her tomboyish spirit.

The twins' parents, Lord and Lady Cresswell had been scholars of some note. They had traveled extensively with their family in Greece, haunting the important spots of the world until "that barbarian Bonaparte," as Lord Cresswell was wont to call him, had driven them home. In fact, they, along with their good friend the Comte de Vaudron, had been of inestimable service to Lord Elgin in ensuring that his priceless marbles were brought to England. Of all the children, Cassie had inherited her parents' scholarly turn of mind. Frances had put her excellent if unusual education to good use as an authoress of children's histories and continued to exercise an excellent mind as a brilliant political hostess and helpmeet to her husband, whose healthy respect for her intelligence made him bring his ideas to her for criticism and advice before he advanced them to the world at large. But it was Cassie who was the true intellectual, and her appetite for knowledge was as insatiable as Ned's. She was as well versed in the classics as he, and her more daring nature led her to question established opinion more readily. She did not hesitate to argue with him and challenge his opinions. To Ned, who rarely found anyone to share his interests, much less discuss them, this was as novel as it was refreshing, and they became fast, though occasionally argumentative, friends.

As time went by, some of the Cresswell exuberance rubbed off on Ned and he became more relaxed and ready to enter into new things. He, in turn, with his greater foresight and more levelheaded approach to life, kept the twins from falling into scrapes so disastrous that adult assistance was required to extricate them. They greatly appreciated this freedom from embarrassment and rewarded their new companion with their respect and occasional requests for advice.

But those busy happy days, for Cassie at any rate, had vanished with the boys. She and Lord Mainwaring had ridden with them up to London, where they had made some final purchases at S. Unwin's General Equipment Warehouse in Lombard Street before stowing their belongings on the ship that was to take them to Bombay. The captain was an acquaintance of Lord Mainwaring's, and Cassie had been glad to think that Freddie and Ned would have at least one friend on the long voyage. She had watched and waved as they sailed with the tide and then returned home, feeling lonelier than she ever had in her entire life. Freddie had always been more than a mere brother. He had been her constant companion, while Ned was the one person in the whole word who truly understood and appreciated her. It was true that Lady Frances encouraged Cassie's studies and her brother-in-law discussed them with her. Both of them included her as an equal in their conversations, but no one took the place of Ned, who teased her and delighted in challenging her ideas and stimulating her mind.

At least she had the mail, but it was slow and unpredictable. It could take ages for her replies to her letters to arrive—letters she had filled with thoughts on her reading, reflections on life in general, and questions about his experiences—but she reveled in his responses when they did come. His style, so very like him, made Ned seem present at the moment she was reading his letter. His reflections and comments, fashioned as they were to address her particular interests and tastes, made what could have been a mere traveler's description spring to life before her eyes. Thus, even though she sorely missed his companionship, she continued to feel the strength of his friendship. He had never mentioned Arabella again, but Cassie knew his sensitive retiring nature too well to think that she had been forgotten. For her part, Cassie had found it extraordinarily difficult even to exchange the politest of commonplaces with Arabella and was quite relieved when the girl had quit the neighborhood for what had been a predictably brilliant Season. Of course she had been hailed as an incomparable. How could anyone so devoted to herself and her toilette have become anything less than a diamond, Cassie had reflected cynically.

A belle who had enjoyed such success could not be expected to leave the scene of such triumph to bury herself in Hampshire, and many of those attending assemblies around Cresswell and Camberly that summer bemoaned the loss of their brightest star. Cassie, however, found such events to be much more enjoyable without Arabella's disturbing presence—a presense that seemed to have fostered nothing but dissension and jealousy as much among her envious female competitors as among vain young men.

Having seen what misery beauty, unaccompanied by heart or wit and bent solely on pursuit of its own pleasure, could cause, Cassie was not inclined to want a come-out of her own, but here she was having some difficulty. Her ordinarily levelheaded and sympathetic sister, who had suffered one miserable Season herself, was adamant that Cassie at least experience the world of the *ton* before condemning it out of hand.

"But Fanny," Cassie had wailed, "how can you, of all

people, insist that I waste my time in society when you were so unhappy there yourself? You thought most of those routs and balls excessively silly. And I daresay that I am less inclined to society than you.''

"Yes, love. You are entirely in the right of it. I was desperately unhappy, but that was my first Season when I was under the aegis of Lady Bingley, who was as feather-headed a female as you could hope to meet. Directly on bringing me to a gathering she would retire to the card room, leaving me to gaze around the room and wish intensely that I could become part of the nearest pillar or bank of flowers. But when I helped Lady Streatham chaperon Kitty, it was altogether different. Lady Streatham's acquaintances were not the empty-headed dowagers that comprised Lady Bingley's coterie; she made every effort to put me as well as Kitty forward and make us feel comfortable. And then the Comte de Vaudron made me see that dressing beautifully and fashionably could be as much an exercise of one's aesthetic sense and taste as any other sort of creative expression and it need not be merely empty competition to see whose dressmaker can make one resemble the most stunning fashion plate in *La Belle Assemblée*. Besides, Julian and his friends are in the *ton* and they certainly discuss more serious subjects than the cut of their coats or their own favored ways of tying a cravat.''

Cassie recognized the truth of this, but while she admitted that Lady Frances Mainwaring and Lady Elizabeth Streatham had found men who could carry more than one thought in their heads at a time, she remained skeptical about the possibility that there were enough such people to make a trip to London worthwhile, especially since two of the few intelligent men were at present on the high seas heading home.

CHAPTER 2

It was the Comte de Vaudron who saved the Season for Cassie as he had once saved it for her elder sister, though not in quite the same way. Cassie was again sitting in the library when the post arrived, but this time it was Frances who came rushing in waving a letter, which unlike the others, was on heavy cream paper and addressed in an elegant flowing script. "It's from the Comte de Vaudron," Frances announced, her eyes sparkling. "And he proposes a scheme that you are certain to like above all things. You know he is cataloging the marbles he and Papa helped Lord Elgin bring back from Greece. Having worked this age on them, he is beginning to realize what an enormous task it is and is feeling a bit overawed at the extent left unfinished. He is hoping that you will be able to help him, or at least act as his amanuensis when we arrive in Town. I rather think this should prove to be just the thing, don't you? Good heavens, the time! I promised Lady Taylor I would meet her at the church to arrange the flowers on the altar. I must dash." And Frances hurried off, leaving her sister to her thoughts. The idea of quitting the freshness, the quiet, and the freedom of the countryside for the frenzied, noisy pace and structured existence of London was detestable to someone whose neighbors had long ago ceased to comment on her long solitary walks with Wellington or her mad dashes across the fields on a horse that everyone from Squire Tilden to Sir Lucius Taylor had declared to be a "mount far too restive and totally unsuitable for a lady." Still, the idea of immersing herself in the beautiful artifacts brought back from Athens

17

did have a certain appeal, and besides, she dearly loved the comte.

Never having had the good fortune of his friend Lord Cresswell, who had found a wife to share his enthusiasm, and being totally uninterested in living the stultified, formal life at Versailles required of France's aristocrats, the Comte de Vaudron had led a solitary existence until he had met the Cresswells. Lord and Lady Cresswell had shared their interests as well as their lively young family with him and he had grown inordinately fond of them all during their Grecian sojourn. When the revolution had made it impossible for him to return to his own country, and Napoleon seemed to be consuming all of Europe at an alarming rate, he had come to London and, after their parents' deaths, had once again established himself as a benevolent uncle to Frances, Cassandra, and Freddie. He had helped Frances enjoy herself during her second Season in London and had assisted her in the creation of her own special style, which had made her blossom into a witty and beautiful woman. While he had always been a favorite of the twins, ready at a moment's notice to get up an interesting excursion for their special amusement, he had not figured as prominately in their lives as he had in their sister's. Now it seemed he was turning his attentions toward Cassie's welfare and she looked forward to having him as a support in the ordeal to come—the intense social round demanded by the *ton* of one of its would-be members.

Her reverie was interrupted by a squelching sound and a brief cough. As she looked around, her gaze encountered three dripping wet and barely recognizable figures in the doorway. Wellington certainly more closely resembled a black Scottish than a white West Highland terrier while the distinctive black stripes of his erstwhile friend and companion, Nelson the Cat, seemed to have merged and spread to cover his white chest and paws. Theodore was distinguished from the other two by being covered in mud only to his waist and he was clutching another lump of mud to his chest, this lump's only distinguished feature being its quack. "We fell in the pond," he explained unnecessarily.

"Arf, arf," Wellington agreed. He was thoroughly enjoying himself. Theodore had proven himself to be a regular Trojan, and sooner than the little dog had dared hope. Today's adventure had been almost as good as any that Freddie and Cassie had tumbled into.

"So I see." As she spoke, Cassie had visions of a series of torn smocks and muddied breeches she and Freddie had presented to Frances in just such a manner.

"Cook said she won't have me in her kitchen, tho I came to the you. She said I'm to go thraight to the pump and take that 'dratted dog and cat' with me. I told her they weren't 'dratted' and she got ever tho red in the fathe and took a broom and here we are."

"Yes. Here you are," Cassie agreed, just beginning to understand the fortitude her sister had exhibited all these years in the face of Freddie's and her exploits. No disaster had been too dirty or bloody to upset her. Feeling the weight of her elder sister's example, she inquired as calmly and with as much interest as she could infuse into her voice, which now threatened to break into laughter, into the reasons for their condition. The trio, which truly did look disreputable, had now begun to appear somewhat shamefaced.

"Well, it was Ethelred's fault," Theodore explained, twisting one foot nervously on the pattern in the carpet.

"Ethelred?" Cassie inquired blankly.

The grubby quacking lump was extended for her inspection, revealing a bill and two small webbed feet. "Yeth. I named him Ethelred because he was unready jutht like the King Ethelred the Unready that Mama told me about."

This explanation clearly wasn't enough for his aunt, who continued to look puzzled. "Well, you thee, Wellington, Nelthon, and I were playing with my boat on the pond and we *truly* were being careful not to get wet, when we heard a crack and some peeping and then thith egg fell into the pond right near uth. Only it wathn't a whole egg becauth Ethelred'th head was thicking out. Then Wellington and

Nelthon ruthed in and tried to catch it but the waves they made jutht puthed in farther from thore, tho I had to wade in. We got him on thore and he got out of hith egg and made thraight for Wellington. There didn't seem to be any duckth around, so I brought him here. Can we keep him, please Aunt Catthie? I think he likes uth." The mingled chorus of quacks, meows and arfs that followed this statement seemed to bear out this assumption.

Cassie smiled. "I expect you'd have a hard time getting rid of Ethelred now, but come along and let's wash all of you and dry you out." She led the trio out of the pump in the stable yard, where, under the watchful eye of John Coachman, they splashed happily until they more nearly resembled their former selves.

"Just like old times, you might say, Miss Cassie," John's weather-beaten face expanded in a warm grin. Like Wellington, he had missed the activity since Freddie had been gone, but being slightly more perceptive than the little terrier, he had worried a great deal that the sparkle had gone out of Miss Cassie when the boys had left. John loved Frances and he was proud of what a fine young man Freddie had become, but Cassie was his true favorite. Ever since she had taken her first spill from a pony at two years old and refused to cry, Cassie had won the critical coachman's heart, though he would have died rather than let on about his devotion. Young Master Theodore is proving to be just the ticket for diverting all of them, he thought, looking at Cassie's animated face and at the animals enthusiastically playing under the pump. Spending his life around them, John had been well aware of Wellington and Nelson's despondency since Freddie's departure. "A good rubdown and you'll be right as rain," he announced, handing one towel to Cassie for Theodore and vigorously patting the rest with another. "But you must ask Nurse to get you some dry clothes, Master Theodore," he directed as he gave a final wipe behind Wellington's ears.

"But what thall we do with Ethelred?" Theodore wondered aloud. Ethelred, who had enjoyed the episode at the pump more than anyone, was quacking merrily and swimming in the barrel under the spigot, but as the others showed signs of leaving, he peeped anxiously and hopped out.

"He shall have a bed right next to Wellington's and Nelson's by the stove in the kitchen," Cassie replied. Seeing the mistrustful look on Theodore's face, she added, "Don't worry, Teddy, Cook does get exasperated when they get underfoot, but she loves them dearly and would miss their companionship sorely. Besides, what would she do with her scraps if she didn't have those two to take care of them for her? She knows that Nelson is the best mouser in Hampshire and Wellington won her heart when he caught the rat gnawing its way into her flour bin."

"All right," Theodore sighed, still somewhat anxious about his new pet's acceptance in the bailwick of such a domestic despot as Cook. "But may I help John make a bed for Ethelred?" he asked.

"Certainly, dear, but you must put on some other clothes first and I shall make sure these three finish drying out." Cassie smiled encouragingly at him as she shepherded the animals toward the kitchen. All were agreeably tired and needed no coaxing to lie quietly in a heap of fur and feathers under the stove while Cassie tried to convince Cook that really one more animal would not disrupt her domain so very much. Cook, who truly did have a soft spot for "her two rascals," demurred briefly before letting herself be won over.

"It's Miss Cassie and Master Freddie all over again," she remarked to no one in particular, shaking her head as she went back to rolling out pastry for a game pie. "Still and all, it's nice to have some activity around here once more," she addressed the kitchen clock, which remained obstinately mute.

Activity of a less drastic and certainly more social nature was the topic of discussion among the three ladies decorating the church for Sunday. Frances, Sir Lucius Taylor's wife, and his youngest daughter, the celebrated and, if Cassie's opinions were to be noted, infamous Arabella, were busily adding greens to complete the handsome arrangements in large vases of the church's rather severe altar.

"Will Cassie be joining you in London this Season?" Lady Taylor inquired, stepping back to admire the effect of a carefully placed sprig of lavender.

"Yes. We shall all be going up this time, though I fear we shall miss Freddie's company dreadfully. Brothers do come so in handy at a time like this—if not for their value as a partner of last resort, then for the friends they bring with them. Not that Cassie is in the least shy, but one always feels safer in numbers at first."

Arabella, always more than willing to discuss the resounding success of her first Season, broke in, "If I said to Mama once, I must have said it a thousand times last year before we left Hampshire, 'If only, dear Mama, you had been fit to provide me with older brothers instead of sisters, I should feel a good deal easier in my mind about my first ball.' I am sure I wished times out of mind that Edwina were an Edward before my first evening at Almack's. She is naturally very dear to me, but as a partner or friend of possible partners she was quite useless." Thus Arabella ruthlessly dismissed one of the *ton*'s most dashing matrons with a shrug of her pretty shoulders. It was a gesture that had once caused one lovelorn swain to label her "Cruel Disdain" and she seized every opportunity to practice it. "At any rate, I learned how to go on in no time at all and I had the most famous time. Didn't I, Mama?"

This was that worthy lady's cue to expound on the brilliance of her daughter's Season: how Lord such-a-one had hailed her as a diamond of the first water, how the Marquess so-and-so had disagreed, calling her instead an incomparable; how young Viscount this-and-that had been instantly struck by her beauty and positively haunted their house in Berkeley Square. All through the recital Arabella looked sweetly conscious until Frances was ready to wring the soft white neck which made such a perfect foil for the dusky curls. She was able to forbear, however, and with a great effort of will, she refrained from inquiring about any suitors, the absence of which had been quite noticeable during Arabella's return to Hampshire.

Such an unfair question would have elicited the gayest of inconsequential laughter and the amused reply that "of course Papa and Mama say I'm far too young to be settling down no matter how hard any gentleman may press his suit." The truth of the matter was that Arabella was aiming higher than any of the eligible but none-too-brilliant matches that had presented themselves. It had been a disappointment not to have netted a truly grand fish, but after all, it had only been her first Season, and these things take time. Arabella was determined to take no less than a marquess. After all, one had to have one's standards. But in spite of enjoying all the advantages of youth, beauty, and wealth, Arabella was laboring under the distinct disadvantage of being the daughter of a minor baronet and a woman who, though prettily enough behaved, had brought to her marriage a great deal of money earned in trade. It would have taken far more address and sophistication than Arabella possessed to erase these two flaws from the mind of a truly brilliant catch.

If Cassie, ensconced once again in her favorite chair in the library, could have been privy to all this, she would have felt a great deal happier about the projected Season, but knowing the type of person Arabella was, and knowing that she had been hailed as a great success in the metropolis, filled her with foreboding. For it seemed to her that a society which admired someone such as Arabella Taylor would never accept someone like Lady Cassandra Cresswell. Nor would she ever feel anything but uncomfortable or bored among such people. If only she had one friend and confidante, it wouldn't be so bad. Of course she did have Fanny and Lord Mainwaring, Ned's sister Lady Kitty Willoughby, and Lord Mainwaring's cousin, Lady Streatham, who had been so supportive of Fanny when she was in London for Kitty's come-out, but having them wasn't the same as having someone of one's own age and experience. It made her miss Ned and Freddie even more dreadfully. But she supposed that Frances was in the right of it. She couldn't molder forever in Hampshire with her books, going out in society less and less until she became nothing but an ape-leader.

Dearly as she loved her aunt Harriet, she could see that the lady's particular quirks and rather prickly personality had developed over the course of the years during her brother's absence in Greece, when she had been alone at Cresswell devoting herself to her orchids. It was not that she had been lonely, because her horticultural interests were her consuming passion. But this passion had led her to ignore all else, and so when she was forced into contact with society at large, she was most uncomfortable. True, she had little use for anyone, and even less use for fools, whom she considered to be the bulk of humanity, but Cassie had often thought it too bad that she didn't seem truly to love anybody. Of course, she cared a great deal about what happened to Frances and the twins, but she did not miss them when they were gone, and was only tangentially involved with them as their paths crossed at meals or during the course of the day. Though she knew Aunt Harriet was perfectly happy with her existence, and though it was a relief to know at least one woman whose entire life did not revolve around men, Cassie sometimes felt sad for her.

Not that her sister Frances's life revolved around men. She continued to write and publish her own books and maintained her own separate existence as an author, but Cassie could see that there were times when she gave up her own work to join Lord Mainwaring or Theodore in something that interested them. If only there were some middle ground between being an eccentric recluse or plunging headlong into society, but there did not seem to be. Men could enter politics or the army and thus pursue an interest among companions of similar dispositions, but there was nothing for someone like Cassie, who remained at a loss about how she was to go on in life. She supposed that Frances was correct, and that having lived buried at Cresswell with her books, she ought to try London to see what the alternatives were.

When Lady Frances returned for tea, Cassie was able to

tell her that having thought it over, she could now be easy in her mind about going to London.

"I'm glad, dear." Frances smiled at her younger sister's wrinkled brow and worried eyes. "I think you'll find enough there to interest you that you won't be forced to devote your entire existence to dressing and promenading at this ball or that rout. After all, Julian and I shall be there, and we have no more patience with worthless fribbles than you do. And not everyone is like Arabella. She came along with her mama this afternoon. What a frivolous thing she is, to be sure! I wonder at her success. But then, the only lips I have heard speak of her triumphs have been hers. At any rate, I shall write the comte directly and then see to it that the household has plenty of time to prepare before we depart. At least I do not have to worry about cajoling Aunt Harriet into coming or wonder how we shall transport her darlings to London as I did when we went up to London for Kitty's come-out. By the by, where are Wellington and Nelson? They never miss an opportunity to chase each other at teatime. Nurse said that Teddy had his tea early. When three such rambunctious characters are so quiet, I begin to have my suspicions."

Cassie regaled her with the afternoon's adventure, much to her sister's amusement.

"I can see that with Nelson and Wellington to egg him on, Tedfdy is bound to fall into as many scrapes as you and Freddie put together. Well, I must go meet this Ethelred, who has already managed to cause such a commotion in a household much accustomed to dealing with upheaval."

CHAPTER 3

Lady Frances' organization being what it was, the entire household was soon ensconced in Mainwaring House in Grosvenor Square. When Frances and Lord Mainwaring had first been married they had lived in the Cresswells' house on Brook Street, leaving his mother, the Dowager Marchioness of Camberly, to reign in state in Grosvenor Square. Lord Mainwaring had been more than happy to vacate what he more often than not termed "that gloomy pile" so his mother could entertain the other town tabbies to tea in style. It was Mainwaring's expressed opinion that more marriages had been made and more reputations launched or ruined in that stately drawing room than in any other in all of England. At this mother's death and upon his assumption of political duties, the marquess had reluctantly moved back—"But only on the condition that you make it fit for human habitation, my love," he had admonished Frances.

Frances, following the taste for simplicity, lightness, and elegance derived from her childhood spent among the glories of classical antiquity, had transformed the somber mansion into a dwelling that combined elegance with graciousness, and created an atmosphere which was both welcoming and restful to all and sundry—politicians, Corinthians, society matrons, and the select few among the Upper Ten Thousand whom the Mainwarings counted among their friends.

It was upon the threshold of this august residence one day in late March that the entourage from Cresswell descended to be welcomed by Higgins the butler and the staff, whom he had assembled in the front hall. "Hurrah! Hurrah! We're here at last," shouted Teddy, who despite having been allowed to ride the entire distance on the box with John Coachman, still possessed an excess of high spirits.

"Arf! Arf!" echoed Wellington, who had also ridden on the box and, like his newly adopted playmate, was in fine fettle. Nelson, having endured the journey nursing a queasy stomach nestled against the squabs of the Mainwarings' beautifully sprung traveling carriage, descended in a more leisurely manner, tail aloft, delicately sniffing and evaluating the town scents which assailed him. At this point, Ethelred, who had slept quietly in a basket on Cassie's lap, woke up and demanded to be set free. With a loud quack and several flaps of yet unformed wings, he hopped down, beady eyes eager to take in all the new sights. Catching sight of their protégé, Wellington and Nelson instantly forgot their delight at being set free in the metropolis and, adopting the most jaded of airs, sauntered in a blasé fashion toward the stables with Ethelred and Teddy in hot pursuit.

"I daresay they shall have the place at sixes and sevens in no short while," Frances observed as she descended, a bandbox in one hand, to greet the staff. Cassie, clutching Ethelred's now deserted basket, followed suit, and with Higgins's assistance the travelers were soon ensconced comfortably in the drawing room in front of a well-laden tea tray and a welcoming fire.

In no short order, Wellington, Nelson, Teddy, and Ethelred appeared. Having explored the nether regions and discovered there that tea had already been sent upstairs, they had lost no time in hastening to the scene. Wellington and Nelson took up their accustomed places on either side of the fire while Ethelred padded around snapping at a curtain tassel here, pecking at a design on the rug there, until he was entirely satisfied with his new surroundings. He then joined his friends by the fireplace, where all three, along with Theodore, concentrated on the tea table.

As Theodore, consuming a hot buttered crumpet, expounded on the wonders of the stables, Frances absently nibbled a scone and perused a stack of gilt-edged invitations. Such abstraction made an ideal situation for the crumb-snatching brigade which watched every gesture of Teddy's that scattered bits of crumpet or every piece of scone that fell unnoticed from Frances's hand as she sorted through the mail. In fact, Cassie was the only one doing justice to the beautiful array that Higgins had brought in.

"Itth a bang up table, Cathie, though it doethn't hold a candle to the one at Crethwell," enthused Teddy, sending an irresistible shower of crumbs in Ethelred's direction. The little duck pecked happily until the other two, unable to restrain themselves, pounced at the same time on a large piece that had dropped beyond his reach under the cake stand.

"Cassie, my love, here is a card for Lady Delamere's rout tomorrow evening. That should do quite well for your first introduction to the *ton*," Frances remarked, not bothering to look up from her correspondence as she automatically caught the cake stand, which teetered precariously after Wellington's dive for the crumb. "Her affairs are always quite brilliant, though it's sure to be a sad crush so early in the Season. There is no time to have Madame Regnery make up anything new for you, but your white gauze with the blue satin pipings that we had made for the Alton assembly should do very well. It was fortunate that the snow made it impossible to attend."

"Teddy, if you eat another crumpet, you'll become ill," Cassie admonished before turning an anxious face toward Frances. "That dress may have done very well in Hampshire, but are you quite certain it will do for London?"

"Of course, love. It's very simple, but the lines are quite elegant and you're so lovely that you don't need rosettes and ruchings to disguise your flaws." Frances smiled fondly at her younger sister.

"Oh, give over, Fanny, do. You know that brunettes are all the rage and blondes sadly out of fashion now. At any rate, blondes are supposed to have complexions of peaches and cream." Cassie made a face in the gilt-framed mirror over the fireplace. "And despite the quantities of almond paste that Rose insists I use on them, my freckles will persist in appearing.'' Here Cassie wrinkled a beautifully straight nose, whose only flaw was its light sprinkling of freckles. Though it was not a face that exhibited the rosebud lips, velvet brown eyes, and delicately rounded chin that were all the rage, it was one that reflected far more character than those commonly encountered. The eyes were a brilliant dark sapphire, revealing a sparkle of humor in their depths which had disconcerted more than one self-satisfied young buck. Her hair was gold rather than blond and showed a definite tendency to break out into curls unless taken severely to task. The chin was a trifle determined for the taste of most amorous swains, but its challenge was softened by a generous mouth that hinted at a passionate nature below the surface. It was a vivacious face, which created a first impression of vitality and interest, and it caught the attention of those sensitive or clever enough to recognize the intelligence and strength of character that lay behind it. But even those who failed to appreciate the promise of a keen mind and a lively sense of humor rated Lady Cassandra Cresswell a very taking thing.

''Papa!'' Teddy leaped up, threatening the equilibrium of the cake stand for the second time.

''Hello, Teddy, my boy. Did you have a good journey?'' Lord Julian Mainwaring, Marquess of Camberly's somewhat forbidding countenance broke into a smile as he surveyed the little group around the fire. Handing his many-caped greatcoat to the hovering Higgins, he strode over to the fire, stepping gingerly around the menagerie.

''Oh yes, Papa! It was splendid and John Coachman let me sit on the box with him the entire way,'' Teddy assured him enthusiastically.

''Did he now? That was a rare treat. How were the new bays handling?'' No one, seeing the fondness in Mainwaring's eyes as he looked at his son, could have guessed that not too many years ago he had considered children to be the worst possible sort of encumbrance. However, marriage to Frances and his necessary involvement with Ned and Freddie had taught him that they were not all little monsters who were

better off seen and not heard. To the contrary, he had
discovered during various outings to the Tower, Astley's
Amphitheatre, and balloon ascensions that childish curiosity
and enthusiasm could be quite enjoyable—enchanting even.
So, much to his friends' astonishment, he had become a
devoted, though by no means doting, parent, participating
personally in much of his son's education and activities.

His son's eyes shone as he reassured his father, "They're
a bang-up pair and John says they're very sweet goers."

"I am delighted to hear that they're all I thought they would
be. Hello, my love," Julian bent to plant a kiss on Frances's
forehead as she handed him a cup of tea. "Everything in
good order when you arrived?"

"Yes. We're settled in nicely, thank you, and John has
been able to find an eager young lad to help out in the stables.
He's a cousin of Lady Streatham's groom Thompson and
seems quite anxious to learn. How was your meeting with
Canning?"

"Excellent. I admired Castlereagh's grasp of affairs on
the Continent, but it's time we took to problems at home,
and George Canning is the man for that. He has a far greater
sense of what must be done in the way of financial reforms.
But he needs support. He lacks the charm of Castlereagh and
there are many who greatly distrust him."

"I am persuaded, Julian, that you, with acquaintances
among both factions, can bring about some understanding."
Frances raised a quizzical eyebrow and handed him the last
remaining crumpet.

"I shall certainly do my utmost, love. But on to more
immediate and pressing matters. I see a stack of invitations
in your lap and I have the foreboding feeling that I am to
be called upon to help ensure that Cassie is successfully
launched toward the dubious pleasure of taking the *ton* by
storm." He grimaced in the mirror at his sister-in-law.
Having seen Lady Frances blossom during a Season from
one who disdained and avoided the fashionable world to one
who could charm it at will, he felt confident that Cassie would

do the same, but he understood and sympathized with her reluctance.

"How fortunate you should mention it, my dear. Lady Delamere holds a rout tomorrow evening. It's sure to prove a dreadful squeeze, but we should attend it," his wife replied, eyeing him hopefully.

"Ecod, catched already. Well, you may count on me to escort you both and to defend you from dandies, fribbles, court cards, overeager young men, and all the other bores that plague these affairs. Furthermore, I shall order Bertie to join us and lend us éclat."

"That would be famous," Cassie thanked him, visibly relieved at the prospect of this support. Bertie Montgomery, longtime family friend of the Cresswells, had been at school with Lord Mainwaring. A perpetual bachelor, possessed of the most discriminating taste and a kind heart, he was an escort to ease the mind of the most nervous of damsels encountering the *ton* for the first time. An exquisite dancer, up on all the latest on-dits, he could be counted on to smooth the most difficult of social encounters and win the hearts of the *ton*'s most demanding dowagers.

"That's settled then," Frances remarked, propping the invitation up on the mantel. "We shall make our first appearance this Season tomorrow night. I must send a note to Elizabeth to ensure her presence and Nigel's." Frances, knowing the perceptive and kindhearted nature of Julian's favorite cousin, Lady Streatham, felt sure that the matron, well aware of the pitfalls awaiting a young woman entering society, would make certain that her son attended and brought along some of his brother officers from the Guards.

CHAPTER 4

So it was that Cassie, mounting the curving staircase at Lady Delamere's imposing residence in Portman Square, was well protected in her first engagement with polite society. His sister and brother-in-law preceded her up the stairway and Bertie Montgomery, resplendent in an exquisitely cut swallowtail coat and satin knee breeches, lent a supporting arm. Surrounded as she was by family and friends, Cassie was not particularly nervous, but as she surveyed the glittering throng she could not identify one among the turbaned dowagers, the overanxious young women, the self-important tulips of the ton whom she would not find a dead bore within no time at all. Sighing inwardly, she made her curtsy to her host and hostess and allowed Bertie to lead her into the set that was forming for the quadrille.

"Don't look so Friday-faced, Cassie. Know you don't like this above half, but it ain't all that bad, you know," admonished Bertie, who, correctly interpreting her thoughts, strove to reassure her. "Most of 'em haven't a thought in their cock lofts beyond cutting a dash or getting leg-shackled, but there's nothing to say you have to join their ranks, and there's nothing to say you can't be amused by it all instead of upset."

A faint smile lit Cassie's features. "You're in the right of it, Bertie," she agreed. "What a gudgeon I am. After all, Frances contrives to keep herself tolerably amused. It's just . . ." Her voice trailed off as she caught sight of Arabella Taylor, who, surrounded by a group of young bucks, was laughing delightedly and flirting behind her fan.

Bertie's eyes followed hers. "That girl may think she's an out-and-outer, but mark my words, none of 'em will come up to scratch," he observed, nodding sagely. "Kirkby will never get caught in the parson's mousetrap. Pierrepont's whole future depends upon his great aunt's fortune and she would never countenance his marrying someone who smelled of the shop, no matter how remote the connection. As for Fortescue, he hasn't a feather to fly with and it would take a larger fortune than Arabella's to keep the duns off his back. Besides which it's one thing to trifle with a pretty ninny-hammer and quite another to marry her. A man wants a woman of sense for his wife." He held up a hand at Cassie's mutinous expression. "Not that serving as a marriage market is all that society has to offer, but that is what Arabella is hoping for, which is why she and others like her can cause a stir—they think of nothing else and devote their energies solely to that." Here the set broke up and he returned her to Lady Frances, who was politely listening to the complaints of a hatchet-faced woman in a towering purple turban.

"Disgraceful!" Lady Buffington exclaimed, her dewlaps fairly jiggling in indignation. "What the young bloods won't do these days! Why we ended up in the ditch all because the stage driver had allowed one of them to take the ribbons. He came through Witney at such a pace that no one could have stopped him. Of course he took the turn at far too great a speed, overset the coach, and forced us off the road. You would never catch my Charles in such tomfoolery." Here she thrust forward a limp youth, declaring that Frances and Cassie must meet her youngest, who had vowed that he refused to rest until he had met Cassie. The unfortunate Charles smiled in a sickly fashion and, after a none-too-subtle push from his mother, asked Cassie to stand up with him.

"Dear Charles, such a good boy." His mother smiled fondly. "Though I worry that some flighty young miss may set her sights on his fortune. He's so tenderhearted that he can never refuse a lady and then he'll marry her so as not to hurt her feelings." She sighed gustily.

Abject fear rather than excessive sensibility seemed to be

"Dear Charles's" overriding emotion as, holding Cassie loosely in a sweaty clasp, he shoved her around the floor. After enduring some minutes of this painful exercise, Cassie could bear the silence no longer. "Have you just arrived in Town, then?" she inquired encouragingly, not caring in the least whether he had or not, but anything was better than this mute shuffling.

"Er . . . um . . . yes," he managed to gasp as, his brow creased in concentration, Charles narrowly missed careening into the couple next to them.

Thinking that perhaps the banality of such small talk had put him off, Cassie tried again, this time with a more leading question, "Have you read *Waverley* yet? I own I am quite partial to Mr. Scott's work."

As this produced no more animated response than the first question, she gave up and allowed herself to be led woodenly around the floor. Keeping Bertie's strictures in mind, she allowed her gaze to travel around the ballroom. There certainly was enough to entertain even the most jaundiced of observers—a plain-whey-faced damsel obviously hoping to compensate for what she lacked in address by adorning herself with rivers of diamonds, an aged dandy who creaked by, his corsets laced to give him a wasp waist that nearly deprived him of breath, a bracket-faced dowager in an immense green turban who fixed each hopeful young woman with an eagle stare and then turned to comment in an audible whisper to her mousy companion.

After what seemed an interminable period she was restored to Frances and Julian. Just then Bertie appeared bearing glasses of ratafia for the ladies and followed by a tall man whose languid air proclaimed him an habitué of such brilliant gatherings.

"Dear Lady Mainwaring, delightful to see you," he drawled, bowing low over Frances's hand. "What ever can have persuaded two such sensible people as you and Julian to subject yourselves to such a crush?"

Frances raised one mobile eyebrow. "But our reasons are unassailable. We are accompanying my younger sister in her first introduction to the *ton*. Allow me to present Lady Cassandra Cresswell. Much more to the purpose is what are you doing here, Lord Dartington?''

"*Touché,* Frances. You always were far too awake on every suit for my poor wit." Lord Dartington looked to be amused. "Is Cassandra as fearful a bluestocking as you, I wonder," he quizzed her.

Frances laughed. "You are doing it much too brown, my lord, but you must find out for yourself."

Lord Dartington smiled at Cassie. "May I have the very great honor, Lady Cassandra," he begged, holding out a slim white hand with a flourish.

"Do go on, Cassie," Bertie urged. "Once you are seen with Dartington, your reputation is assured. Only think of it! Why, being seen to amuse him for the duration of a boulanger is worth your successful appearance at several soirees. You may now absent yourself from these affairs for the next fortnight and still be remembered as a *succès fou.*"

The sardonic gleam in Lord Dartington's eye gave Cassie a moment's unease, but being one who could never resist a challenge, she put up her chin and replied in a dampening tone, "You are too kind, sir."

"Like your sister, you are unimpressed with such frippery fellows as we who haunt London's ballrooms," he teased as he led her on to the floor.

"That depends entirely upon the way you occupy your time outside of such hallowed halls," Cassie retorted. There was something in his tolerant air that piqued her and she resolved to remain unimpressed by one who clearly considered himself to be a nonpareil.

"Well met, young Cassandra," he responded. The kindling look in her eyes warned him that he had gone too far and he relented, adding in a kinder tone, "I am not an ogre, you know. But if one doesn't appear to be completely bored with everyone one encounters, one runs the risk of being accosted by every encroaching mushroom and toad-eater who ever aspired to establish himself in society. A cut direct here and there, a general air of cynical boredom, and

I am left entirely free to choose my friends as I will. If Frances had followed my lead, she would never have had to endure a half an hour's conversation with that odious Lady Buffington, nor would you have been forced to risk life and limb on the floor with the young whelp she so fondly refers to as 'my youngest.' " Here he imitated the patronizing accents of the doting mother with such accuracy that Cassie could not help laughing. "Much better," he approved. "Think of the damage to my character if a mere green girl had remained poker-faced during the entire dance with me."

Cassie relaxed to some degree and found herself relating the perils of sharing a closed carriage with a dog, a cat, and a duck, all of whom seemed to feel entitled to space equal to or larger than that allotted to the human occupants.

He laughed in turn. "And now you have amused me, for which I thank you." Dartington guided her skillfully around. "When the two tabbies pounce on me, I shall pronounce you 'refreshing' and your success is ensured. Never forget, my dear, that no matter how many male hearts are laid at your feet, you are not assured of a place in this world until you thaw that organ in one of the icy dowagers who rules it." With these sage words, he restored her to her companions, who joined by Kitty and her husband Lord Willoughby, made a gay little coterie. Cassie was delighted to see these reinforcements, but the sight of Kitty, recalling as it did the thought of the absent Ned and Freddie, brought a lump to her throat.

"La, Cassie, how prodigious elegant you look—the first stare of fashion and you've not yet been on the Town a week," Kitty greeted her enthusiastically.

Cassie would happily have sat out the next few dances to exchange news of friends and hear about Kitty's new baby, "the sweetest thing you can imagine, Cassie," but they were interrupted by the arrival of a portly young man whose fussily tied cravat threatened to strangle him.

"Ah, Willoughby. I haven't seen you this age. Been rusticating, old man?" the young man inquired, subjecting Cassie to a thorough scrutiny that began with the wreath of flowers in her hair and traveled insolently to the tips of her white satin slippers. Cassie flushed angrily and turned away as much as possible to concentrate more on the conversation with Kitty. "You simply must introduce me to your charming friend," he continued, fixing Lord Willoughby with a meaningful stare.

Looking acutely uncomfortable, Kitty's husband bowed to the inevitable and muttered, "An old school acqaintance, Basil Weatherby, Lady Cassandra Cresswell."

"Utterly charming. Lady Cassandra cannot have long been on the Town, I am sure as I should have instantly been aware of such beauty come amongst us. I really must have this dance," he drawled.

Though Lord Willoughby looked not to be best pleased and Cassie was less than enthusiastic, there was no help for it but to be led out to the floor. Cassie needn't have worried that she would not have a thing to say to such an insufferable young man. In his own estimation, Basil Weatherby needed no one else to carry on a brilliant conversation. He seemed to feel it incumbent upon him to point out the ridiculous quirks in the leaders of the *ton*, winking knowingly as he spoke of Lord Petersham's collection of snuffboxes and repeating Lord Alvanley's latest witticism as though it had been addressed solely to him. In short, he did his best to intimate that he rubbed shoulders with the very tulips of the *ton* and that no social gathering would be complete without "Wily Weatherby"—here he smiled in a knowing way and contrived to stroke Cassie's hand while gripping it tighter in his fleshy palm.

The dance seemed endless. No matter where Cassie looked, he managed to bring his face with its pulpy lips and protuberant eyes into view. After what seemed an eternity they headed toward Cassie's group, which had now been joined by Lord and Lady Streatham and their son Nigel. Divining Cassie's ill-concealed distaste for her partner, Lady Streatham, a perceptive and kindhearted soul, immediately rushed forward, exclaiming, "Cassie, my dear, how delightful to see you! You must come tell us about Freddie. Nigel is absolutely dying to hear his latest adventures."

Cassie smiled gratefully, took a gulp of air, and began to share the latest news of her twin. After the dreadful Basil and the inarticulate Charles it was a relief to see Nigel's bluff open-faced countenance and take a moment to share the descriptions of the splendor of maharajahs' palaces, villainous thugs, murderous dacoits, perilous tiger hunts, and all the other exotic details she had gleaned from Ned and Freddie's correspondence.

Nigel, who was between Freddie and Ned in age, had been their constant companion when they were all in London. Being with him was almost as good as being with her brother and Ned. He was a cheerful giant given to claiming that he made up in size for what he lacked in his brain box. He was perfectly happy to leave the thinking to clever fellows like Ned, and though he wouldn't have been caught dead with a book, he had inordinate respect for Cassie and Ned, who not only read them, but actually enjoyed them.

"You're looking bang up to the nines, Cassie. I hardly recognized you in such fancy toggery. I see that old Basil was trying his best to charm you. That man gives me a pain in the bread basket. Fancies himself an out-of-door, does old 'Wily Weatherby,' but I must say I don't like him above half—nasty weasely sort of fellow," Ned remarked.

"He's the most odious toad," Cassie rejoined hotly. "Trying to make out that he's all the crack and condescending to me as though I were a complete rustic, and all the time ogling me as though I were some prime bit of blood. Disgusting!"

"Don't fly into the boughs, Cassie," Nigel soothed. "We'll keep a weather eye out for him next time. I expect he caught poor Willoughby off guard and there was nothing else he could do but introduce you. Basil will make a good catch for someone who can stomach him. He's well breeched. Got a wealthy aunt who dotes on him, but to my mind he's a nasty piece of work. Trouble is he's such an eligible bachelor, he gets invited everywhere.'' Here Nigel caught a meaningful look from his mother. ''Ahem, Cassie, would you like to dance,'' he asked, responding dutifully to his mother's unspoken urging.

Cassie, who had intercepted the look from Lady Streatham, smiled and replied, ''Thank you, Nigel, but I would just as soon sit this one out.'' When she saw the relief on his face, her smile deepened, ''Let's sit down and you can tell me all about life in the Guards, which is sure to be more interesting than anything I have encountered at Cresswell or here at the Marriage Mart.''

While Nigel was not an extraordinarily bright young man, he was kind, and he detected the wistful note in Cassie's voice. ''Is it too dreadful having to attend all these routs and balls and things? I should hate it. Lord, one quadrille and I'm done for. But I thought females like that sort of thing— not that you're like other females—thank goodness. You're a great gun, Cassie. If I could find someone like you, it wouldn't be half bad to go to these sorts of things.'' His brow furrowed as a thought struck him. ''You wouldn't like to get married, would you, Cassie? If you would, then neither one of us would have to stand this nonsense. You've got more pluck than most men. We could have a bang-up time. And . . .''—he added the clincher in a rush—''I don't know anyone who's a more bruising rider or a better judge of horseflesh.''

Cassie smiled fondly at him, replying gently, ''That's very sweet of you, Nigel, and you're a dear to think of me, but I really don't want to be married, and neither do you.'' Her quick eyes caught the barely perceptible relaxation of his posture at her reply and the slight sigh of relief as he realized his narrow escape, and she had to struggle to keep her countenance. ''But I hope you will stand my friend and rescue me as you did tonight. Now tell me, did you purchase that bay you saw at Tattersall's not long ago?''

Thus engaged in one of their favorite pastimes, comparing

the points of various bits of blood they had known or seen and describing the ground over which they had been on diverse hunts, Nigel and Cassie managed to wile away the remainder of the evening most enjoyably.

CHAPTER 5

The next day Cassie was awakened by Frances hard on the heels of the maid who brought in the morning chocolate. Having correctly interpreted Cassie's reactions to her various partners the previous evening, Frances thought it time to call upon the Comte de Vaudron before her younger sister's opinion of London and the *ton* descended so low as to be irredeemable.

"Cassie, my love," Frances began, pulling her wrapper closer as she settled herself at the foot of Cassie's bed. "We must call on the comte as soon as possible. Today bids to be fair and I think we should beg Julian to drive us around the park and drop us off at the comte's before repairing to Brooks's. What do you say?"

Cassie, who had been somewhat daunted by visions of galas similar to that of the previous evening stretching endlessly, cheered up considerably. Her face regained some of its former animation and she replied, "I should like that of all things."

"It's done then. As soon as you're dressed, we shall be off," Frances concluded briskly, rising from the bed and making for the door.

Inspired, Cassie instructed Rose to select her newest walking dress. Indeed, she looked quite charming when she descended sometime later. The lavender tint of her zephyrine silk pelisse intensified the blue of her eyes and the lace-trimmed capuchin brim of her bonnet framed her curls, which, ordinarily kept ruthlessly smoothed and pulled into a knot, were allowed to escape in golden profusion. Even

41

Lord Mainwaring, that noted connoisseur of feminine
fashion, remarked that she looked complete to a shade as
he handed her into his curricle.

Wellington, who fancied himself a coaching dog, had run
out eagerly when the elegant equipage was brought around
to the door. Hating to disappoint him, Cassie did her best
to explain why he wasn't being lifted onto the driver's seat.
"Not today, Wellington, we're not going for a long ride,
you know. We're off to visit some very dull friezes which
wouldn't interest you in the least." The little dog's ears and
tail drooped but were soon restored to their usual perky
posture when Nelson, who had been sunning himself on the
front step, reminded him that Cook had just finished making
a game pie and there were sure to be some delicious scraps.
With a farewell arf, Wellington sent them on their way and
trotted around to the kitchen to see what he and Nelson could
round up. Besides, he consoled himself, on such a fine day
Theodore was certain to ask John to take him to the park
on his pony and he was bound to invite Wellington along.

The curricle bowled through the park, pausing briefly as
they exchanged salutations with Nigel and some brother
officers then stopped to speak to his mother, who was taking
the air more sedately in her carriage. "You're up betimes
for someone who just survived her first ball," she greeted
Cassie warmly. "I'm only sorry you were subjected to so
many poisonous partners. I shall instruct Nigel to keep an
eagle eye on you." Under no illusions about her offspring,
she added, "He doesn't like dancing above half, but he must
learn and he'd as lief have you as a partner as anyone else.
Girls who simper alarm him intensely and he's likely to tread
on their toes or, worse yet, their gowns. And his brother
officers, though they are rather more ill at ease on the dance
floor than they are in the saddle, can be relied upon to make
pleasant enough partners. At any rate, they are not likely
to try to lead you into some secluded alcove as I'll be bound
young Weatherby would have." She smiled in sympathy at
Cassie's involuntary shudder of revulsion. "Exactly, my

dear. He's a nasty character, make no mistake. You did well to keep him at arm's length.''

Bidding adieu to Lady Streatham, they drove toward Hanover Square, Mainwaring deftly maneuvering among the crush of carriages. The comte was delighted to see them. *''Ma cheré* Fanny *et ma très chère* Cassie, *comme je suis enchanté de vous voir,''* he exclaimed, bending over their hands. ''But come, I am eager to have you see my work and the proof of the most pressing need I have for the assistance of my brilliant Cassandra.'' He led them to a library littered with books and papers, the odd fragment of a frieze or statue scattered here and there among them.

A young man rose to greet them as they entered. ''Ah, I must introduce you to my other assistant. Horace here has had the great good sense to resist all his family's attempts to provide him with a military career. He had decided to become a classicist instead. I have told him that from my experience I find it to be a far more rewarding and undoubtedly a safer form of existence since I should certainly have been one of Madame Guillotine's first lovers had I not been more enamored of the glories of Athens. Lady Mainwaring and Lady Cassandra Cresswell, may I present the Honorable Horace Wilbraham.''

Cassie found herself liking the square-jawed serious face and steady gray eyes of the young man who took her hand. Her heart was further won by his next words. ''I have been longing to meet the daughters of so noted a scholar as your father. I have read everything Lord Charles Cresswell ever wrote and I am a fervent admirer of his. How I envy your upbringing,'' he concluded with a wistful note that Cassie found somehow quite touching.

''The Earl of Amberly is undoubtedly a man of excellent principles, but he does not understand a son who prefers books to sport,'' the comte explained. ''Horace, show Cassie what we have been doing while I inveigle news of that young rapscallion brother of hers out of Fanny.''

Horace led Cassie over to a pile of papers at which he had

been working. "We are describing everything Lord Elgin brought over. It is a monumental task, but so rewarding. You, who have been there, cannot imagine the feeling it gives me to be able to touch the past and to try to capture the magnificence of these marbles in words so that others may share them. We hope to be able to publish a catalog which will be of inestimable value to scholars everywhere."

Here, the comte interrupted scornfully, "Yes, Fosbroke claims that his *Encyclopaedia of Antiquities, and Elements of Archaeology, Classical and Medieval* is the first of its kind, but it is a mere compendium. We intend to produce a work of much greater detail and thus of far greater use to scholars than his desultory attempt."

"Ours is a truly enormous enterprise," Horace continued enthusiastically, "and having someone such as you to assist us will be the greatest help imaginable. The comte speaks very highly of your accomplishments, Lady Cassandra." Horace's eagerness was infectious and Cassie found herself warming to this earnest young scholar, so different from anyone else she knew—except, of course, for Ned, but Ned was special.

"Do call me Cassie, please," she begged, smiling at him. "And do show me how you have been proceeding. Papa would be so pleased to see that his work was being carried on so carefully by such authorities."

The next two hours flew by as Horace and the comte explained what they had done, what they hoped to accomplish, and the process they had been through thus far. Cassie found herself relaxing and entering into the conversation in a way she had not since the departure of Ned and Freddie. Indeed, Horace was as learned as Ned and certainly far less argumentative—a point which stood greatly in his favor. The awe in which he held Lord Charles seemed to extend to all the Cresswells and the admiration in his eyes as he listened to Cassie was balm to her lonely spirit. They discussed not only the cataloguing of Lord Elgin's marbles, but the new edition of *Tacquot's Latin Scholar's Guide* and various translations of Homer, though they both agreed that Chapman's remained the best.

"It is wonderful to find a lady who thinks of something beyond the latest drawings in Ackermann's *Repository* or *La Belle Assemblée*. In general, I have no conversation. I never seem to find anything to say at the routs and balls my mother insists I escort her to. My presence never adds anything and it continually reminds her what a disappointment I am to them," he confided.

Cassie snorted. "You must find it equally difficult to converse with men as well because I find that if they have anything in their heads beyond sport, it has to do with the set of their coats or the intricacies of their cravats. It would be amusing if one were allowed merely to remain in the background observing, but no one allows one to do that." She sighed audibly.

Horace nodded. "Very true," he agreed. "Though I admit to being a mere observer at Lady Delamere's rout. I saw you there and thought how very elegant you looked without all the fussy frills and silly gewgaws that most women seem to need to wear to lend themselves consequence."

At this Cassie turned quite pink with pleasure. She was not a stranger to flattery, but this speech was delivered with such ingenuousness that she felt truly complimented. "Why thank you. It is wonderful to be recognized as an individual in such a situation when one is ordinarily judged by one's social address or position."

"I know. I realize that I am more often the second son of the Earl of Amberly at these affairs than I am Horace Wilbraham, scholar, though I suppose it makes little difference because most people would rather know the former than the latter," Horace concluded somewhat gloomily.

"I find Horace Wilbraham infinitely preferable to and far more interesting than the second son of the Earl of Amberly," Cassie declared stoutly.

"How kind you are," Horace thanked her, smiling gratefully.

"And have you two decided how you would like to divide up your work? I have more than enough for the three of us, and if we ever finish with Lord Elgin's collection, we should do the same with the Towneley Marbles and the sculptures from Bassae," the comte remarked as he and Lady Frances strolled over to the window where Cassie and Horace were sitting.

"Come, Cassie. John should be here shortly. I instructed him to call for us before nuncheon. I daren't leave Teddy, Ethelred, Wellington, and Nelson alone together for too long a stretch. Cook and Nurse are worth their weights in gold, but neither one of them has the strength of character to resist the blandishments of those four," remarked Frances as she pulled on her lemon kid gloves.

Cassie agreed ruefully. "Nor the resourcefulness or strength of character to rescue them from the scrapes they are likely to fall into."

The butler came in to announce the arrival of the ladies' carriage, and after arranging to come the next day and gratefully accepting Horace's invitation to escort them to a concert at the Academy of Ancient Music, they departed, well satisfied with the morning's outing.

Lady Frances, sneaking a glance at her sister's profile, was pleased to see a happier look than had been on her face for some time, but refrained from any comment. She was correct in her observations. Cassie was delighted. After having endured so many dull and pointless conversations she had found it refreshing and revitalizing to share her deepest interests with someone who could appreciate them. She looked forward with pleasure to the next evening and to the days ahead, which no longer seemed to stretch emptily and endlessly before her.

CHAPTER 6

Cassie's expectations were not disappointed. She truly enjoyed the concert, but what made it even more delightful was having Horace there. He was so attentive to her slightest wish, making certain she was comfortably placed in the most advantageous seat possible. Occasionally during the performance she caught him glancing at her to reassure himself that she was enjoying herself to the utmost. No one, except Ned, had ever paid such attention to her wishes or had seemed to be so concerned for her happiness. She felt immensely touched and flattered by such thoughtfulness, particularly since it provided such a marked contrast to the treatment she had received at the hands of her dancing partners at Lady Delamere's rout. It heightened her enjoyment that much more when in the carriage on the way home he inquired in an endearingly diffident way, "I do hope the concert pleased you?"

"Oh, yes. It was entirely delightful. I do so love music, but I have had little chance to hear anything but ill-rendered pianoforte recitals performed more for the opportunity they afford to demonstrate that the performer would make someone a delightful and accomplished companion than for the sake of the music. Thank you ever so much," she replied gratefully.

He laughed. "You are too critical, Cassandra. That poor young woman undoubtedly has nothing else to show for herself, but I, too, have endured too many similar tedious evenings to be much in sympathy with the performers. It is one of the true delights of the Town to be able to hear pieces as they should be played. I attend many such evenings. They give me such a great deal of pleasure that I am afraid I must admit them to be one of my true vices. My parents often accuse me of neglecting my social responsibilities for such evenings of self-indulgence. I hope I shall be able to convince you to join me again. But what did you think of the Handel?''

''I especially delighted in that. One rarely gets an opportunity to hear it so well performed. But here we are. Thank you so much. I enjoyed myself tremendously.'' Cassie had been so engrossed in their discussion that she was astounded to find the carriage had come to a stop and the footman was waiting patiently to hand her down.

Not all evenings could be as certain to appeal to Cassie as the one with Horace. Certainly she looked forward to her first appearance at Almack's with a notable lack of enthusiasm. ''It is certainly less elegant than any other gathering you'll be asked to attend,'' Frances warned. ''It makes up in the selectness of its elected guests what it lacks in amenities. Truly, the entire experience is a study in the pretensions of anyone with social aspirations. If the tastes of its patronesses were not so omnipotent, it would be a dead bore. But their social hegemony so governs the imagination of the *ton* that it becomes extraordinarily amusing to see how people allow themselves to be affected by entry to its hallowed portals and the whims of those who rule it. Those who dominate in the political or military arenas become putty in their hands and are properly subservient. The Iron Duke himself was sent home to change into proper attire before being allowed admittance and he submitted without a word of protest.''

Cassie looked doubtful. ''I don't see the slightest need to make a push for the approval of such people. After all, I don't intend to spend my life in the *ton*, so its opinion matters very little to me.''

''That's as may be,'' Frances agreed. ''But the patron-esses' approval can do you no harm and their sanction allows you the opportunity to appear at any social function you should wish, thus giving you the liberty of selecting whomever you will as social companions. And besides, such acceptance becomes a social cachet to your own special activities and interests, which might otherwise not be found to be socially acceptable.''

Begrudgingly Cassie acknowledged the wisdom of her elder sister's views. Personally, she would have preferred to do without such ceremony, but she was realistic enough to be aware that such social recognition could smooth her way in other areas more dear to her heart. So, with as much enthusiasm as she could muster, she instructed Rose to select her the approved raiment of a young lady in her first Season—a white muslin gown with cerulean blue trimming— and allowed her to dress her hair in the simplest of styles with a matching wreath of blue flowers.

The rooms were already crowded when they arrived, and the Mainwarings were immediately hailed by several acquaintances as they made their way through the crush. Lord Mainwaring's political crony Lord Charlton, looking most uncomfortable and out of place, hovered awkwardly near a capable-looking woman conversing animatedly with Princess Esterhazy and a blushing young damsel who seemed on the verge of expiring at being recognized by such an august personage. ''Ah, Julian''—he greeted Lord Mainwaring with the eagerness of a drowning man seizing a buoyant object— ''have you seen Canning lately? I know you and Castlereagh were as thick as thieves in Vienna, but mark my words, George Canning is your man for the moment. With your views on our financial situation, I should think you and he should rub along happily together.'' He drew Julian aside, leaving Frances and Cassie to shift for themselves, a situation which was soon remedied by the appearance of the Streathams.

Nigel was the picture of discomfort as he towered over his vivacious mother. Cassie, correctly interpreting the emotions at war within him—a desire to please his mother by partnering Cassie and his loathing for the dance floor— burst out laughing. He reddened self-consciously. ''Relax, Nigel,'' she reassured him. ''I shall be more than happy if you procure me a glass of that dreadful lemonade and then share your latest adventures with me.''

Relieved, Nigel practically stumbled over himself in his eagerness to cater to her wishes. They spent the next half hour exchanging reminiscences and ignoring the quizzical glances sent their way by the inveterate matchmakers who frequented the place.

Their *tête-à-tête* was brought to an end by Nigel's exasperated mother, who turned from observing the dance floor to exclaim, ''Really, Nigel, it's too bad in you. Cassie will never lack for partners. You must stop monopolizing her and ask Amanda Billingsley to dance. She's such a dab of a girl, no one will notice her unless someone makes an effort. Off with you. There's a good boy.'' A firm hand in the small of his back accompanied these words. Nigel rose dutifully and lumbered over to the corner where Miss Billingsley, keeping close to her mama, was timidly observing the scene.

Once Nigel had departed, Cassie found herself approached by several young gallants eager to discover all they could about one of the Season's more attractive new faces. She conversed dutifully with them, but her mind was on a thousand other things—the latest piece of work she was doing for the comte, a scratch on her horse's fetlock which seemed to be developing an infection—and all of her partners remained an indistinct blur to her. At last she was able to welcome a moment of respite between dances when she could stand quietly in the shadows and observe the throng around her. The lights and the crush of people made her yearn for the green fields of Hampshire and the exhilarating feelings of freshness and freedom as she galloped across them. How she longed for that solitude. In no time at all the moment of peace was interrupted by conversation behind her.

''My dear, you must tell me who that divine man is,'' drawled an affected voice.

''I have not the remotest idea, but he looks just like Byron's Corsair. Do let us stroll in that direction,'' replied her companion with a fashionable lisp easily identified as belonging to Arabella Taylor.

Try as she might, Cassie could not refrain from glancing toward the end of the room where something appeared to have attracted a throng of people. Involuntarily she found herself drawn toward the center of the commotion, which she judged to be a tall dark-haired man whose broad-shouldered back was toward her. He was speaking to Lady Jersey, but as Cassie approached he turned toward the center of the room and she found herself looking at a tanned hawklike face whose swarthiness was rendered even more striking by the dark blue eyes under black brows. Their gaze alighted on Cassie and a singularly attractive smile erased the cynical lines around the well-shaped mouth and softened his somewhat sardonic expression. "Cassie," he exclaimed, holding out a hand.

Bereft of speech, Cassie extended hers, wondering how this stranger could possibly know her. The mystery was solved in an instant as another much beloved face appeared at the stranger's elbow. "Freddie, Ned," she shouted joyfully, gripping the hand that lifted hers to his lips.

One eyebrow lifted quizzically. "Am I that changed then, best of playmates?" Ned inquired in an amused voice.

"N-no, not exactly," stammered Cassie in an unusual state of confusion. But he was changed! True, the shock of dark hair that *would* fall over his forehead seemed in danger of doing so again despite his elegant crop. The eager, intelligent glance remained, but it was altered somehow by an ironic gleam that seemed to mock its owner as much as it did the company around him. The finely chiseled lips were firmer and less inclined to smile, while the lines at either side indicated that most of these smiles were more likely to result from derision than genuine amusement.

Ned, looking down at his companion, found a less physically noticeable but equally disconcerting transformation. The hair, done *à la couronne*, a style much admired by Horace, seemed too severe for the unruly curls he remembered. The teasing sparkle in the eyes had been replaced by a more serious, almost somber expression. Ned found himself wondering what could have happened to quench the rebellious spirit he remembered.

This mutual examination was broken by an exuberant Bertie Montgomery, who strode over exclaiming jubilantly as he wrung Freddie's hand, "Freddie, my boy!" He nodded in Ned's direction. "Wonderful to see you both. Quite the nabobs, I hear. London will be agog to learn of your exploits. Do let me be the first to hear 'em, as then I shall be lionized and shall be able to lord it over all the rest."

At that, the world, or at least the world of the *ton*, closed in around them. Lord Mainwaring shook their hands, wondering how they'd left everything in India. Lady Frances kissed Ned and clung to Freddie, remarking that since they were in evening attire, they must have been at Mainwaring House and wondering if Cook had given them anything to eat.

Freddie smiled fondly at his sister. "Lord, Fran, can you imagine my even bidding good day to Cook and not having some tasty morsel thrust upon me? In fact, Ned and I would have been here hours earlier if John Coachman hadn't fussed so over the horses, or if Higgins hadn't insisted on unearthing Mainwaring's best port." This last was said with an apologetic look toward his brother-in-law. "And Cook. Cook knew for certain that we'd been existing on 'that outlandish heathen fare' for so long that she insisted we have at least one good English meal inside us before we went gallivanting all over Town. So, you see, we have been a good deal delayed in paying our respects to you all." Freddie indicated the rest of the fashionable world, which had by now joined the crowd, with a breezy wave of his hand.

During this interchange, Lady Jersey, always alive to an attractive young man with an interesting background, had managed to wean Ned away to partner her in a waltz. And Horace, who had eschewed such useless social gatherings until he had met Cassie, suddenly noticed that the object of his attention was bereft of company and led her off into a quiet corner where they could discuss the merits of the translation of Euripides which had just appeared in Acker-mann's *Repository*.

Cassie was naturally delighted to see Horace, but despite her consuming interest in the topic, she discovered she could not keep her mind on it. Try though she would to concentrate on Horace's eloquent and admirable defense of someone whose works he had heard Cassie criticize severely, she found her eyes wandering to the center of the room, where Ned, a teasing smile on his lips, was bending over Lady Jersey, apparently enthralled by the latest on-dits that "Silence" was recounting in her own inimitable fashion. Where had the shy and self-effacing Ned acquired such an assured and positively flirtatious manner? That aside, where had those broad shoulders and the confident manner come from? Struggling to analyze the transformation, Cassie could barely muster the monosyllables to answer Horace. "Very true," or "Of course," or "Without a doubt," she rejoined at appropriate moments, trying to nod sagely, while the entire time her mind was in a whirl.

Cassie was not the only one to be taken aback at the changes in the two travelers. Limpetlike, Arabella Taylor clung to Freddie Cresswell's arm as he strode over to claim his sister as a partner. "Oh, Freddie, you're so very grown up!" she cooed. "What exotic scenes you and Ned must have encountered! Why, I should never have recognized either one of you if you hadn't appeared together and sought out the Mainwarings. You're both so brown! I expect that dealing with all those heathens has made men out of both of you." She sighed audibly. "I am so tired of the same old beaux one finds in Town. All they think about is their tailors. There is not a true man to be found among them. I grant you I have been paid some very pretty compliments by leaders of the *ton*"—here she blushed becomingly and lowered her eyes. "But one becomes bored with such trifles and longs to meet someone who is a man of strength and a leader in society instead of a mere hanger-on."

Her eyes followed Ned as he restored a laughing Lady Jersey to her coterie. Freddie and Arabella were just close enough to hear her as she tapped his cheek with her fan, scolding him coquettishly, "Naughty boy. Your travels have taught you wicked ways. You must take me for a drive in the park and tell me more."

"And," pursued Arabella, keeping a close eye on Ned as he leaned over to respond to Lady Jersey's latest sally, "I've heard you have both become disgustingly plump in the pocket, veritable Golden Balls, if ballroom gossip is to be believed."

"Don't believe a word of it, Bella," admonished Freddie, trying desperately to pry himself loose from her clutches. "You know what the town tabbies are." He at last succeeded in pulling away from her to join his sister, whom he greeted with visible relief. "Cassie, at last! Will you grant a poor fellow, desperate for intelligent female companionship of any sort, even if it is his sister's, this dance?"

Cassie laughed. "Of course, Freddie, with all the pleasure in the world." The two strolled off, leaving Arabella and Horace to deal with each other as best they could.

CHAPTER 7

It would have been a gross exaggeration to say that all of London was intrigued by the reappearance of the two travelers, but their return certainly formed the main topic of conversation the next day in several select drawing rooms. The floor of one of these in particular was littered with exotic trifles as Freddie distributed acquisitions from his travels to his nearest and dearest. "Freddie, how lovely! You are rigging me out in the latest fashion whether I will or no," exclaimed Cassie, surveying the effect of a cashmere shawl draped artistically over her shoulders while Frances slid numerous delicate gold bracelets onto her wrist. Theodore, totally entranced by a set of elephants and their mahouts beautifully carved in ivory, was arranging them on the floor before an interested audience. Nelson, Wellington, and Ethelred were divided in their opinions—Nelson wishing to bat the pieces around on the carpet, Wellington feeling it would be more amusing to chew them, while Ethelred, unready as usual, sat regarding them suspiciously with beady black eyes.

Lord Mainwaring was ensconced in a chair by the fire reviewing the reports Freddie had brought back. Agreeably surprised by the thoroughness of the observation and the degree of detail with which they were recorded, he remarked, "Well done, Freddie. Your recommendations about replacing the *banyans*, who can charge what they will for their services as brokers of goods to unsuspecting foreigners, with knowledgeable Englishmen is certainly well founded. I hope you will help me in effecting the change."

Freddie, accustomed to holding his formidable brother-in-law in some degree of awe, flushed with pleasure, replying modestly. "That's very kind of you, sir, but even the veriest neophyte can see how these men are able to take advantage of those unfamiliar with the commodities so as to charge whatever price they wish and exact whatever-percent commission they desire."

Cassie, beaming proudly at her brother, disagreed. "That's as may be, Freddie, and I daresay that's a common enough topic in the coffee rooms all over India, but your suggestion of setting up an exchange where such abuses can be remedied shows an active intelligence that is lacking in so many people who merely listen to hearsay and add their own complaints to the general conversation but do not bestir themselves to discover a solution."

Unused to such praise in a family whose talents usually outshone his, Freddie was visibly flattered but disclaimed any credit in his most offhand manner. "Oh it was nothing, Cassie. Any gudgeon could see what needed to be done."

Cassie refused to be convinced. "You are far too modest, Freddie, truly. You must make a push to ensure that your recommendations are heard." Privately she was relieved to hear how well her twin had conducted himself. Cassie had always had faith that he had more bottom and sense than his peers. Even though his talents had failed to assert themselves during his school years, she had remained certain that given the proper opportunity, Freddie would prove himself brighter and more steady than he was credited by most people, who were inclined to dismiss him as a lovable chap but sporting mad and devoted to nothing more serious than his stable.

This reverie was broken by Higgins, who announced, "Lady Taylor, Miss Arabella Taylor."

Cassie gave a start of surprise. Never intimate with Arabella in the country, she had not sought her out in the city, and had been annoyed at herself for being piqued at Arabella's failure to acknowledge her existence when their paths had crossed at various social functions. Wise enough in the ways of the world to recognize that Arabella never entered into friendships that did not profit her, Cassie perfectly understood that someone determined to be labeled an incomparable would rather die than admit a connection to a young woman who, to all intents and purposes, was a country nobody and content to remain exactly that. Furthermore, running an eye recently educated in the shops of Bond Street modistes over Arabella's walking dress of jaconet muslin under a richly worked open robe with a mulberry-colored spencer that showed off to perfection the flawless skin and dark eyes, Cassie was puzzled by the visit and the obvious care Arabella had lavished on her toilette. The plaited front of the gown enhanced a generous figure and the cornette of lace under her hat framed her face delightfully.

"La, Cassandra, you are looking vastly elegant, I am sure," Arabella declared, tripping across the room. Modifying this uncharacteristically generous praise, she continued, "I vow I wouldn't have recognized you at all."

A casual observer might have been pardoned for being confused over the intended recipient of this speech as Arabella, ostensibly addressing Cassie, never looked in her direction but smiled and dimpled at Freddie instead the entire time she was speaking.

"You must think I showed a sad lack of conduct in not calling on you directly you arrived in Town. I am sure I meant to call times out of mind, but one has so many engagements, so many pressing social obligations . . ." She trailed off, hoping to be asked to elaborate on these.

Cassie, who found more to comment on in this sudden appearance than in her neglect, was cudgeling her brains for an explanation for this sudden solicitude and wondering how best to discover the reason for the visit in order to bring it to a close as expeditiously as possible. Town bronze, in her opinion, had done nothing to improve the dubious charms of Hampshire's reigning belle. "Do not refine too much on it, Arabella. Having been about a bit, I can see that someone as sought after as you must have many more urgent engagements," Cassie replied, adopting what she hoped was an interested enough tone of voice to encourage Arabella to state the purpose of her visit.

However, Arabella was not to be led. Her eyes surveying the room, she disposed herself elegantly upon a chair and smiled intimately at Freddie, remarking, "What a stir you and Ned caused at Almack's! Everyone has a different story to explain how you made your fortunes and what you plan to do to dazzle us with your wealth. Do tell me all your adventures. I feel certain you and he outshone everyone there. You certainly did last evening—both of you brown as natives and looking as though you had a hundred hair-raising tales to relate. Do tell me." She looked up expectantly, her whole being expressive of eager anticipation—an attitude that had won the hearts of numerous swains happy to recount the least little exploit to such a charming listener.

Freddie had known Arabella too long to be overwhelmed by the thought of so much charm and beauty waiting breathlessly to hang on his every word. Like his sister, he was extremely curious as to what really lay behind the unexpected call. Whatever it was, it had not been accomplished, because Arabella's eyes never left off their restless inspection of the room. In the midst of a truly gripping account of stalking a man-eating tiger, he became aware that her wandering attention was occupied elsewhere. "And so, the mahout and I climbed down from the elephant and I was able to dispatch the wounded tiger with a bullet between the eyes," Freddie concluded.

"Very interesting. I am sure you did yourself proud," Arabella replied vaguely with a notable lack of enthusiasm. "Was Ned with you? I vow he is vastly changed since I saw him last. I overheard Lady Jersey telling Countess Lieven that he left a trail of broken hearts in India and Europe. Such a man of the world is sure to cast the other pinks of the *ton* into the shade, such dull lives as they lead. Did you say he stays with his sister?"

At last Freddie understood the impetus behind the visit and was highly amused by it.

Cassie, on the other hand, was incensed. She could barely keep from ringing a peal over their visitor and was debating the wisdom of depressing their visitor's ill-concealed interest in Ned with a sharp retort when the object of all this interest himself was announced.

Ned Mainwaring in riding clothes was even more arresting than Ned Mainwaring in evening attire. The exquisite cut of his coat showed off his broad shoulders to advantage and the close-fitting breeches emphasized the powerful long legs that made him tower over other men. This height, which had made him a gangly and somewhat self-conscious youth, now gave him an air of command, which was further accentuated by his piercing blue eyes and resolute jaw.

"Hello, sir," he greeted Julian, extending a lean tanned hand to his former guardian and mentor.

"Ned, my lad. It's wonderful to see you. I hope you have come to enlighten us on the true state of things behind the undoubtedly highly embellished tales with which Freddie has been regaling us," Lord Mainwaring greeted his nephew with quizzically raised brows.

Ned barely had the opportunity to shake his hand and bend over Lady Frances's before Arabella pounced.

"Ned! How delightful to have you back. We've missed you this age. London has been sadly flat," she declared as she swept gracefully across the room, extending a hand and smiling at him in such a way that he received the full effect of charming dimples and pearly teeth.

Behind Cassie, Freddie, who was enjoying the scene hugely, snorted, "What a bouncer!"

And Cassie, unable to contain herself, gasped, "Why she never paid the least mind to him in Hampshire, let alone London!"

The subject of all this attention appeared unaware of it as he smiled broadly down at Arabella. "Arabella, you are as exquisite as I remember you. Though absent from London's salons, I have nevertheless heard news that you have taken the *ton* by storm."

If Freddie had snorted before, he fairly gagged now. Ned

was the best of good fellows and someone you could count on in the most desperate of situations, but this was doing it much too brown.

Cassie, too, was taken aback. How could Ned, her simple, direct, awkward Ned, speak such fustian?

Arabella, who did not share the twins' critical point of view, scolded him archly as he bent over her hand. "Flatterer. You know you never gave a rap about the latest on-dits."

Ned raised a mobile eyebrow, rejoining, "You will not let me forget the gaucheries of my past, I see, but where the on-dits concern you, I assure you, I listened very carefully."

This bantering exchange could have continued for some time, delighting some and boring others, if Lady Taylor had not recalled with a start their appointment with the dressmaker. "Arabella, come my dear, we must be off," she announced, rising majestically. "Lady Frances, I shall be sending cards for an affair we're having—nothing elaborate, you understand—just a pleasant evening with a card party for us and some dancing for the young people."

Cassie, who could barely keep her own lip from quivering at the thought of Frances and Lord Mainwaring relegated to the card room with the likes of Sir Lucius and Lady Taylor, wondered how her sister was able to keep her countenance. A surreptitious glance over her shoulder at her twin revealed that Freddie, quietly convulsed behind her, was even less successful than she at containing his mirth.

Arabella did not look best pleased to have her *tête-à-tête* interrupted, but she recovered quickly and followed her mother to the door. Just as Higgins was preparing to usher the ladies to their carriage she stopped and, as if struck by a sudden thought, exclaimed, "Ned, why do you not accompany us? Our appointment is not so pressing that we may not take a turn around the park before consigning ourselves to an afternoon with Madame Celestine."

If Ned was somewhat taken aback at being invited to leave directly he had arrived, he did not exhibit the least sign of discomposure. Instead he assisted each of the ladies into the carriage, remarking, "It has been so long since I have been in such a salubrious climate that I welcome every opportunity to enjoy it, especially in the company of two such charming companions."

Arabella simpered complacently and even her mother's somewhat wooden countenance relaxed into the semblance of a smile.

Those left behind in the drawing room were left to react as they would to Arabella's stratagems. "Well, of all the impudent . . ." Cassie sputtered. "She never gave Ned the slightest opportunity to speak for himself."

"Arf," agreed Wellington, whose own nose had been put slightly out of joint because his old friend had been so occupied by that fussy Arabella who had never liked dogs that he had not even acknowledged Wellington's furiously wagging tail and smile of greeting. "I should have barked to get his attention," he confided to Nelson. "But that would have displeased Frances." With a gusty sigh he dropped his nose between his paws and stared into the fire.

"Don't refine upon it too much, Cass," admonished Freddie. "He didn't seem to be the least put out."

"His wits must have gone begging then," Cassie snapped as she went to collect her bonnet and pelisse before seeking the more rational companionship of Horace and the comte.

CHAPTER *8*

Cassie's spirits, which had been somewhat dampened by the alacrity with which Ned had gone off with Arabella, were restored by the warmth of her reception in Hanover Square.

"*Ma cherè* Cassie, how happy we are to see you!" exclaimed the comte as his general factotum, the lugubrious Jacques, ushered her into the study. "We have been arguing . . . no, discussing, the theme represented on this frieze. I believe it it be a procession from the celebration of the Panathenaea, but Horace here has his doubts."

Picking her way carefully among the bits of frieze here, a torso there, Cassie made her way slowly to the one clear patch of floor that the comte and Horace had left for themselves. Horace, who had been frowning in concentration over a section of frieze, looked up as she approached, remarking, "I don't believe it could be the Panathenaea because nowhere is there any representation of the olive wood figure of Athena which was essential to the ceremony. Furthermore, there are too many male figures for it to be the procession."

Cassie studied the figures, stepping first to one side and then the other and moving away from it as far back as the clutter would allow. For some time she remained deep in thought, her eyes fixed on the figure of a child handing something to an adult. Horace, glancing surreptitiously at her face, thought the way she bit her lip in concentration infinitely more charming than all the dimpled smiles and simpers cast his way at the various social affairs his mother had forced him to attend. He was far more attracted to her in her total absorption in the frieze than he had ever been

to any woman, even those who had lavished their most
seductive attentions on him. Here was someone as oblivious
as he to the rest of the world, someone who was not only
as uninterested as he was in the vagaries of fashion or the
latest on-dits, but whose concentration was fixed on the same
concerns as his. In all his years of study he had only found
one person who shared his passiojn for antiquity—the Comte
de Vaudron. For Horace, misunderstood by his family and
ignored by his peers, this friendship had provided the most
rewarding companionship he had ever known. Now here was
someone his own age who, in addition to understanding his
enthusiasm, entered into it as wholeheartedly as he. To
Horace such a state of affairs was nothing short of a miracle
and he regarded Cassie with a mixture of reverence and awe
that he had never felt before in his life.

"Ah, yes." Cassie's brows cleared and she replied, "I
regret that I agree with the comte, Horace. Surely this figure
is that of a girl handing the new *peplos,* woven to cover the
image of Athena, to a magistrate. I am sorry to disagree with
you." Here Cassie flashed such a charming, apologetic smile
at the young man sitting at her feet that it quite took his breath
away. The admiration he'd felt toward a revered scholar's
daughter suddenly metamorphosed into something more
potent, and for the first time he was fully aware of Cassandra
as a beautiful, vital woman. He sat stunned by the intensity
of these new emotions.

Meanwhile, Cassie, oblivious to the powerful effect she
was having, turned to the comte for confirmation of her
theory as she speculated, "It is true that the figure could be
either male or female, but the form looks to be more
feminine, don't you think?"

The comte smiled at his protégé. "I had not previously
thought of that as being the *peplos,* but that is an excellent
interpretation. I quite agree with you *ma chère.*" He was
looking at Cassie as he answered, but as his glance fell on
Horace, transfixed by his private revelations, the smile
deepened to one of amused contemplation. Aha, we have here
the beginning of a passion for something other than the dust

of antiquity, he muttered silently to himself. Such a situation will bear some watching.

Cassie took up a pen, looking expectantly at the comte. "How would you wish this described in the catalog, then?"

He waved a hand toward the manuscript of the catalog, responding airily, "Oh, I absolutely leave it to you, *ma chère,* as your reasoning behind your attribution of it as the Panathenaic procession has far more merit than our humble interpretations. Write what you wish." Turning to Horace with an impish twinkle, he remarked, "This Cassie is a scholar, *non*? I warned you she would put us on our mettle." A blank look was all the response he elicited, so he continued, "We must not get on our high ropes merely because she arrives and answers in a few minutes the question that has been dominating our discussion the entire morning, *hein*?"

"Yeeeeeees," Horace responded vaguely as he slowly returned to reality. He continued in a more punctilious tone, "But surely we should discuss this with others who are equally well read in these matters. It would be most disadvantageous to put forth such an interpretation without having consulted many more sources and explored every avenue of thought in a work that is to serve as a guide for future generations."

"Relax, *mon brave,*" adjured the comte. "Who is more well informed than we? Who has spent more time with these *chefs d'oeuvres* than we? Remember"—he held up a cautionary hand—"the best, most judicious interpretations are those that mingle instinct with learning, and emotion with intellect. Cassandra and I looked at the figure presenting the object and both of us instinctively *felt* it was a girl. This then led us to the more refined and rational conclusion that it was a *peplos* that was being offered. You, on the other hand, looked at the procession and, applying only your knowledge, assumed the procession to be dominantly male and therefore could not explain the reason for such a procession or interpret the identity of the object. This is not to say, of course, that ours is necessarily the correct interpretation,'' he continued fair-mindedly, ''but our trust in our immediate responses gave us perhaps a richer interpretation.''

He laid a reassuring hand on the young man's shoulder, adding, ''I can see you are disturbed. Do not distress yourself, *mon ami*. To cultivate the mind is all very well, but one must not do so at the expense of the other faculties. I think now we require some refreshment, *non*?'' After ringing unsuccessfully for Jacques, the comte strolled off in search of him while Horace, prey to a variety of conflicting emotions, turned to stare out the window.

He was not the only one staring vacantly at the gardens outside the library. Cassie, who had been scribbling furiously at the onset of their discussion, had written progressively more slowly as unwelcome thoughts from earlier in the day returned. At first at a loss to explain her general malaise, she began to examine her feelings more closely and realized, much to her surprise, that she felt betrayed. She should have been glad that Arabella, who had so callously spurned someone as fine as Ned, should now be so eager to capture his attention. And you *are* glad, she admonished herself severely. He deserves, he always deserved, admiration. But how can he be taken in by such an about-face? she wondered. Surely he must see that she only wants his attention because he is the *ton*'s latest sensation. Can't he see that she is constant only as long as friendship brings social distinction? How can he not be disgusted by a nature that is only interested in someone who will lend social cachet to her.

But Ned had not only been disgusted, he had actually looked at Arabella with admiration. That was where the sense of betrayal arose. It came from the fact that someone as intelligent and sensitive as Ned, who had been her constant intellectual companion and ally at countless dull engagements, now seemed as taken in as all the rest by a beautiful countenance, a coquettish manner, and a frivolous mind. Did he value his own mind and interests so little that he would forgo them for the dubious excitement of a flirtation with a pretty ninnyhammer? His pursuit of Arabella seemed to be a rejection of all they had once appreciated and shared. Not only was Cassie genuinely puzzled by his fascination with someone whose existence was so antithetical to his former interests, she felt horribly alone—abandoned in some respects—by someone she had counted on above everyone else for understanding and sympathy.

So lost in thought was she that she did not hear Horace approach, nor did she hear his tenative, "Cassandra?" He tried again, a little more loudly this time.

Cassie came to with a start. "Oh, I do beg your pardon. I'm dreadfully sorry, Horace. I didn't hear you. I was wool-gathering, I'm afraid," she apologized.

Horace, still coping with his newfound appreciation of her, had crossed the room to invite her to Mr. Glover's recently opened exhibition of oils and watercolors in Bond Street, but the words died on his lips as she turned to apologize to him. The bright light streaming from the window behind her turned her hair to a golden halo framing a face whose half-amused, half-rueful expression at having been so distracted coupled with the remorse at having ignored him made her seem all at once so beautiful and so dear that he was overwhelmed with tenderness. Horace was ordinarily the most punctilious and reserved of men, but before he could stop himself, he had seized her inky hand and pressed it reverently to his lips.

Cassie was stunned. Though she had eschewed much of society and the attendant opportunities for flirtation, she had received her share of compliments. Ordinarily she dismissed such admiration as purely groundless flattery, but Horace had shaken her. The intensity of the genuine admiration she read in his eyes and the fervor with which he devoured her hand with kisses were something she had never before experienced. It was a novel and disturbing sensation to be the object of such attention. Her knees felt weak and she found it difficult to catch her breath.

Horace was the first to recall himself to his surroundings. Flushing a deep scarlet, he gasped, "Please forgive me . . .

I never meant to . . . I wouldn't for the world cause you distress. I can't think how I came to forget myself. It is just that I admire you so greatly, Lady Cassandra, and you looked so beautiful . . .'' He blushed even more deeply, if such a thing were possible, and stumbled on, ''I apologize for allowing my feelings to run away with me and subjecting you to such a vulgar display.''

Cassie, once she had a chance to recover from the shock of it all, found herself wishing he would stop disavowing his actions. The idea of being truly admired by one whose mind was generally occupied by higher things was an appealing one and she found it most intriguing to be the subject of such passionate protests from a young man who, if the comte and others were to be believed, had hitherto had no thoughts for anything but his work.

Fortunately for both Cassie and Horace, struggling in the grip of new and strangely intense emotions, the comte and Jacques returned, bringing welcome distraction. Tea was set out and the bustle of serving allowed them time to recover their equanimity, but not before the shrewd eyes of the comte had taken in the entire scene and reconstructed with amazing accuracy the events that must have led up to it. So, the little Cassie is becoming a woman, he thought to himself. *Bon.* It will do her a great deal of good to be distracted from her books. Perhaps she will begin to be a little more pleasure seeking, and Horace, too. He smiled in satisfaction as he accepted a cup of tea from Jacques.

CHAPTER 9

Ned astride Brutus, a high-spirited bay that was the envy of all those who had seen him purchase it at Tattersall's immediately upon his return, was savoring the pleasure of accompanying the Taylor ladies through the park on such a fine day. The flowers were in full bloom, the air was newly washed from an early-morning shower, and the whole world seemed lush and filled with promise. Once again Ned was struck, as he had been so many times since his return, with how fresh and green it all looked. He reveled in it and all the wonderful smells of England in the spring, which, after the heat and dust of India, made it seem an even more wonderful season than it had before his departure.

"La, Ned, your wits are wandering a thousand miles away, I do believe." Arabella's liquid laughter broke into his reverie.

He glanced down at the face whose mischievous, teasing look only added to its charm.

"People will certainly wonder that I am unable to keep the attention of my old playmate for even a short drive in the park. What a lowering thought. I shall very likely go into a decline if you don't tell me immediately all your adventures. They are certain to be vastly amusing and far more interesting than the same tired *on-dits* the tulips of the *ton* trot out again and again in an effort to keep us all entertained. It must have been all so very different from anything here that I hardly know where to ask you to begin. Where did you live? Did you have armies of servants to cater to your every whim? Do the Hindu wives truly throw

68

themselves on their husbands' funeral pryes as we have heard? What a dreadful thought." She shuddered artistically.

"Stop, stop," Ned protested, somewhat taken aback by the barrage of questions. However, he reflected cynically, he ought to be enjoying this. Previously, Arabella had never shown the least sign of interest in any of the many more valuable topics of conversation he could have discussed at length, but now that he had something exotic to offer, some information which, if repeated, could set her apart from the *ton* and cause a stir, she was agog with interest. Still, Ned was not inhuman and the idea of a beautiful, sought-after woman demanding his attention and hanging on his every word would have won the heart of the most hardened of men, much less one who had spent more hot nights than he cared to remember recalling every feature of her lovely face, every charming little gesture, and dreaming of just such moments as this. So he began by recounting the voyage out, describing their slow progress around the cape with occasional stops at exotic ports, his eccentric shipmates, and his final arrival in Calcutta, where he had immediately been plunged into a world whose multitudinous, colorful population, bright hot sun, and pungent foreign smells had threatened to overwhelm him.

Arabella's eyes grew rounder and rounder as he painted a vivid picture of teeming bazaars crowded with vendors of every sort, and he found himself enjoying her rapt attention as he brought to life ponderous bullocks with their painted horns pulling rudely constructed carts, temple processions bearing flower-bedecked statues, and women dressed in flowing saris balancing unwieldy bundles on their heads.

"You must be exceedingly adventurous to visit such a place. How ever did you go on, surrounded as you were by so many strange people? No doubt they thought you some god," Arabella exclaimed.

Ned explained that the longer he remained, the better he understood their customs and the better he was able to function and accomplish what he had set himself to do. He could see that as soon as he began to discuss his research into the customs of the country and the mentality of its inhabitants with a view to comprehending them, her eyes glazed over and she lost interest.

"Oh, there is Sir Brian Brandon waving at us. We must stop, Ned. He is truly one of the leaders of the *ton* and I do so want you to meet him. He is a special friend of mine," she confided in an undertone as a handsome Corinthian on a powerful gray approached them.

Ned, who had his own ideas about whose social advancement would be furthered by such an encounter, allowed himself to be introduced. Nevertheless, if he, as the latest sensation, could make Arabella happy by dancing attendance on her and adding to her consequence, it amused him to do so.

"Arabella, my dear, you look more lovely every day," observed Sir Brian as he leaned down to kiss the dainty hand that was extended to him. "Lady Taylor," he acknowledged Arabella's mother briefly before returning his attention to her daughter who was urging Ned forward.

"Sir Brian, you may have heard of my very dear friend Ned Mainwaring, who was just returned from a sojourn in India where he conducted himself with great distinction." Arabella spoke as though entirely familiar with the events which had conferred fame and fortune upon Ned and Freddie and she presented him with the air of one solely responsible for the discovery and introduction of such an exciting person to society.

Not best pleased to be so quickly claimed as Arabella's exclusive property, Ned extended his hand with a distinct air of hauteur.

"Another of Arabella's famous protégés," Sir Brian inquired as he surveyed Ned with rueful sympathy. "I heard Crockford speaking of your exploits at the club last evening. It seems you and young Cresswell were involved in some extremely delicate negotiations. You must have had the upper hand in the affair, as I find it extremely difficult to picture old Rough-and-Tumble Cresswell in the role of peacemaker.

I should be most interested in hearing the details," he invited, leading Ned a little apart from the others as he spoke.

Pleasantly surprised to find Arabella intimate with a man of obvious sense and interests beyond the petty concerns of the *ton,* Ned allowed himself to be drawn into conversation on the complexities of dealing with an Indian rajah.

Absorbed in their discussion, the two men rode on, oblivious to the person who had introduced them. Arabella, who had completely failed in her object of becoming the focus of attention of two gentlemen instead of one and thus engendering a spirit of rivalry between them, leaned back in the carriage. A distinct pout obscured her dimples and wrinkled her brow in a most unattractive manner. However, she had not been a toast of London for nothing, and squaring her shoulders, she urged the coachman to catch up to the two men. With a tinkling laugh she turned to her mother, saying, "I am certain you are in the right of it, Mama. Times out of mind you have warned me that once men begin talking about affairs, they become deaf and dumb to the world around them. Such a glorious day should not be wasted in a discussion of the tedious machinations of some foreign potentate. Ned, here is all of England waiting to welcome you home and you can talk of nothing but the dirt, dust, and heat you left behind. And you, Sir Brian, are dreadfully provoking to force him to recall all those uncomfortable things when there are ever so many other more cheerful topics to discuss," Arabella scolded the two men archly as she tapped Ned's hand playfully with the ivory point of her parasol.

Once she had succeeded in attracting their attention, she unfurled this concoction so as to soften the unforgiving glare of the sun and cast a flattering pink light on her delicate features. Satisfied that she was presenting as delightful a picture as possible, she prattled on, dividing her dimpled smiles and silvery laugh equally between the two men, contriving in her own inimitable way to make each one feel that he alone was the focus of her attention. Juggling admiring

swains was an art to which Arabella had devoted a great deal
of effort until she was able to bring it off perfectly just as
she was doing now. Even her mother, who had spent years
studying the evolution of such a technique, found herself
constantly amazed at her daughter's ability to keep two men
completely engrossed.

By this time the little party had reached the edge of the
park and Sir Brian, who was being eagerly hailed by some
young bucks mounted on prime bits of blood, took his leave
after securing a waltz with Arabella at the Countess of
Wakefield's upcoming ball.

"I am so delighted you were able to meet him, Ned. If
he takes a liking to you, you are certain to move in the first
circles of fashion," Arabella remarked eagerly as she placed
a gloved hand on Ned's arm and rewarded him with her most
enchanting smile.

He raised one dark brow, demanding in an amused tone,
"And am I destined to move in the first circles of fashion?
I am not at all sure that I wish to."

A delicious little frown appeared as she pouted at him.
"Ned, you are quite dreadful. Of *course* you wish to. Don't
you want everyone to see how important you have become?
And surely you would want your childhood companions to
be proud of you."

Ned laughed. "When you put it so charmingly, how can
anyone resist you?"

Sure of herself now, the beauty spoke earnestly, "Ned,
you know you are destined to do great things. I feel certain
of it. But you must be seen as intimate with those who are
the leaders of the *ton* in order to succeed. I could see that
Sir Brian was most taken with you and he has the most
exacting standards."

Ned smiled down at her. "He must have if he chooses you
as an object of his attention."

"Your travels have taught you to be a dreadful flatterer,"
protested Arabella happily as she blushed and did her best
to look disconcerted.

She succeeded admirably. Ned had encountered coquettes

of every description on his travels and recognized a mistress of the art of flirtation. He was under no illusions as to Arabella's character, but he was forced to admit to himself that despite what must have been a great deal of practice, she still managed to look adorable. He grinned appreciatively, reined in his horse, dismounted, and tossed the reins to an eager young lad who was loitering near Madame Celestine's establishment for just such a purpose. He held out his hand to help her alight from the carriage, remarking as he did so, "I can see you are determined to advance my career. Very well, then, I resign myself into those dainty, but capable hands." He then kissed each one of them before turning to assist her mother.

Arabella was somewhat taken aback. She had always been confident of her ability to twist Ned Mainwaring around her thumb and had been delighted to discover that her former devoted admirer had acquired a delicious air of sophistication on his travels. But she had not expected him to be so accomplished in the art of dalliance. There was a disturbing glint in those dark blue eyes that made her less than certain of her ability to rule him, and the suspicion entered her mind, ever so briefly, that perhaps the tables had been turned.

CHAPTER 10

The understanding that had sprung up between Cassie and Horace deepened in the following weeks and they were seen a great deal in each other's company, attending the more intellectual social events the metropolis had to offer. The visit to Mr. Glover's exhibition was a great success. Cassie would have enjoyed the exhibit anyway, as she preferred landscapes to portraits and thought the *Ruins of Adrian's Villa, in the Campgna, Italy* particularly fine, but it added to her pleasure immensely to be able to discuss it with Horace. He had spent some time in Italy on his Grand Tour and was able to add information and an expanded critical view, which increased her knowledge, and therefore her appreciation, of the artist's skill. In fact, Cassie had been so much taken by this exhibition that Horace, who insisted that these paintings closely resembled the celebrated Mr. Wilson's works, offered to take her to visit Lord Humphrey Wycombe, an old family friend who collected the works of Wilson, Constable, and other landscape painters.

They made an outing of it, including Kitty and Frances in the expedition to their host's country seat, where they enjoyed a wonderful luncheon al fresco and a walk through his notable Italian gardens as well as viewing his truly magnificent collection of paintings.

Cassie was pleased to see Lord Wycombe's obvious enjoyment of Horace's conversation and the serious attention the old man gave to the younger's opinions. Later, strolling around the gardens with her host, she was highly gratified when he confided in her, "Horace is a very good lad. It is the greatest of pities that he receives no encourgement from his family. Why, if I had a son such as he, I should spare no effort or expense to help him pursue his studies. As it is now, he constantly meets with resistance from his parents and they allow him the merest pittance for his scholarly pursuits. If he were to become as enamored at faro or hazard as he is of Homer, he would have the family fortune, considerable as it is, at his disposal. What a waste."

His look of disgust brightened as he patted Cassie's hand, continuing, "Allow me the privilege of an old man who loves Horace more deeply than his own father does and let me say, my dear, that I am thoroughly delighted that he has found as fine and intelligent a companion as you. It does my heart good to see how much happier he is since he has had you as a friend." Noting Cassie's confusion, he added, "That is all I shall ever say on the matter except for one more thing. I knew both of your parents well enough to know they would be infinitely proud of such a bright and charming daughter as you are."

Cassie was too overcome to do much more than stammer, "Thank you." It was so rare that someone outside her family circle recognized and appreciated her talents that she felt a little overwhelmed at his praise.

Horace also squired the ladies from Mainwaring house to the opera several times while Lord Mainwaring was out of Town tending to political concerns. Though she appreciated his escorting her, Lady Frances was a trifle dismayed by his constant attendance. She was delighted that her sister had discovered someone she enjoyed, but Frances, a high stickler where the happiness of her family was concerned, found herself wishing that Horace was not quite so prosy. Cassie had always been one whose high spirits and sense of fun could be counted on to enliven the dullest of surroundings. Now these seem to have disappeared. It was true that Freddie's absence had deprived her of her source of support for her escapades, but Frances had noticed that since the beginning of her friendship with Horace, Cassie had devoted herself even more earnestly to intellectual pursuits at the expense of the lighter side of her nature.

Accustomed to the brilliant political circles in which she and Lord Mainwaring moved, Lady Frances knew very well that a powerful intellect did not necessarily preclude a sense of fun or humor. In point of fact, she would have staunchly maintained that for all his vaunted scholarly interests, the Honorable Horace Wilbraham was far less intelligent than Lady Cassandra Cresswell. At the same time, he seemed to feel far more certain of his intellectual superiority than she did.

Yes, Frances concluded, Horace was eminently suitable as a companion for her sister, but she was concerned lest Cassie, surrounded as she was by empty-headed tulips of the *ton,* give Horace more credit for intelligence than was his due and come to view him as something more than a companion. Having caught that young man, blissfully unaware of anyone's scrutiny, gazing adoringly at Cassie, Frances realized that he was besotted with her sister and she felt certain that he would soon be approaching Lord Mainwaring to ask for her hand. The prospect did not precisely displease Frances, but by the same token it did not please her either. Somehow she had hoped that the return of Ned and Freddie would liven things up, but Freddie was too busy reestablishing ties with his cronies and Ned seemed bent on breaking most, if not all, the female hearts in London. If he could be said to be spending time with anyone, it was with Arabella Taylor. Often he could be seen riding beside her carriage in the park, and if her expression were any indication, his conversation was extraordinarily gratifying to that young woman.

Cassie had also noted this interesting development of events, and far from being pleased at her former playmate's pursuit of the woman he had wooed so long in vain, she felt rather put out by the affair. As they had entered their box at the opera she had happened to glance over at the couple several boxes away from them just as Ned had leaned over

to whisper something that had produced a most coy look and
a playful tap on the cheek from Arabella's fan. Cassie had
looked quickly away, but not before Frances had caught the
expression of disgust on her sister's face. Cassie had
remained rather quiet and abstracted the rest of the evening,
though normally she would have been completely enthralled
by Mozart's music.

It was not too many evenings later, at the Countess of
Wakefield's ball, when Cassie, never one to mince words—
especially when addressing someone she had known since
childhood—articulated this disgust to Ned himself. Frances,
also privy to the little scene, would have been as amused
as always by watching the sparks fly between these two
particularly strong-minded people, except that this time a
more serious note had crept into their argument, though to
do Cassie justice, it had been Ned who had precipitated the
quarrel.

After spending much of the evening with Horace quietly
discussing the relative merits of Mr. Gillies's translation of
Aristotle, Cassie had been lured into an energetic country
dance by her brother, who had begged, "Please, Cass, dance
this one with me. Amanda Billingsley's mother keeps looking
at me in the most meaningful way. It's not that I don't feel
sorry for someone as dish-faced as she is, but must she simper
and make eyes at me just because I give her a nod now and
then?"

"Surely it was only a friendly smile such as she would
direct at anyone she has known for some time," Cassie
suggested.

"Perhaps," Freddie replied, though he did not sound the
least convinced. "But does she have to look so desperate?
It makes a fellow feel dashed uncomfortable, I can tell you."

Here Cassie noticed Ned in conversation with a dashing
redhead who looked to be a good deal amused and gratified
with their *tête-à-tête*. At any rate, she kept hanging on to
his arm in the most intimate way, Cassie reflected huffily.

Not too much later, after Freddie had left her to ask a friend
about a matched pair of grays he was eager to acquire, Cassie

looked about for Horace, who had gone off to the card room
to find his mother. As her glance swept the crowded ballroom
it landed again on Ned, this time with Lady Jersey. That
renowned coquette was positively draping herself all over
him and he seemed to be enjoying it hugely.

Thus, she was not in the best of humors when he strode
across the floor to her just as a waltz was struck up. Bending
over her hand, he looked up at her, quirking one dark brow
and asked, "Would you grant a poor supplicant the very great
honor, Cassie?"

Annoyed though she was, Cassie found it impossible to
resist the appeal in his dark blue eyes and, giving him her
hand, allowed herself to be led onto the floor. As they whirled
around the room she found herself wondering again at the
change in her old gawky Ned, who bore not the least
resemblance to the tall powerful man now guiding her skillfully among the maze of couples.

However, it was the same old Ned who broke into her
thoughts some minutes later in his usual direct manner.
"Now, Cassie, what's this I hear about your lending a hand
to the Comte de Vaudron? I should think that you would like
it above all things. And you, with the background Frances
gave you in history, as well as your own knowledge of Greek,
will do the thing right. Why, if some moldly old pedant got
hold of those marbles, he would want to bury them away
so only the most devoted scholars among us would have the
right to view them just as they have done with the zoological
collection at the British Museum. It don't bear thinking of."
Ned paused and regarded his partner thoughtfully. She was
in many ways lovelier than ever, but somehow the spark that
had made her what she was—awake on all suits and ready
for any adventure—seemed to have disappeared. The
thoughtful look on his face vanished as quickly as it had
appeared and he continued in a rallying tone, "And speaking
of pedants, I hear Wilbraham has joined the comte's
entourage. Take care, Cass, lest you cast him in the shade.
He doesn't take too kindly to competition, especially when
it comes from someone with true intellectual attainments."

Cassie did not look to be best pleased at this remark, and she defended her fellow scholar in a decidedly frosty tone. "I consider Horace Wilbraham to be quite the brightest young man of my acquaintance."

Ned snorted, "Freddie and I didn't return a moment too soon if you are forced to make do for companionship with that pompous—"

The calm disdain which Cassie had hitherto displayed dissolved in an instant as she retorted in a furious undertone, "Horace, at least, possesses a mind devoted to serious subjects, for which I admire him. He is concerned with higher things than causing a stir in the ballroom or at the opera. I am thankful to know someone who does not waste his time, as so many do, flitting from one person to the next, squandering his intelligence on idle flirtation and frivolous chatter. If there is a better man around, I am sure—"

"You don't know," Ned finished. His brows snapped together and now, equally furious, he took up the battle. "Have a care, Cassie," he warned, "or you will become as much of a dead bore as he is."

"Well, of all the wickedly unjust things," Cassie gasped. Too angry now for caution, she continued, "I should far rather be a bore than a silly heartless flirt like Arabella Taylor, whose only thought is to amuse herself, whatever the cost. I wish you joy of her."

"Thank you. I am sure I shall receive it from a woman who at least knows how to enjoy herself and entertain others," Ned answered grimly.

By now they were well within earshot of Frances and Kitty and somehow they managed to finish the waltz in hostile silence. With a curt nod to these two ladies, Ned restored his partner to her coterie and then, without a backward glance at Cassie, strode off, leaving them all openmouthed.

Frances was the first to recover. Seeing her sister's distress, she came quickly to her aid, saying, "Horace has come to tell me that as his mother is feeling a trifle fatigued he is taking her home." Privately she thought it was less fatigue which motivated Lady Wilbraham than a desire to make her son cater to her every little whim, but at the moment it suited Frances to believe this fiction. "She has the right idea," she continued. "This has become a sad crush and I would just as soon leave now that we have paid our respects to the countess. Besides, Teddy seemed fretful tonight and I am worried that he has caught something from the stableboy he has been spending time with."

Ordinarily, Cassie would have recognized this last farrago of nonsense as a stratagem of the most obvious sort—Lady Frances being a practical mother and never one to be unduly dismayed by the normal misfortunes of childhood—but she was far too upset to think clearly, much less recognize the ruses employed for her protection. With a grateful sigh she acquiesced and allowed herself to return to Grosvenor Square, where she sought the sanctuary of her dressing room as quickly as possible.

CHAPTER 11

Though escape from the crowds in the ballroom afforded her peace and quiet, it meant that Cassie had ample time to reflect on the entire scene that had passed and she spent a sleepless night going over and over again her contretemps with Ned. Try as she might, she could not erase the final image she had of him, his face taut with anger, blue eyes blazing as he accused her of being a bore. I am not in the least a bore, she told herself defiantly. I can discuss a vaster array of subjects than most of my acquaintances and I am truly interested in almost any topic. Well, most topics of a serious nature, she amended, remembering how insipid she found the conversation of Arabella and other damsels like her.

It is *he* who has changed. But irrefutable though her logic might be, she found herself wondering doubtfully if Ned might not be right. Perhaps her devotion to scholarly pursuits was making her rather serious and dull. Thus in the following weeks the two men laboring over metopes from the Parthenon in Hanover Square saw very little of Cassie. Instead, she threw herself into an orgy of activity.

It would have been too much to expect that she frequented every social event that was offered, but in her time off from serious endeavors, she took the opportunity to allay another worry of hers, which was that she had been neglecting Theodore. With this in mind, and remembering her own days in London when Frances had seen Kitty through her come-out, she inveigled Freddie and Nigel into taking her and Teddy to Sadlers Wells, where they spent several delicious hours under the spell of Grimaldi. The famous clown was

a good deal older than he had been when Freddie and Cassie
had last seen him perform, but his antics were as amusing
as ever, and Teddy was enchanted.

Watching him as he sat enthralled, Cassie realized that it
had been some time since she had done anything for the sheer
pleasure of it. True, she loved the work she was doing with
the comte. It was intriguing, challenging, and rewarding,
but there was always a purpose behind it. Reflecting further,
she became more conscious of the fact that everything she
did in her life had some well-conceived reason behind it.
Even the more frivolous activities of her come-out were for
a purpose and became, therefore, duties which she felt it
incumbent upon herself to fulfill. Thus she had found herself
at balls and routs conscientiously asking herself if she had
taken adequate advantage of each event to expand and enlarge
her acquaintance, never giving a thought to enjoying herself.
In fact she had, on the basis of her limited experience with
the assemblies in Hampshir, journeyed to London with the
expectation that the social events of the Season would be
larger but equally mindless versions of these country gatherings. With this preconception she had not even stopped to
consider the possibility that they might be entertaining or
amusing, and thus they had not afforded her much amusement
or entertainment. Nor had she, bearing Ned's criticism in
mind, afforded much amusement or entertainment to those
she encountered there, she reflected.

As always, Ned Mainwaring, with his keen perception and
his ability to get straight to the heart of the matter, had started
her thinking, and Cassie was far too fair-minded to let her
anger or her disapproval of his behavior keep her from
appreciating his insight. The very thought of losing Ned as
a friend, a distinct possibility given the heated nature of their
discussion at the Countess of Wakefield's, made her vow
to scrutinize her own behavior and work to make amends,
if possible.

Much the same thoughts that occupied Cassie were preying
on Ned as well. He had returned home seething with rage
at the condescending tone with which Cassie had criticized

a childhood playmate who could be accused of doing nothing worse than the rest of the *beau monde*—dressing, flirting, chatting, and generally enjoying herself. A bottle of port later, some of the rage had subsided and the chief impression that remained, hazy though it was by this time, of the unpleasant scene in the ballroom was the hurt look in Cassie's eyes along with the sense that somehow he had let her down. Damn it, I don't owe her an explanation of my behavior, he fumed. And Horace Wilbraham *is* a pedant of the worst sort. But somehow, no matter how he vindicated his conduct, it didn't justify the pain he seemed to have caused an old friend. I shall make it up to her tomorrow, he resolved. It's been years since we went to Astley's. Certainly Horace won't have taken her there, he would not be caught dead frequenting such a place. And besides, Teddy would enjoy it. Feeling a trifle comforted by this decision, he promptly fell into a deep sleep.

It was with this laudable purpose in mind that he presented himself quite early one morning in Grosvenor Square only to find the place in a minor turmoil.

"Good morning, sir," the venerable Higgins greeted Ned with his usual stately demeanor, but Ned retained the distinct impression that he had come from somewhere in a great hurry. This feeling was just establishing itself in his mind when Teddy came tearing around the corner and screeched to an abrupt halt when he caught sight of a visitor in the hall.

Seeing who it was, he relaxed visibly exclaiming, "Oh, famous! You're jutht the person we want. You thee, Papa and Mama are out riding in the park and Freddie ith at Tatterthallth, and thereth jutht Cathie and me and I'm not tall enough." As Ned persisted in looking blank despite this illuminating explanation, Theodore, looking slightly exasperated at the occasional and inopportune obtuseness of adults, summed up the problem in a word. "It'th Ethelred."

At that moment, Wellington and Nelson came racing around the corner in the direction from which Theodore had appeared. Recognizing an old friend and source of aid, Wellington smiled his most gracious smile and plopped himself directly in front of Ned's gleaming Hessians. "Arf, arf," he barked significantly before getting up again and heading back around the corner, pausing to look meaningfully over his shoulder at Ned and Theodore. Considering it beneath him to dash around in such an undignified hurry, Nelson strode off in the same direction with the same significant backward look at them. Recognizing an imperative summons when he saw one, Ned followed the two messengers and Theodore with alacrity.

The reason for all this commotion at his arrival became immediately apparent as he descended to the walled garden behind the breakfast room. There was Cassie, a picture of the fashionable young lady in a morning dress of shaded yellow jaconet muslin with sleeves *en bouffants* perched precariously on top of the wall clutching a distressed Ethelred.

Entirely forgetting the unfortunate nature of their last encounter, she greeted Ned with obvious relief. "Ned, the very one! You have no notion how delighted I am to see you."

An appreciative smile lit up his tanned features as he strode over to the wall, remarking, "On the contrary, Cassie, I have a very fair idea of exactly how glad you are to see me. Oh, do be quiet, I shall get you down." This last, obviously addressed to Ethelred, seemed to reassure both parties. "Here, hand him to me," he directed. Taking the frightened duck in a firm grasp, he smoothed his feathers and managed to calm him down before restoring him to his friends on the ground and turning to assist Cassie.

"Pooh, I am not such a poor creature," she remarked indignantly, ignoring his hand and climbing down the thick vines which must have provided her the means of scaling the wall in the first place. "You see, Lady Telfair's odious pug somehow got into the garden and took great exception to Ethelred, in his own garden, if you can imagine such effontery. I daresay you think it's amusing"—Cassie fired up as Ned's eyes began to dance—"but you wouldn't if you were Ethelred, and it is truly a *nasty* little dog."

"Arf, arf," Wellington agreed wholeheartedly. Nelson declined to comment, but the look of disdain on his face provided ample evidence of his opinion on their neighbor.

"At any rate, neither Nelson nor Wellington was around to protect him, so, taking fright, he flew to the top of the wall, but he's not much of a flier. So he panicked, and began quacking dreadfully. This brought Teddy, Nelson, and Wellington, who routed the pug but could do nothing to rescue Ethelred. They went for James the footman, but it was beneath his dignity to rescue a duck—"

"But not beneath yours, I see," Ned interrupted. "I thought it would not take long before the true Cassandra Cresswell emerged from the proper young lady of the *ton* that I found upon my return." The air of injured dignity which Cassie invariably assumed at being caught in a scrape descended upon her countenance. Ned grinned and proffered one tan hand. "Cry friends, then, Cass," he begged.

Cassie's infectious smile lit her face as she in turn extended a slightly grimy one. "Friends, Ned," she agreed.

This satisfactory resolution to their quarrel was interrupted by Teddy, who insisted on discussing the finer points of Ned's bay with him. "He lookth to be a high-mettled, prime bit of blood," he observed, nodding his head with all the sagacity of a dedicated frequenter of Tattersall's.

Ned's eyes twinkled as he nodded. "Oh he is, I was assured of the purity of his lineage. He's a Thoroughbred from ear to hoof, and though highly strung, there's not an ounce of vice in him," he agreed. Recognizing the light of a fanatic in the boy's eyes, he offered, "Would you like to examine him yourself?"

"Oh, yeth," breathed Teddy, glad to see his belief that Ned must be a right one confirmed. He and Wellington began to head to the stables, where Higgins, seeing that Ned's visit was going to be protracted, had ordered the horse to be taken.

Teddy's headlong rush was stopped midflight by Ned, who suggested that his aunt, who was credited to be no mean judge of horseflesh herself, might like to accompany them. Teddy looked somewhat crestfallen at having the purely masculine nature of the party vitiated. Seeing this, Ned was quick to point out that many people, Nigel Streatham included, considered Cassie to be a far better judge of the finer points of equine quality than her brother. This was a piece of news, indeed, to Teddy, who looked curiously at Cassie for confirmation of this interesting opinion.

"Well, Freddie has been known to be more impressed by the more showy points of a horse than I am and he is sometimes less critical," she acknowledged, loath to disparage her twin.

"Cut line, Cassie," Ned commented. "You know if it weren't for you, he would have bought that gelding from Ponsonby and been taken for a complete flat. You saw immediately that it was spavined."

Cassie grinned at the memory of Freddie bouncing along on the gelding's back after she had suggested that it might be wise to put it through its paces before purchasing it. "You are right, as always, Ned. Freddie was certain he was striking a bargain. He insisted that Ponsonby was at the low-water mark and needed the blunt. He was, too, and it was a shame we weren't able to help him by buying the horse, but the price was too high to pay for that bonesetter."

Teddy looked from one to the other, round-eyed at these revelations concerning an uncle he had always considered to be something of a demigod, at least as far as the sporting world was concerned. Despite his high regard for Cassie's intelligence, he tended, like all boys, to dismiss female opinion, particularly in these matters, as so much chatter, and he was much struck by Ned's obvious regard for her horse sense. At this point they reached the stables and he became totally immersed in examining the horse, talking to it gently as he rubbed its nose and ran a remarkably experienced eye for one so young over it.

Watching Teddy and Brutus, Ned was recalled to the original purpose of his visit. "I say, Cass, remember how much we enjoyed ourselves at Astley's? How would you like it if I escorted you and Teddy there soon?" he inquired.

"Why, what a capital notion, Ned!" Cassie responded enthusiastically. "I am sure Teddy would enjoy it above all things." She smiled shyly and added, "And I should like it a great deal, too."

Looking down at her, Ned saw the little girl he had once known peeping out from behind the severely intellectual facade she seemed to have adopted and he felt a great rush of tenderness toward her. "It's agreed, then. I shall ask Freddie if he would like to join us and it will be just like old times," he said, surprised himself at how much he was looking forward to the outing all of a sudden.

CHAPTER 12

It was just like old times, Cassie reflected, as several days later the four of them were ensconced at Astley's Amphitheatre, except that Philip Astley was no longer there to perform. As they witnessed one equestrian feat after another she couldn't recall when she'd enjoyed herself more. It was so comfortable to be with Freddie and Ned again, laughing and joking. She felt none of the constraint she sometimes did with Horace when, amused at some ridiculous pretension, she would laugh or make some sarcastic remark only to find him looking at her with a puzzled or faintly disapproving air. In fact, until now, completely at ease and accompanied by her oldest friends, she had been unaware that she had felt this way and she wondered at it. Loyalty to Horace immediately asserted itself and she banished such thoughts, recalling instead the intellectual stimulation she always enjoyed during their discussions.

"Cathie, Cathie," Teddy cried, tugging at her sleeve and recalling her to the scene at hand. "Do look at the way he standth on the horth ath it goeth. How doth he do it?" he wondered.

The small boy was totally entranced, and watching his absorption, Cassie could see that she would soon be hard put to keep him from emulating the famous trick rider Andrew Ducrow. Remembering another boy who had sat enraptured in much the same way many years ago, Cassie tried to save her nephew from disastrous experiences by cautioning him about the difficulties involved in attempting this particular feat. "I once knew someone who gave his head a nasty crack trying to do that very trick and he was in bed for weeks as a result," she warned him.

"You did?" Teddy looked up inquiringly. "Who was it?"

Cassie quirked a teasing eyebrow at Freddie. He grinned guiltily, admitting, "I was certain that it was easily done and tried it one day on Prince when no one was around to stop me. Unfortunately, it was in the stable yard, and when I slipped off his back, I hit my head on the cobbles. Everything went black, and when I awoke with a blinding headache, I found myself in bed, surrounded by anxious and disapproving adults. I was laid up for some time and was most uncomfortable, I assure you. But Cassie felt for me in my plight. She read adventure stories to me by the hour and was a famous nurse. Actually, old Ned here was a Trojan, too, because he retrieved his toy soldiers from Camberly, and when I was a bit better, Nigel was allowed to visit me with his and we had some famous battles. So you see, I was tolerably amused, but it was difficult being confined to a bed during such fine weather."

Seeing the disappointed look on her nephew's face, Cassie hastened to add, "But when we returned to Cresswell where there was nice soft grass, we practiced endlessly. And"— she smiled impishly—"I expect we could do the same thing now when we return to Cresswell."

"We could?" Teddy asked eagerly. "Would you help me?"

"Certainly," she replied. "I was able to ride several times around the paddock standing on Prince's back with no help and without falling. I should think I could do it again. I don't expect, after all, that once one has learned something like that, one forgets it very easily."

Looking over at her animated face as she discussed this with Teddy, Ned reflected how few of the women he had flirted with and encountered in society would have given a second thought to the pleasure of a small boy, much less have entered into it as wholeheartedly as Cassie did. Her unaffected enthusiasm had always attracted him, but now the contrast she presented to the sophisticated women of the *ton*

made him cherish her even more. He was glad once again
that the unpleasantness of the Countess of Wakefield's ball
had not spoiled their friendship. Being an avid horseman
himself, Ned was enjoying the evening as much as anybody.
The horses were magnificent specimens, their riders no less
so. He leaned over to Teddy, who, after this evening and
the episode with Brutus, was now his ardent admirer, and
explained to him how the equestrians were able to practice
and to accomplish what seemed to be impossible feats.

Watching the rapt expression on Teddy's face as he listened
to Ned, Cassie recalled an evening when she and Freddie
had looked just such a way at Lord Mainwaring as he had
introduced them to the marvels of Astley's. It was a rare man
who was able to offer such a treat to a child, she reflected,
and once again she was struck, as she had been so many times
before, with Ned's kind and sensitive nature. The shock of
seeing him as a man of the world—handsome, assured,
sought after by ladies of all ages and descriptions—had wiped
this original conception of him from her mind and she was
glad to have it restored.

Thus it was that when he turned to her, a half-quizzical,
half-amused expression on his face, and asked, "Enjoying
yourself?" she thanked him warmly, her entire face glowing
with enthusiasm. Looking down at her, Ned realized, as he
had from time to time in the past, that his tomboy playmate
was also quite a lovely young woman. And later, driving
home, as Cassie continued to tease Freddie with his past
adventures, Ned decided that he could not recall when he
had enjoyed an evening more.

"What a bouncer, Freddie! You most certainly did *not*
succeed in riding the entire way 'round the paddock at
Cresswell the first time we tried standing on Prince's back,"
Cassie protested, laughing at her twin's extravagant claims
that after his accident he had immediately mastered the art.
She turned to appeal to Ned. "Don't you recall that you tore
your second-best breeches when you fell off and that I didn't
fall nearly as many times as Freddie?"

Ned, however, was not one to be completely won by feminine appeals. "Now Cassie, if you don't remember, I do, several pinafores that were all over grass stains," he argued.

She frowned, but remained undaunted as she asserted, "That may be true, but I only *slid* off. Freddie *fell.*"

Ned choked, "You never could bear to be anything less than the best where horses were concerned." A darkling look from Cassie made her pause and admit, "Very well. You were in the right of it. Freddie did fall more times than you."

"There! You see, Ned agrees with me," Cassie crowed triumphantly as she turned to her crestfallen twin.

"Well, if that don't beat all," spluttered Freddie. "You defend a friend through thick and thin over all parts of the globe and at the least argument from a woman he betrays you."

Ned laid a palliative hand on his shoulder as he admonished, "Calm down, my boy. Cassie may have fallen fewer times, but you stayed on longer."

Cassie was outraged. "Why you traitor!" she blurted. "You know that's not true!"

By this time Ned was laughing so hard he could argue no longer. He held up a hand as he gasped, "Peace, you two. You'll be the death of me. I always swore you would be, and you will if you don't give over."

Theodore, scrunched into a corner of the carriage, was enjoying himself hugely. He had never seen adults scrapping like this before. Why, they were no different from him and Jem, Cresswell's stableboy, when they got into an argument. This had truly been a most instructional evening!

The night's experiences proved to be illuminating to more than one of the party's members, though their particular enlightenment dawned on Ned and Cassie later than it had on Teddy.

Ned had ample opportunity to reflect on Cassie's original, open, and friendly nature as he escorted Arabella to Lady Allsop's the next evening. As always, she was a vision of loveliness. When he came to collect her and her mother, the sight of her quite took his breath away. In a dress of aerophane crepe over a white satin slip the silver Vandyke trimming on her short sleeves matching the border of the skirt also edged in silver, and pearls threaded through her hair as well as at her throat, she looked like an angel as she descended the staircase. Her smile as she took Ned's arm was devastating, and the melting look that accompanied her seductively murmured, "Oh Ned, you *do* look dashing," would have captivated a far less susceptible man than Ned Mainwaring, who, despite his treatment at her hands and a series of torrid *affaires de coeur* in the capital cities of Europe, was predisposed to admire his former love.

However, as the evening advanced, it began to be borne in on him that Arabella had allowed him to escort her as much for who he was—the latest sensation in a Season that already promised to be sadly flat—as for the pleasure she might be expected to derive from his company. It was true that she stood up with him for more than one dance and that she had laughingly accorded him, from among all the eager admirers clamoring for it, her hand in the waltz. But as he whirled her around the floor he was aware that as much as she gazed meaningfully into his eyes, she was constantly glancing around the room to see just how many people were aware of how very devoted the wealthy and extremely eligible Ned Mainwaring was to the lovely Arabella Taylor.

Just as this slightly cynical thought entered his head she looked up, cheeks flushed, dark eyes alight with happiness, a bewitching smile beginning at the corners of her mouth, and sighed. "Ned, you waltz divinely. Why, not even Sir Brian Brandon dances as well as you and he is acknowledged to be one of the best."

Ned, who had not the slightest wish to cut a dash either on the dance floor or in society, did not know whether to be flattered or concerned at being favorably compared to so notable a Corinthian. His dark blue eyes twinkling with amusement, he raised one mobile black brow remarking sardonically, "I am certainly now set for life, for surely no one could aspire to greater heights of glory than that."

Arabella nodded. "Oh no, certainly not," she agreed seriously. "For he is top of the trees, you know," she assured him.

Ned's amusement faded as he realized that she was entirely in earnest. "I collect this means you now consider me to be an eligible *parti*," he commented ironically.

His acid tone was completely lost on Arabella, who looked up in astonishment. "But of course!" she exclaimed in some surprise that he should even be in doubt of such a thing.

Finding himself at a loss, he soon escaped to go in search of refreshments, leaving her in the eager hands of young Ponsonby, who was quite desperate to lead her in the quadrille. As he crossed the ballroom he found himself wishing that Cassie were there. He could just picture the way her big blue eyes would brim with amusement when he told her that he'd been adjudged a worthy member of the Corinthian set by no less a social devotee than Arabella. He could even hear the laughter gurgle in her throat as she protested, "Oh Ned, not even *Arabella* could be such a gudgeon!"

"And what has put such a cynical expression on the face of one so young and debonair?" a voice at his elbow inquired. Ned looked down into the dancing eyes of Lady Jersey. Here, at least, was someone witty enough to see the amusing side.

His teeth gleaming in his tan face, he replied, "I have just been informed that I can now consider myself a Corinthian."

Lady Jersey's eyes wandered to the other side of the room, where a besotted Ponsonby was gazing adoringly at Arabella. "But most assuredly, *mon brave,*" she murmured wickedly. "Surely you don't think the fair Arabella would allow herself to be led in a waltz by anyone less than a nonpareil?" she inquired.

It was truly turning out to be an evening of revelations. Ned had never before viewed himself in this light, but he could tell from the alacrity with which his invitations to dance were accepted that he was apparently the last person in this ballroom to realize that he was an extremely desirable partner.

Arabella, who was keeping as eagle an eye on Ned's conquests as much as she was counting her own, was flushed with pride. So pleased was she at his success and the glory his attentions reflected on her that she allowed herself to squeeze his hand as he helped her into the carriage. "I told you that Sir Brian would have to look to his laurels with you around," she cooed delightedly.

Meanwhile, Cassie was undergoing an equally revelatory experience that evening at the theater. Horace, having heard her express a wish to see Kean's *Richard III,* had escorted her and Frances to Drury Lane. At first, Cassie had thought the famous actor to be somewhat melodramatic, but as the play progressed, she fell more and more under his spell until she became totally immersed in the action of the play, only to be brought rudely back to earth by Horace's whispered comment that he thought Kean a frippery fellow who rolled his eyes too much. Forgetting her first reaction to the actor, Cassie protested, "How can you say so? I think it is a most sensitive interpretation."

"My dear Cassandra," Horace began in a tone that to Cassie sounded almost patronizing, "the entire performance is sensational in the extreme. Shakespeare's language is overblown enough as it is, and this fellow exploits it for all he is worth. I am astonished that you can like it. For my part, I find it to be quite vulgar."

Cassie's mouth, which had dropped open in astonishment, shut with a snap as she turned her attention to the stage, totally ignoring Horace, who had been about to launch into a dissertation on the superiority of Greek tragedy. He subsided into hurt and angry silence. Frances, an interested bystander to the scene, was not sorry that he had revealed this side of his nature to Cassie. It would do her good to see just how stubborn and opinionated Horace Wilbraham could be. For her part, Cassie had never felt so out of charity with her companion. She was quite glad when Horace finally deposited the ladies at Grosvenor Square and she was free to discuss the performance with a more open-minded and stimulating conversationalist. She and Frances agreed that while Kean did tend toward the histrionic, his sensitive rendition of the hunchback had made them view the play and the characters in a slightly different light than they had before.

CHAPTER *13*

The next day when Cassie arrived at the comte's, her acknowledgment of Horace's greeting was rather frosty, but she was almost immediately mollified by his next words. "Cassandra, I had not the least intention of offending you last evening," he apologized. "I realize that I am inclined to be carried away by my enthusiams. You must forgive me if I react so strongly, but drama, and tragedy in particular, is one of my ruling passions and I find I cannot be lukewarm about it."

Cassie smiled as she replied, "Think nothing of it. I certainly shall not."

He heaved an obvious sigh of relief before turning back to the marbles he had been examining. Cassie was fast becoming an obsession with him. He had never been able to converse with a woman who comprehended what he was saying and could therefore truly appreciate him. That someone as lovely as Cassie paid attention to him and understood him was quite wonderful. Lately, he had begun to contemplate asking her to marry him. The more he thought about it, the idea of spending his life with this exquisite creature who would cherish his work and admire him made him quite drunk with happiness. Her coldness the previous evening had threatened this beatific vision and struck terror into his heart. Without understanding the cause of it, he was determined to overcome her displeasure. Her gracious acceptance of his apology convinced him once more that he was truly blessed in his friendship with her and he was more determined than ever to make her his.

Cassie, moving over to the materials she had been working on, was contemplating a less rosy picture of the future than was her companion, for it had occurred to her that while he had apologized for upsetting her, Horace did not in the least comprehend what he had said to do so. It was not that she was made uncomfortable because he did not completely share her opinions. After all, she and Ned had disagreed times out of mind and had spent many happy hours arguing with each other over an entire range of subjects. What bothered her was Horace's utter lack of appreciation for the myriad and conflicting emotions which Kean's performance, overdone through it may have been, revealed, as well as his total obliviousness to the sympathetic emotional response the actor managed to elicit from the audience. That he could be so caught up in the mechanics of the play's presentation as to ignore completely and absolutely its fundamental drama revealed a rather unsympathetic side to his character of which she had previously been unaware. This, coupled with his obstinate refusal to appreciate any of the good points at all in the performance simply because he had one criticism of it made him seem slightly narrow-minded.

To top it off, he had entirely misunderstood the cause of her displeasure. That he should assume that she would naturally be in complete agreement with any opinion of his and ascribe her distress merely to the fact that he expressed his opinions with such ardor thoroughly annoyed her. The more she thought about it, the more Cassie was angered by his blatant disregard for her individual critical faculties and taste. She remained in a most pensive mood for the rest of the day despite the fact that she was working on a truly exquisite section of frieze.

Over in his corner of the library, the comte, observing the angry set of Cassie's jaw, nodded sagely and thought to himself, She has spirit, that one. It will take someone with a stronger and more adventurous nature than Horace Wilbraham's to appreciate someone such as she. He is a good lad, but something of a dull dog and his mind is no match for hers. He certainly lacks the quick wit and charming

conversation. We must see what we can do to find Cassie
an intellectual companion worthy of her.

Much the same thoughts were going through Lady Kitty
Willoughby's mind as she observed her brother and Arabella
Taylor. Arabella had called at the Willoughbys on the
slimmest of pretexts. She and her maid were on their way
shopping and she simply *had* to know the name of the shop
where Kitty had procured the perfectly ravishing ribbons for
the bonnet she had been wearing in the park the other day.

Kitty was nobody's fool and was thus not the least surprised
when Ned walked in, obviously dressed for a ride in the park,
that a girl who not two minutes before had been determined
to unearth the exact duplicate of Lady Willoughby's ribbons
now had no thought in her mind beyond a refreshing stroll
through Hyde Park.

Glancing coyly up at Ned from under the brim of a
charming cottage-shaped straw bonnet, she laid one lavender
kid-gloved hand on his arm, begging, "Do join your sister
and me in the park. I had been planning to make some small
purchases in Bond Street, but it is far too fine a day to waste.
I should infinitely prefer taking the air and sharing some
elegant conversation with some charming companions."

Kitty, far too well bred to reveal the least dismay at this
abrupt change in plan, yielded to superior strategy as gracefully as she could, adding her voice to Arabella's. "That
is a delightful idea. I shall just go and fetch my bonnet."
And that, she fumed as she quitted the drawing room, leaves
that scheming little hussy with Ned all to herself. No doubt
she is counting on having the good quarter of an hour alone
with him that it would take her to primp herself to perfection.
Well, she shan't have it! Snatching a bonnet with more haste
than usual, Kitty slapped it on her head without even
consulting the mirror. No doubt I shall look the perfect quiz,
she thought, but I won't leave poor Ned in her clutches a
minute longer than necessary.

"Poor Ned," in fact, was tolerably amused by the entire
situation. Knowing that Arabella bore no great friendship
for his sister, who, as a dashing young matron, was apt to

offer more competition than Arabella liked to encounter, he had surmised as he entered the drawing room that Kitty had been the victim of some stratagem.

It only remained to establish the exact nature of the vague excuse Arabella had invented to explain her unexpected visit. Ned had been too aware of the possessive light in Arabella's eyes as they had lighted on him to doubt that he was her real quarry. Watching her take in the significance of his attire and change her plans accordingly had been a very real entertainment. Consequently, he leaned his broad shoulders against the mantel, awaiting developments.

Arabella looked admiringly at these same shoulders, noticed that they were shaking suspiciously. Tilting her head at him coquettishly, she inquired, "Are you laughing at me?"

Unable to contain himself, Ned burst into laughter. "You enchanting little witch! Confess, you had not the least notion of going for a walk when you came here."

An uncertain look flitted across her features before she gurgled merrily and admitted, "Of course not, you silly creature. But you men are so elusive, we poor women are forced to adopt the feeblest of excuses in order to win your escort."

He heaved himself from the mantel and strode over to capture one small hand. Raising it gracefully to his lips, he murmured, "I should be loath to put you to such trouble and I doubt very much that so beautiful a creature as you is at all familiar with the shifts mere ordinary women are put to."

His tone was earnest, but Arabella saw the quizzical gleam in his blue eyes. "You are a dreadful creature to tease me so," she said, pouting.

He smiled at her. "And you know your pout is as enchanting as your smile, so I refuse to feel the least compunction at causing it to appear. But come, I hear my sister on the stairs."

As they sauntered along in the sunshine, Arabella chattering happily of this musicale and that ridotto, of the shocking quiz of a turban that Lady Ullapool wore to the opera and the truly ravishing riding habit Amanda St. Clair had ordered, Kitty saw the boredom begin to creep into Ned's eyes. She noted the mechanical responses that appeared to satisfy Arabella while her escort appraised the points of Lord Alvanley's hack, cast an experienced eye over the showy chestnuts drawing the barouche of a noted barque of frailty, and generally kept his mind occupied while leaving Arabella under the impression that he was attending solely to her.

This won't do, Kitty told herself. No matter how besotted he had been in the past, or how attracted he is now, he would be bored with her within a week and ready to strangle her within a fortnight. Confronted with a situation similar to that of the comte's, she arrived at the same conclusion—such intelligence and wit should not be condemned to pass the rest of its existence with mediocrity and self-centeredness as its companion.

CHAPTER 14

While some of their nearest and dearest were cudgeling their brains for ways to help Cassie and Ned recognize and free themselves from entanglements that were unlikely to prove enriching to either one, the two principals were continuing to pursue these same relationships with varying degrees of satisfaction.

A dreadfully boring evening at Lady Heatherstone's rout, where there was such a dearth of conversation between sets that Cassie would have been grateful for a partner who even wanted to discuss something as mundane as his shirt points or the weather, had left Cassie wondering if she had not perhaps been too critical of Horace.

Meanwhile, that young man, desperate at the coolness with which Cassie had been treating him lately, was inspired to more active and more sensitive behavior than was customary for his rather self-centered nature. Driven nearly to distraction at the thought that she might be losing her interest in him, he even included Teddy and Wellington in his next invitation, though he normally detested children and pets—lumping them all into the same category as noisy nuisances that were to be avoided at any cost.

However, he knew Cassie's fondness for her young nephew and he resolved to make the truly handsome sacrifice of taking her, Teddy, and any other companions for an outing in the park. That this generous gesture would also confirm the world's opinion that Lady Cassandra Cresswell and Horace Wilbraham were an "item" was an added advantage to the outing that was not lost on Horace, scornful though he might be of society and its predilection for gossip.

So it was that the next sunny day he presented himself at Grovenor Square. "I thought that since it was such fine weather you and Master Theodore might like to take the air with me in the park," he stammered hesitantly in response to the inquiring look Cassie directed at him as Higgins ushered him into the drawing room.

He was instantly rewarded with a brilliant smile. "The very thing!" Cassie exclaimed, jumping up. She had been penning, without much enthusiasm, a letter to Aunt Harriet, who, casual though she was about her nearest relatives, did like to hear from time to time how they were rubbing along. After relating everyone's general health, Cassie had been having great difficulty selecting a topic of mutual interest. Her aunt, who possessed unbridled intellectual curiosity in horticultural matters, was totally uninterested in any aspect of classical antiquity, and even less so in the fashionable happenings in London society at the moment. Knowing Aunt Harriet to be at least on speaking terms with the Comte de Vaudron, one of the three males of her acquaintance—the other two being Lord Julian Mainwaring and Ned Mainwaring—that she did not label a complete nodcock, Cassie filled a great deal of the letter describing his household and his current endeavors. She had written herself to a standstill, however, and had been gazing wistfully out the window at the sunlit square when Horace was announced. The prospect of a walk drove all the previous uncharitable thoughts she had harbored toward him from her mind and she accepted his proposal with alacrity.

Horace further endeared himself to her by suggesting that she might like to invite Theodore and any other interested parties to accompany them. At the first mention of an outing Wellington, who had been resting his chin comfortably on Cassie's slippered foot, perked up his ears. When he heard the full extent of the invitation, he bounced happily out of the room to go in search of Theodore.

Cassie smiled gratefully at Horace. "How kind of you to remember Teddy and include him. He amuses himself quite wonderfully here, but I am persuaded that the delights to be found in London pale in comparison to the freedom he has to explore the woods and ponds at Cresswell and Camberly.''

Horace was both charmed and relieved by her appreciation of his scheme and was just about to suggest that young Theodore was exceedingly fortunate in having an aunt so devoted to his welfare when Theodore himself appeared with Wellington at his heels.

"Did you with to thee me, Aunt Cathie,'' he asked, looking Horace over with all the unabashed curiosity of a five-year-old.

Horace, unaccustomed to enduring the candid scrutiny of the very young, fidgeted and looked the other way, only to encounter an equally appraising stare from Wellington's bright shoe-button eyes. The little dog, sensing the stranger's unease, smiled encouragingly, but as this seemed to render the visitor even more nervous, he gave up and looked at Cassie expectantly instead.

"Yes, dear, I did want to see you, though Wellington was beforehand in summoning you. Mr. Wilbraham has very kindly invited us to join him for a walk in the park.''

To Theodore, accustomed as he was to such noted Corinthians as Lord Mainwaring, Ned, and Freddie, the prospect of sauntering sedately through the park with someone he had no hesitation in stigmatizing as a very dull dog, was less than inviting, but he mustered as much enthusiasm as he could and accepted with tolerably good grace. "Thank you, thir. That ith motht kind of you. May Wellington come, too?''

"Yes, my lad. Of course. Most certainly,'' Horace replied ingratiatingly, well aware that it behooved him in his courtship of Cassie to ensure that Theodore and Wellington were his allies.

Wellington, like Theodore, preferred the more invigorating company of such bucks as Freddie, Nigel Streatham, Ned, or Lord Mainwaring, even Bertie Montgomery, who, despite his not being a sporting man, was enough of a nonpareil to lend an air of fashion to any party, but he was grateful for the chance to be out of doors. He trotted off happily to collect Nelson and Ethelred while Cassie went to don her pelisse and exchange her slippers for half boots and Theodore went to retrieve his new sailboat, recently purchased by an indulgent Uncle Freddie.

Horace looked to be a bit taken aback at the size and composition of the party when they assembled sometime later in the hall, but seeing Cassie's happy expectant look, he was more than satisfied. As Cassie's maid Rose accompanied them, neither he nor Cassie was obliged to pay close attention to the more motley part of the group and Horace was free to devote himself to retrieving his position with the object of his adoration.

He set about to do this immediately, discussing the report recently published by the trustees of the British Museum in the *Edinburgh Review* and soliciting her opinion with becoming eagerness.

Cassie, who had also read the report, was delighted to comment on it, agreeing wholeheartedly with its author's belief in the need for more care in the display and preservation of zoological specimens. Thus she was in a charitable frame of mind toward her escort by the time they reached the recently erected statue of Achilles. Here, Cassie stopped to explain to an openmouthed Theodore that it had been cast from cannons captured from Napoleon at Toulouse, Salamanca, Vittoria, and Waterloo and donated "By the women of England to Arthur, Duke of Wellington." At the mention of his namesake, Wellington, who had been sniffing the statue with an entirely different interest, perked up and regarded it with new respect.

Theodore, who had marched many of his toy soldiers through some of these same famous battles, walked 'round and 'round, envisioning the fields of glory that the lump of metal must have seen. He was brought quickly back to reality by a loud quack from Ethelred, who had spied the Serpentine and was making directly for it.

"Your friend seems to prefer aquatic adventure to history.

Shall we follow him? Perhaps I can help you with your boat,''
Horace offered kindly.

He was immediately rewarded with a brilliant smile from
Cassie and a rather subdued "Thank you, thir" from
Theodore. Theodore, having observed Horace precariously
balancing teacups and looking nervously at the prime bits
of blood that happened to come close to him, had little
expectation that he would be of the least use, but he
acquiesced. He and Wellington watched in some amusement
as Horace managed to tangle the string in the riggings and
to capsize the boat as he set it in the water, but they held
their tongues until he had quite finished and turned to address
Cassie.

"Now we can really sail it and have some fun," Theodore
confided to the little terrier.

"Arf. Arf," Wellington barked as he ran precariously
along the edge, watching as the little craft caught the wind
and gained speed.

"Quack. Quack," Ethelred proudly escorted the sailboat
around the pond.

All was going famously until an unexpected and violent
puff of wind tore at the sails, causing the little craft to shoot
forward so rapidly that the string attaching it to Theodore
broke and it sailed proudly into the middle of the Serpentine.
"Oh, no!" Theodore wailed. "Cathie, Cathie, my boat.
What shall we do?"

"Never mind, love," Cassie comforted him. "We shall
look for a gardener and see if he can help us."

"You mustn't sail in such heavy weather, young Master
Theodore," Horace commented with ponderous humor.

Meanwhile, Wellington was surveying the scene,
disgustedly thinking to himself that if it were left to his
landlubbing companions, they would never retrieve the boat.
Without a moment's hesitation the little dog hurled himself
into the pond with a terrific splash.

"Quack. Quack." Ethelred steamed up, intrigued by all
the commotion and enchanted to be able to share quite the

most delightful thing he'd seen in London with his best friend.

In no time at all, Wellington had paddled out to the craft, which was now becalmed in the very center of the Serpentine. Seizing the frayed end of the string in his strong terrier jaws, he paddled back to what was now a crowd of spectators surrounding Cassie and Horace on the bank. Always one to appreciate an audience, the little terrier found himself in somewhat of a dilemma as he found it impossible to smile winningly at the onlookers and keep the string between his teeth. He settled instead for adopting a valiant expression as he towed the boat to shore, Ethelred behind him, quacking encouragement all the way.

His efforts were rewarded by Teddy, who clapped gleefully before grabbing the string and praising him. "I knew you could do it, Wellington. You're smarter than all the dogs at Astley's Amphitheater put together."

Wellington smiled modestly, but when a fashionably clad young buck exclaimed to his friend, "Gad, did you see that? What spirit. Damme, that dog's a regular Trojan!" he was ready to burst with pride. With a mighty shove, he clambered up the wall and onto the bank, where he was greeted enthusiastically.

"Quack! Quack!" Ethelred cheered, beaming praise from his bright little eyes.

"Well done, Wellington!" Cassie congratulated him as she sought a dry spot on his head to pat. The little dog was so drenched that it was rather difficult to locate one, and unfortunately for her, he decided at that moment to shake himself dry. Spraying muddy water in all directions, he thoroughly spattered Cassie's gray kerseymere pelisse. As she was trying to wipe the spots off with her pocket handkerchief, Ethelred hopped out and waddled over to her, shaking out his feathers and indicating in no uncertain terms that he was tired and wanted to be picked up. Never one to refuse a friend, Cassie stooped over and lifted him in her arms.

At this moment, an amused voice intruded on the scene.

"I should have known when I heard the commotion and saw a crowd gathered that somehow Cassie would be at the bottom of it," remarked Ned, sauntering up with Arabella on his arm.

Cassie had been conscious, even as she had donned it that morning, that though the gray pelisse with ruby trim was infinitely becoming, it was definitely outmoded. Now, seeing Arabella's exquisite silk pelisse in the latest shade of *peau de papillon* with the delicate ruff and sleeves *à l'Espagnole* which emphasized her dainty beauty, Cassie felt doubly aware of her dowdy appearance.

Her humiliation was complete when Arabella fluted, "Oh, Cassie, how perfectly dreadful! You're soaked and your pelisse is all over mud. I wonder that you bear it so calmly." Arabella laid a hand on her arm with a meltingly sympathetic look which, Cassie thought to herself, was all for Ned's benefit. She doesn't care a rap how I look, only that she looks a great deal better. In spite of this salutary little speech to herself, Cassie could not help feeling like a scrub of a schoolgirl, thus confronted by her elegant friends.

Help came from an unexpected quarter. "Cassandra always looks beautiful," Horace defended her. "She has an elegance of mind and spirit that render her beautiful no matter how she is clad."

"Why, thank you, Horace," Cassie exclaimed in surprise, her smile appearing like the sun after a shower.

Arabella's jaw shut with a snap, making her mouth an unbecomingly thin line in her face. She was not accustomed to hearing others than herself praised with such gallantry and it did not please her in the least.

But Theodore spoke staunchly in defense of his aunt. "Cathie ith the most beautiful lady I know, and what's more, she'th a great gun, too."

"Arf! Arf!" Wellington joined in, not one to be outdone by a couple of humans when the reputation of his mistress was at stake.

"Well done, all of you," drawled Ned, highly amused at the spirited defense accorded his playmate.

Arabella, mightily put out by the turn events were taking, interrupted sweetly, "Why yes. With such good friends as these, one doesn't need to be fashionable or win the approval of the *ton*. And speaking of the *ton,* I am certain I see Sir Brian waving to us. We should leave Cassie to go home and change into some dry clothes." Laying a possessive hand on Ned's arm, she led him off toward the spot where Sir Brian, astride a magnificent gray, was conversing with Lady Jersey and her companions in an elegant barouche.

The schoolroom party wended their way home, where no one was the least surprised at their dishevelment, Higgins having welcomed Cassie and Freddie over the years in far grubbier attire than anyone was in now. Without blinking an eye, the butler instructed them, "You go on into the drawing room. I shall have a fire lit there and tea brought in to you directly." Cheered at the prospect, the entire party hurried upstairs.

In no time at all, tea and cakes were brought in and Frances, who had appeared from an hour spent with the dressmaker, was regaled with tales of Wellington's quick thinking and heroic action. The little dog sat blissfully munching a cake surreptitiously slipped to him by Theodore, and allowed himself to be led to the best spot in front of the fire and generally fussed over.

"We saw Ned and Arabella, too," Theodore volunteered, "and I mutht thay, I don't think she wath very nice to Cathie. She didn't say anything particularly nathty, but they had mean eyeth."

Here, Horace deemed it prudent to interrupt. "You're looking much more the thing, Cassandra. I confess to some relief at that. I had meant to give you an outing that would afford you some relaxation, but instead it became far more taxing than the writing you were engaged in when I appeared."

The darkling look that had appeared on Cassie's face at the mention of Ned and Araballa vanished and she smiled warmly. "Oh no, Horace, I had a lovely time," she contradicted him. Then, lowering her voice confidentially, she admitted, "I do so enjoy a bit of adventure, you know."

Privately, Horace thought that someone as elegant as Lady Cassandra Cresswell should avoid adventure at all costs, but unwilling to disrupt their reestablished harmony, he contented himself with remarking simply, "I'm glad."

"Thank you so much for thinking of it and including all of us, especially when we proved to be more of a charge than you anticipated." Laying a hand on his arm, Cassie smiled gratefully at him.

She looked so charming and Horace had felt such a thrill of pride at her gratitude when he had championed her in the face of Arabella's comments that he resolved to speak to Lord Mainwaring at the soonest possible moment. He then took his leave, but not before securing the first waltz at the upcoming ball in Cassie's honor.

Horace sauntered home, will satisfied with the day's events, picturing himself the center of attention at intellectual soirees with a beautiful vivacious wife on his arm. At first he had been so taken with Cassie that he had not thought beyond his attraction, but later, as he had observed her at various social gatherings, it had been borne in on him that having such a woman as his wife would do a great deal to further his advancement in the scholarly community. Having realized that, he frequently congratulated himself on having had the forethought to be attracted to the daughter of such noted classicists as Lord and Lady Cresswell.

CHAPTER 15

Cassie was not the only one to see her companion through slightly different eyes. Ned, reflecting on his latest experience, however, was coming to view his in a less propitious light. Beginning with his first youthful adoration of Arabella, he had suffered disillusionment. But the several intervening years that he had not seen her had dimmed the first sharp pangs of disappointment and he had come to see her as Cassie had first characterized her—a social creature who craved gaiety. Picturing Arabella in that light, he had taken some of the blame for his dismissal upon himself, realizing that a raw, reserved, and serious youth such as he had been could hardly have appealed to someone who aspired to the pinnacles of social success. As he had moved from one princely court to another in India, Ned had acquired diplomatic skills and social polish. This, and the fact that as a single, attractive male in a foreign land he was much sought after as a companion by the ladies connected with the British enclave, had given him a great deal of experience in the art of dalliance and increased his self-confidence enormously.

He had gradaully lost the natural shyness and reserve which had obscured a keen wit and charming conversation and discovered that he was someone who could entertain and be entertained by society. Added experience in the capitals of Europe, where his facility with languages and his sensitive nature recommended him to some of Europe's most beguiling coquettes, had turned him into a man who was admired by women of taste everywhere. By the time he returned to

London, Ned was so much the master of any social situation that he had entirely forgotten his pettish resolve to prove himself to Arabella Taylor.

The ease with which he had captured her interest had amused him. Never one to rate himself very high, he was under no illusions that it was his character or intellect that attracted her. Full well Ned realized that he was one of the Season's sensations and that it was in this role that he commanded Arabella's attention. He had so far recovered from his infatuation with her that he could be amused by her transparent attempts to win him as her cicisbeo, being well aware that as soon as another, more fashionable conquest presented itself, he would lose much of his attraction for her. There was not the slightest doubt that Arabella was a very beautiful, very skilled young woman who could be counted on to charm any escort and to make him feel as though he were the very center of her existence. So, Ned had acquiesced in all her various schemes and, though fully cognizant of her machinations, had allowed himself to be taken in by all her little ploys, viewing them as diverting but harmless manifestations of her devotion to fashion. It frequently amused him to see how important the opinion of the *ton* was to her, and though he considered this slavish worship of the tenets of the beau monde to be a weakness in her, it was, nevertheless, a weakness which rendered her charming.

All this had changed, however, when he witnessed her encounter with Cassie in the park. What had been a charming, if frivolous, propensity for following fashion's lead suddenly appeared a selfish desire to be the sole focus of attention whatever the cost. The self-centeredness that had heretofore seemed amusingly childlike now became unattractive at best, not to mention unkind.

Disgusted at himself as well as Arabella, Ned began to eschew social gatherings, concentrating instead on furthering his political aspirations. Having experienced firsthand in India the way England's mercantile interests influenced her foreign policy and military affairs, he had become quite concerned that these far-flung mercantile interests be given the proper attention and direction by the government at home. The advent of Canning and Huskisson in the government, men who were scrutinizing colonial policy and reappraising the Navigation Acts, encouraged him to believe that there were people in power who shared his interests.

Convinced that he was too young and too reserved to be successful in Parliament, Ned concentrated on attaching himself to the proper people. He was decidedly fortunate to have Lord Julian Mainwaring as an uncle, for not only did the marquess move in the correct political circles and have the ears of the most influential men, he was able to offer a fair assessment of Ned's character and capabilities to these political allies.

Thus Ned became a more frequent visitor in Grosvenor Square and at Brooks's, where Lord Mainwaring had been kind enough to sponsor him. There, he found, thanks to his connection with Lord Mainwaring, that some of the government's leading lights were increasingly happy to include him in their discussions. Even Lord Charlton, a man whose enormous power was usually hidden from the view of the uninitiated, favored him with his opinions one day after a large repast.

Strolling over to the table where Ned was regaling some of the younger men with colorful descriptions of his more lurid exploits, Lord Charlton launched without ceremony into a political discussion. "Fenton tells me that you're in favor of the relaxation of the Navigation Acts," he charged.

Ned nodded a cautious assent.

"Are you daft, lad? With Spain allowing the world to trade with her colonies and the opening of Brazilian ports we need to protect ourselves against competition," he insisted.

"That is true, sir, but keeping the Navigation Acts as they are won't accomplish that. Portugal, Prussia, and the Netherlands are benefiting from trade with Brazil, San Domingo, and the others, but in order to protect themselves, they are raising their dues against British vessels. This will not only injure us, but worse, it hinders our colonial trade," Ned defended himself.

"You may have a point there, my boy. Fenton warned me that you were almost as extreme as Bentham on the subject of the Colonies," Lord Charlton remarked, wagging an admonitory finger at him.

Ned laughed, "Never that, sir. But I do believe that we must rid ourselves of the notion that the acts exist purely for the profit of the mother country. We ought to recognize that what is in the Colonies' best interests will ultimately be in our own best interests and act accordingly."

"Good lad," Lord Charlton approved. "I was merely teasing you, though. Bentham is a fine man with high ideals, but he sometimes becomes so involved in what should be that he completely loses sight of what is."

Ned nodded. "We need high-minded men with vision to keep us headed in the right direction, but we also need others with a more pragmatic bent to ensure that these reforms are carried out."

"I agree. I agree. It's all very well to carry on about the need for reform in government, but most of those who advocate it so strongly haven't the least notion how to go about accomplishing it. We need men like you who are intelligent enough to grasp the theories, and the principles of these improvements, but whose experience has trained them to succeed in getting such changes carried out. From what I hear, you and young Freddie Cresswell were able to make a goodly number of changes in India without setting up anyone's back and causing resistance. We need young men like you. I must make sure to introduce you to Canning one day. He's a busy man, but not so busy that he doesn't realize he needs supporters—especially bright young men who are too few and far between these days for my liking. Everyone is too caught up in cutting a dash for himself in society to worry about politics or the state of affairs here and in the Colonies. Now that Boney's no longer a threat, they seem to have forgotten that such things as governments and armies exist, much less realize that they need people to run them. But I won't run on. You must come and see me. I shall see what I can do to bring you to Canning's attention."

"Thank you ever so much, sir." Ned was visibly gratified at this unexpected vote of confidence and support. In fact, he was so elated at the prospect of moving in such exalted political circles that he quitted Brooks's immediately after Lord Charlton and strode over to Grosvenor Square to share the news of this propitious encounter.

He would have preferred to share it with Cassie, who had been privy to all his political aspirations through their correspondence, but since the episode in the park, she appeared to have been avoiding him. And when she did encounter him, she was noticeably cool in her manner. In all likelihood, Ned reflected disgustedly, she would be off somewhere with that tiresome fellow, Horace Wilbraham. Being entirely correct in his assumptions, he was forced to content himself with relating it all to Freddie, who, though he listened with interest, was not as fully conversant with Ned's ideas and dreams as his sister.

Aware of the importance of Lord Charlton, though, he was suitably enthusiastic. "Most impressive, Neddie boy!" he exclaimed, giving Ned a hearty buffet on the shoulder. "In no time at all you'll be moving in such exclusive circles you'll be quite above my touch."

Ned quirked an amused eyebrow at him. "You always were given to exaggeration, Freddie. After all, you and I are interested in accomplishing the same things, and you have your own ideas as to what should be done."

Freddie looked skeptical, protesting, "That's as may be, Ned, but I haven't got nearly as much in the old cock loft as you. Why, if you hadn't gone gallivanting off to India with me, you'd be at Oxford now ruining your eyesight, your nose eternally in some musty old tome like the rest of those scholarly fellows." A darkling look settled on his normally sunny features as he continued, "And speaking of scholarly fellows, I wish I knew what Cassie saw in Wilbraham. Fellow haunts the place. I tell you, that disapproving studious look he constantly wears is enough to put anybody off. To tell you the truth, Cassie is becoming almost as bad as he is.

She says she enjoys his company because it improves her mind. Hah! If you ask me, I don't think he's half as bright as you or Cassie. All he is, is a prosy old windbag.'' He lowered his voice conspiratorially. "I can tell you, Fanny doesn't like the connection above half either. Of course she doesn't *say* anything, but you can see it, nevertheless. Why even Teddy and Wellington don't care for him in the least.''

Cathing Ned's amused glance, he defended himself. "Laugh all you want to, but Teddy and Wellington know a right 'un when they see him. If you ask me, there's something dashed smoky about him. Can't put my finger on it at the moment, but there's something queer there, I'll be bound.''

Further commentary on the character of the unfortunate and defenseless Horace was interrupted by the headlong entrance of Teddy, closely followed by Wellington, Nelson, and Ethelred. "Uncle Freddie, Uncle Freddie,'' Teddy burst out. Catching sight of his idol, he came to a screeching halt, causing the companions following close behind him to tumble into a disorganized heap of fur and feathers. "How glad I am to thee you, thir,'' he exclaimed. "Did you ride Brututh? May I go thee him? I promith you Wellington won't bother him. He'th ever tho good with hortheth,'' Theodore begged, looking worshipfully up at Ned.

Ned laughed, but he was touched by the blatant admiration he saw in Teddy's eyes. "It's Ned, Teddy. And, yes, I did ride Brutus and of course you may go see him. I expect he would enjoy it as I have been a rather dull companion to him lately.''

"Oh, thank you, thir . . . I mean Ned,'' Teddy added shyly. On the point of a departure as precipitate as his entrance, he recalled his original errand and turned back to Freddie, asking, "Uncle Freddie, could you come and pitch for me? I want to try my new cricket bat, but John Coachman can't spare Jim at the moment, tho . . .'' Teddy's voice trailed off disconsolately.

"I'm sorry, Teddy,'' Freddie began apologetically,

glancing at the clock on the mantel, "but I promised Fortescue I would meet him at Tattersall's. Why don't you ask Cassie?"

"Cathie?" Teddy sounded doubtful.

"She's a much better pitcher than I am, you know," Freddie admitted generously. Always loath to let his twin take all the glory, he couldn't resist adding, "But she's hopelessly cow-handed with a bat."

Teddy remained looking dubious until Ned added, "Don't underestimate your aunt Cassie. She and Freddie played together as children and she always could do everything he did—sometimes better." He grinned at the sputtering sound behind him.

Convinced that if his hero said it, it must be so, Teddy wasted no time in racing off in search of his aunt while Wellington, Nelson, and Ethelred, having learned from their recent experience, followed at a more judicious distance.

CHAPTER 16

As Ned had surmised, Cassie was with Horace busily working at the Comte de Vaudron's. Feeling guilty about having abstained from visiting the comte because she had wished to avoid Horace, Cassie had thrown herself back into their endeavor with renewed energy and had happily spent her morning amid friezes and fragments of statues. She enjoyed the quiet of the comte's library after the constant bustle of Mainwaring House, but even more, she enjoyed the feeling of silent companionship as she, Horace, and the comte sat working, each absorbed in his or her own particular project.

There had been more commotion than usual in Grosvenor Square that morning as Mainwaring House girded its loins for the ball in honor of Cassie's come-out. Frances, ordinarily the least ostentatious of hostesses and the most sympathetic of sisters, this time had turned a deaf ear to Cassie's remonstrances.

"Fanny, there's not the least need to go to all that bother," Cassie protested. "I've been introduced to most of the *ton* already. They know and I know I shall never cut a dash, so there's really no need to bring me to their attention further. I've met enough of them to feel certain that I don't wish to spend my entire life in society. I'm happy as I am, so a ball is really to no purpose." She did not add, though she might have, that since she also had an extremely eligible prospect, there was no longer any reason for her to be introduced to marriageable young men. It was common knowledge in the household that since Lord Mainwaring's return, Horace had been assiduous in his efforts to seek the marquess out but had met with little success. With unerring instinct he always seemed to arrive at Grosvenor Square just minutes after Julian had left.

"And a good thing, too," Higgins commented, unbending a little to confide in Cook. Ordinarily the most dignified of mortals, who would never indulge in anything so far beneath him as to gossip, especially with his inferiors, Higgins found this matter to be of such serious concern that he relaxed his rigid principles. "This Horace Wilbraham is not the match for her. Our Cassie wants someone who's awake on every suit. He is far too dull for her. She would be bored within a month and she could never get along for long with someone made as nervous by horses as he is."

Cook nodded sagely as she handed him another slice of plum cake. "Aye, you're in the right of it, Mr. Higgins. Our Miss Cassie's much too lively for the likes of him. She wants someone who knows all about them Greek fellows she's so interested in as well as someone who will help her cut a dash. Leastways, she's much too pretty to waste her life as a spinster. She needs a man who is adventurous as Master Freddie but with a little more in the brain box." She paused for a moment, fixing a ruminative stare on the remains of the plum cake. "She needs someone like Master Ned," she announced at last.

Higgins appeared to be much struck by this idea. "Master Ned," he murmured thoughtfully. "You may have something there, Mrs. Wilkins. I must see what I can discover about this situation. Certainly the prospect of young Mr. Wilbraham as a husband for Miss Cassie doesn't bear thinking of."

But for the time being Higgins had to set aside this concern for his young mistress's future as he was far too busy doing his best to ensure that the ball to be given in honor of Lady Cassandra Cresswell would be the most talked of event of the Season. He threw himself into the supervision of silver polishing and chandelier washing, spending more time than he cared to think of ordering the proper quantities of champagne and flowers, making sure there were enough link boys engaged, and worrying over the procurement of the miles of red carpet to be laid out to the street. And though he left the preparation of the quantities of lobster patties, jellies, chantillies, ices, and sweetmeats to Cook, he kept a proprietary interest in it all and made certain, having spent much time discussing such matters over a pint of ale with contemporaries from other great houses, that nothing but the best was being served at Mainwaring House.

On a smaller scale, Rose, Cassie's maid, was putting forth her best efforts to make sure that Cassie was in her best looks for the big event. She watched her mistress with a more observant eye than usual to make certain that she didn't set a foot out of doors without a bonnet and a parasol. "Because you know Miss Cassie," she confided in Lady Frances's maid, more intimately known to Rose as her eldest sister Daisy. "If I didn't keep a sharp eye on her, she would forget either one or both and be brown as an Indian in no time."

It was at Rose's urging that a protesting Cassie went more than her usual one time to Madame Regnery to be fitted. When Cassie pointed out to her that Madame knew her figure and all its flaws better than its owner did, Rose turned mulish. "It's as much as my position is worth, Miss Cassie, to see that you do us all proud. It is already outside of enough the airs and graces Miss Arabella Taylor's Susan puts on. I've borne with them for years because we all know your mind is on higher things, but allowing her to have the least cause to put on airs because her mistress criticizes your toilette at your own ball is something I will not do, no matter how much it displeases you. I have my pride, after all, and no mistress of mine is going to be outdone by that creature."

"Very well, Rose," Cassie sighed. "I had no notion I was such a trial to you, but I can see that you have had to put up with a good deal all these years."

"Not at all, Miss Cassie," Rose contradicted her stoutly. "You're far more beautiful than Miss Araballa. Aye, you may stare, brunettes being all the rage, but your nose is much better and your chin won't run to fat the way hers will, mark my words. What's more, your skin and curls owe nothing to art.'' Seeing Cassie's look of patent disbelief, Rose defended herself. ''Well, everyone is aware that she paints . . . or at the very least she uses the rouge pot and blackens her lashes. It's common enough knowledge, but Susan is forever complaining of the hours she has to spend with all sorts of lotions and powders, making her mistress look her best. Why you would be astounded at the goings-on.''

''Arabella?'' Cassie was horrified. The idea of painting conjured up an image of a sophisticated woman far more exciting than the person she had seen skin her knees and fall off her pony times out of mind.

''Yes, Miss Arabella,'' Rose maintained firmly. ''And what's more, her curls aren't natural either.'' Again Cassie appeared to be completely taken aback by this revelation. ''The amount of time Susan spends to make those ringlets would make your head spin. Why her hair is as straight as a board!'' Rose shook her head.

''Gracious, this certainly has been a most enlightening afternoon,'' Cassie commented. Still too bemused by this surprising information to absorb it all, she allowed herself to be helped into her pelisse and hustled off to Madame Regnery's elegant establishment on South Moulton Street, where she meekly endured a tedious hour of being pushed and prodded while Madame's minions draped and pinned.

CHAPTER 17

The extraordinary efforts of all the staff were well worth it, and those waiting to be helped out of carriages the next evening in front of a Mainwaring House ablaze with the light from quantities of flambeaux were already labeling it a dreadful squeeze even before they mounted the great marble staircase. There was such a crush of vehicles that the link boys, John Coachman, and the lads from several of the neighboring stables had their hands full helping the carriages maneuver up to the doorway to deposit their occupants.

Cassie, standing at the head of the stairs with Frances and Lord Mainwaring, couldn't remember when Mainwaring House had looked so elegant.

"It certainly outdoes the way it looked for my come-out," Lady Kitty Willoughby assured her as she greeted Cassie warmly. "And that was voted the event of the Season."

Cassie was astounded at the sheer numbers of beautifully clad women, their shoulders glittering with splendid jewels, accompanied by elegant men in satin knee breeches who mounted the stairway to greet them before proceeding to the ballroom, where the banks of flowers, masses of candles, and musicians all contrived to overwhelm the senses.

Rose finally had her way, and Cassie who had submitted to many more hours in the preparation of her toilette than she would have ordinarily allowed, was in her best looks. Wearing a round dress of Urling's net over a white satin slip, the skirt trimmed with flounces of lace, she looked ethereal and innocent among the brightly colored assemblage. Her mother's magnificent baroque pearls emphasized the creamy

121

smoothness of her skin. Pearls also anchored the lozenges of her corsage and were sewn in the rouleaux of satin that trimmed the short puffed sleeves. Rose had prevailed upon her to allow her hair to be dressed in a more elaborate style than the simple ones preferred by Horace. At Cassie's protests that these were the types he favored, Rose had snorted, "Hah! And what does Master Horace know, I'd like to know. He's head over heels in love with you as it is. Besides, it's the ladies you want to impress. They're the ones who gossip. Except for a few very elegant gentlemen like Mr. Bertie Montgomery, men don't give a fig for such things, but they do notice them if a woman points out to them, and rest assured, people like Miss Arabella Taylor take every opportunity to do so."

So Cassie had given in and permitted Rose to dress her hair in the French style with the back hair brought up to the top of her head and held in place with a garland of white roses, while a profusion of curls, "nat'ral, every one of them," Rose had declared with satisfaction, framed her face. "Just you watch, Miss Cassie," she had admonished her mistress, "if that Miss Arabella dares to wear curls this evening, they'll go limp with all the heat, because it's bound to be a sad crush." With that, she had given a final pat to her mistress's coiffeur, twitched a flounce on her dress, and sent her on her way.

If she had been able to see her mistress leading off the first dance with Lord Mainwaring, Rose would have been reassured that her ministrations had not been in vain. Though she did not rate it high on her favorite list of activities, Cassie was possessed of a natural grace and coordination which made her a beautiful dancer. To see her coupled with as adept a partner as Lord Mainwaring, whose powerful frame elegantly clad in black evening clothes provided the perfect foil for her slim figure encased in shimmering white, quite took the breath away of even the most casual of observers. No matter that brunettes were all the rage, Cassie's cloud of golden hair and her dark blue eyes fringed with dark lashes only emphasized the freshness of her complexion. Compared

with the gaudy sophisticates around her, whose faces were
pictures of weary boredom or self-interest, she presented such
a contrast of innocence and vitality that it caused the pulses
of more than one male bystander to quicken.

Even Freddie, who ordinarily remained blithely unaware
of the competitive spirit rampant in the fashionable world,
remarked to his twin as he led her through the quadrille,
"You're looking fine as fivepence, Cass."

"Why thank you, Freddie," she responded, surprised and
touched by this brotherly encomium.

Freddie nodded as sagely as if he had been an acute
observer of the social scene for years instead of the past hour.
"Tell you what, you take the shine out of every lady here.
Even Fortescue told me he thought you looked to be in prime
twig, and you know Forty, you have to be a horse, and a
sweet goer at that, to rate such praise from him," he
volunteered.

"That is praise indeed. I am truly overcome," Cassie
agreed, her eyes dancing. "If you say any more, I shall fear
you're offering me Spanish coin and that you're angling for
something like borrowing my horse Chiron or wanting me
to do some disagreeable task such as writing a letter for you."

Freddie looked aggrieved. "Lord, Cass, can't a fellow
offer you a compliment without your being so blasted
suspicious?"

His sister laughed. "Forgive me, Freddie. It's just that
you are so much in the way of pointing out what's wrong
with my seat as I take a jump or the way I hold a cricket
bat that I'm not accustomed to your praise and I don't know
how to react properly. I *do* appreciate it, and your approval
means more to me than most because you are often odiously
candid about my flaws. Thank you."

"Now *that's* more the spirit a compliment should be
received in," her twin remarked, accepting this handsome
apology with an air of noble condescension.

Their *tête-à-tête* was interrupted by Ned, who strolled over
to claim his dance. He led Cassie so energetically around
the floor that she was quite out of breath when Bertie

appeared to claim her in the waltz he had reserved the minute he had received the gilt-edged invitation.

Casting an experienced eye over her toilette, he nodded approvingly. "That's an exceedingly elegant rig, Cassie. Madame Regnery outdid herself this time . . . not that she didn't have an inspiring model."

"Why thank you, Bertie," Cassie responded in a highly gratified tone. "Coming from such an *exacting* arbiter of taste and fashion as you, that is high praise indeed!" And Cassie was flattered. Constant and true a friend though he might be, Bertie Montgomery never allowed his exquisite sensibilities to be blinded by loyalty. Indeed, he considered that the several occasions he had rendered the greatest assistance to his friends had been when his obstinate criticism had helped them to avert sartorial disasters.

He shuddered even now to think how close old Ponsonby had actually been to wearing a waistcoast of a particularly violent shade of yellow had not Bertie fortuitously appeared just as he was leaving the house in Curzon Street. Even such a nonpareil as Lord Julian Mainwaring, Bertie's oldest friend and schoolmate, had been known to have second thoughts when Bertie, upon encountering him, had looked vaguely troubled and asked, "Are you sure you want to be seen in that cravat, old man?" Thus his approbation was an accolade of which Cassie could justifiably be proud, and though she normally did not devote a great deal of thought to her appearance once she had dressed, she did feel a glow of confidence knowing that the others considered her to be in her best looks.

The exertions on the dance floor added a becoming flush to her cheeks and the humidity of the crowded ballroom made the few golden tendrils escaping from her coiffeur curl so delightfully around her animated face that more than one bracket-faced dowager remarked that the youngest of Belinda Carstairs's daughters was a remarkably pretty gel. And among the male observers, bored by Seasons of new faces entering society, more than one young buck was heard to say that Freddie Cresswell's sister was turning into a "demmed beauty."

By the end of the dance, Cassie was breathless and her feet were beginning to ache, so it was with relief that she realized her next dance was promised to Horace. She knew he could be counted on to prefer sitting quietly on the sidelines to maneuvering around a crowded floor. But when Bertie, casting an eye around the ballroom, remarked, "And now, having had the great honor of dancing with the belle of the ball, I shall take you to your next partner, wherever he is," Horace was nowhere to be seen.

After searching the assemblage for some minutes, Cassie finally identified him amid a clump of men earnestly discussing something intriguing enough to render them totally oblivious to their surroundings and their social obligations. "There," she pointed him out to Bertie.

"Well, I call that pretty cavalier behavior," Bertie commented, taking her arm. "Yes, and foolish, too. If he don't take care, one of the many pinks of the *ton* who's been admiring you all evening is likely to steal you from under his nose. Horace always was a slow top."

Cassie laughed. Nevertheless, she flushed with pleasure as she replied, "Doing it much too brown, Bertie. I'm no incomparable, but you certainly make me feel like one."

It was Bertie's turn to blush, but he was saved from making any response as they had reached the group that contained Horace, Ned, that noted classicist and president of the Society of Antiquaries, the Earl of Aberdeen, and several others whom Cassie did not recognize.

"Ah, *ma chère* Cassie," exclaimed the comte, turning to take her hand. "Come, you must take my place. Milord has been asking how our work progresses. You must tell him while I go in search of Lady Montague, to whom I promised a waltz."

The Earl greeted Cassie courteously. "I heard that you are following in the footsteps of your estimable father and mother. You were fortunate in having such diligent and devoted scholars as parents. They were an inspiration to us all and we miss them sorely. But at least we have someone equally brilliant in the Comte de Vaudron to carry on their valuable work. And your colleague, Horace here, bids fair to joining their select group. He has been telling me how his interpretation of the object on one of the friezes as a *peplos* establishes the sex of a previously unidentified figure and thus makes it clear that the procession represented is a celebration of the Panathenaea. A brilliant piece of deduction. I saw the frieze myself and was at a loss, but now, applying Horace's theory, I see it makes perfect sense.''

All thoughts of her gay surroundings vanished and Cassie felt a cold chill wash over her. A knot hardened in her stomach. She felt as she once had when Freddie, in one of their few true fights, had sought to tip her a leveler and had punched her in the stomach instead, knocking the wind out of her. The shock of Horace's deceit and betrayal left her cold and shaking. Mustering all her courage, she gritted her teeth, smiled brilliantly, and replied, ''Yes we discussed it at some length and it does seem to be the most reasonable way to look at it. Horace is very quick to adopt new ideas.'' She looked around, desperately searching for some excuse to leave, but seeing none, fixed her eyes on a pillar, remarking, ''But I see my sister beckoning me. I must go to her. I do apologize for leaving such an interesting discussion.'' With this she fled as precipitately as possible, trying not to reveal her anger or her pressing wish to be somewhere by herself.

The only escape lay in the garden. Glancing quickly around to assure herself that no one would notice or remark on her exit, she slipped through the open French window and into the peace and quiet outside. The glow from the ballroom made the obscurity of the yew-lined walk around the perimeter walls appear even darker than usual. It was here she fled to lean against the cold mossy wall, her breath coming in gasps as she clenched and unclenched her hands and tried to blink back the tears of rage that sprang to her eyes.

Her disappearance had been swift and quiet enough to escape everyone's notice except that of someone whose quick perception and sensitivity had seen her first start of surprise and had hazarded a fairly accurate guess as to its cause. Years of debating intellectual arguments with Cassie had closely attuned Ned to her mind and her ways of thinking. He had been several years ahead of Horace Wilbraham in school, where he had known him as an earnest, but plodding student who lacked the intellectual brilliance and creativity or the curiosity to become a true scholar. Familiar with the pedantic and unoriginal cast of his mind, Ned had been more than a little surprised that he had come up with such a well-constructed and intriguing interpretation of the frieze. In fact, Ned had just been criticizing himself for having judged Horace too quickly when he happened to catch sight of Cassie's face. One glance and he knew the reason for the look of shock and betrayal registered there. His initial disgust at such intellectual dishonesty faded quickly when she left, replaced by an urgent desire to catch up with her and assure her that *he,* at least, recognized the stamp of her intellect even if others did not.

Waving to an imaginary acquaintance across the room, Ned bowed to the group and headed for the French windows, where a swirl of white flounce was all that gave away Cassie's place of retreat.

He stepped across the threshold and into the shadows. "Cassie?" he called softly, walking toward the farthest corner of the garden. "Cassie?" He tried again with no success. This time, though, he heard a faint rustle and saw the vague gleam of pearls caught in the light from the ballroom. As he approached, he heard the gasps and saw the shaking of the delicate shoulders as Cassie fought for control.

Ned's heart went out to her. One swift step brought him to her and he pulled the slender form into his arms. For some time he held her there, stroking her hair and murmuring over and over, "My poor girl. Hush, Cassie."

The sobbing subsided. Cassie gave a gulp, pulled herself

away, and looked up, apologizing angrily, "I can't think why I was so overcome. I'm usually not such a poor creature. It's just that—"

A lean bronzed hand reached out to push back a stray tendril as Ned soothed, "I know. I know. You couldn't fathom how anyone could lay claim so baldly to your ideas."

The dark blue eyes bright with unshed tears regarded him in astonishment. "But how did you know?" she demanded with some surprise.

Ned smiled fondly down at her. "Cassie, my girl, I know your mind as well as I know my own, and I also know Horace Wilbraham's. You were at daggers drawn with me once for casting doubt on his capabilities, but he doesn't hold a candle to you in any field. He no more could have dreamed up that interpretation than he could ride Chiron."

She smiled weakly at him. "Will you forgive me for being so angry at you that time I acknowledged that perhaps you were in the right of it?"

An answering smile glimmered as Ned raised his eyebrows in disbelief, exclaiming, "An apology! From the redoubtable Cassandra? You must be more distraught than I had realized."

This sally was rewarded with a watery chuckle.

"That's better, my girl. It takes more than a poor pedant to get the better of Lady Cassandra Cresswell."

Cassie's smile was erased as another thought came to her. Eyes dark with hurt and anger, she looked up at Ned as she wondered aloud, "But how could he . . . how could he lie like that?"

And take the credit from someone he professed to admire so extravagantly and pursued with such dogged determination, Ned remarked privately in disgust. But he kept his thoughts to himself, saying instead as he took her hands in a firm but gentle clasp, "I don't know why, Cassie." A flash of grin broke the gravity of his expression. "But it's a brilliant interpretation. You can hardly blame the poor fellow for wishing he'd thought of it," he conceded.

She smiled shyly at him. "Thank you, Ned. How kind of you to say so."

Looking unwontedly serious, he cupped her chin in his hand and gazed deep into her eyes. "It's not kindness, my girl. It's the truth. You have a mind filled with ideas that can compete with the best of them," he assured her.

She returned his look gravely, questioningly.

They stood some time gazing at one another until a burst of laughter from the ballroom recalled them to their surroundings.

"Will you be all right?" Ned asked in some concern, gathering both her hands gently in his.

Cassie dropped her eyes to look at her slim white fingers linked with his long tanned ones and nodded.

A tender look stole into Ned's eyes. He dropped a light kiss onto the golden curls. "That's my Cassie. Come." He drew her hand through his arm. "It wouldn't do for someone to be missing too long at her own ball, much as she considers such things to be the most frippery of occupations." This last remark, spoken as it was in a rallying tone, restored some modicum of vivacity to Cassie's countenance.

"That's the ticket," Ned approved. "Come. Waltz with me. It's the thing to do, you know. Sally Jersey vows I am the best waltz partner this side of the Channel." He quizzed her wickedly as he led her onto the floor.

To those who cared to observe, Lady Cassandra Cresswell, having danced continuously that evening, was now being whirled gaily around the room by one of the Season's biggest matrimonial prizes and enjoying herself immensely.

CHAPTER *18*

For Cassie the rest of the evening passed in a blur of assorted partners and conversations. Freddie and Bertie kept her plied with glasses of champagne and delicacies from the supper room, but she could no more than take a sip here and a nibble there. Somehow, she was not quite sure how, she managed to smile and nod in the appropriate places. Certainly she was able to satisfy eager partners or doting mamas with her conversation. At any rate, Arabella, who had magically appeared at Frances's elbow the moment Ned led Cassie back to the Mainwarings' coterie after their dance, seemed to find Cassie's abstracted response of, "Yes, lovely . . . no, truly, did she?" to her questions about the elegance of her own toilette and the raptures of Madame Celestine over her favorite partroness entirely satisfactory.

At last the evening ended and she was able to fall into bed, alone at last and at peace, to try to marshal the welter of thoughts, impressions, and emotions that had occupied her mind the latter part of the evening.

First and foremost were anger and disgust at Horace's appropriation of her ideas as his own. She then fell prey to a variety of emotions ranging from abhorrence of his duplicity and his sycophantic need for admiration whatever the cost, to hurt pride at his assumption that she would not notice or care that her inspiration fed his glory, to disillusionment at the discovery of dishonesty in someone she had admired and given her friendship to, to rage at her own stupidity at having been so blind to his weaknesses.

But thoughts of that dreadful moment in the ballroom when

130

revelation struck her also brought with them the memory of Ned's kindness. And the feelings stirred by that were even more varied and complicated than those precipitated by Horace's betrayal. She had always thought of Ned Mainwaring as an ordinary part of her life just as she had considered Freddie, Frances, Julian, and Teddy to be, but his sudden appearance in the garden had changed all that. He had invariably been extraordinarily sensitive to her moods and needs, and on the occasions when Freddie's bracing "Buck up, Cassie," had not had the desired effect, his sympathetic ear and advice had always brought solace. But this time something had been different. At first when he had taken her in his arms, she had felt nothing more than the comfort and security she had felt when as a child she had run to her parents or to Frances with a skinned knee. But as he had stroked her hair and comforted her, she had relaxed, and other, different feelings had washed over her.

Gradually she had become aware of his lean strength, the solidity of his chest, and the tightening of the muscles in his arms underneath the material of his jacket as he held her. When he had looked down at her, encouraging her and rallying her back into better spirits so she could reenter the ballroom with some degree of equanimity, she had realized for the first time what a singularly attractive man her old playmate had become. There had been an intensity in the dark blue eyes that she had not seen before and this had evoked a quiver of response in her that she could not quite place. All of a sudden she had become vividly aware of his nearness, of the warmth of his fingers on her bare arms and the feel of his breath in her hair. When he had kissed the top of her head, the response became a warm languorous tide sweeping over her and threatening to suffocate her. It had subsided somewhat by the time they returned to the ballroom, but her heightened awareness of Ned had not. During their waltz she had been conscious of nothing so much as the warm hand at her waist holding her, guiding her, and the agility with which he moved as he led her deftly around the floor.

Cassie lay awake for some time recalling in precise detail all these feelings and the moment that had brought about each one of these new sensations as she tried to identify and analyze the responses they evoked. But cogitate as she would, she could not come up with any satisfactory explanations for the puzzling sense of vague disquiet which excited her and made her extremely anxious all at the same time. She at last fell asleep just as the first rays of sunshine stole between the curtains, but it was a restless sleep, and it was not long before she woke, impatient to see if the daylight and quotidian duties would prove these new sensations to be mere figments of her imagination.

On his part, Ned was just as disquieted. Though no less confused than Cassie, having had more worldly experience than she, he was somewhat less in the dark as to the causes of the intense emotions he had experienced that evening. Unlike Cassie, he had not even made any attempts to go to bed or to seek the oblivion of sleep, but instead had sat in front of the fire swirling a glass of brandy in one hand and staring into the flames. When he had returned from his travels, having moved in society in India and Europe as well as London, Ned had begun to see Cassie from a more social perspective and to realize that she had become a lovely young woman. He had become more accustomed to this new picture of his former playmate as an attractive member of the opposite sex than Cassie had.

The revelations he was undergoing now were not of that nature, but they were no less disconcerting. Despite an initial sense of shock, Ned had gradually adjusted to the idea of a beautiful grown-up Cassie, but he had continued to regard her in this light as a fond brother might have. When she looked particularly elegant or charming, he had felt nothing more than the pride that Freddie or Frances might feel that their sister was admired, and he had been pleased to see her so well accepted by the *ton*. He had been less pleased by her attachment to Horace Wilbraham, but again, that had been the same feeling of disgust that Freddie experienced seeing his sister wasting her attention on someone who was inferior to her in every way.

However, when Ned had pulled Cassie into his arms that evening, something had occurred to make him realize that Cassie affected him in a way that had nothing to do with brotherly affection.

The vision of her, his intrepid playmate, trying desperately to stifle heartbroken sobs, had torn at his heart, and as he stared into the flames, it continued to move him. Because she had always been so ready to take on any challenge or adventure that Freddie, Nigel, or Ned could devise, Ned had always pictured Cassie as stronger and larger than she really was. It had been a shock to discover as he had pulled her close to him how small and fragile she felt in his arms. As he had looked down into her tear-filled eyes, huge in her delicate face, an overwhelming surge of protective rage had swept over him. He wanted to hold her close and do battle with anyone or anything that threatened her equanimity. The fact that, independent as she was, Cassie would have scorned to accept such protection made him doubly eager to spring to her defense and act as her champion.

As the sobs had subsided and Ned's immediate concern for her distress had lessened, he had gradually become aware of how she felt in his arms—the softness of her skin under his hands, the delicate scent of her hair brushing his chin— and he had wanted to pull her even closer to him, to hold her there forever, reveling in the depth of tenderness that welled up within him. He had held many other women in his arms, a good number of them more seductive and more voluptuous than Cassie Cresswell, but the feel of her body against his, lithe, slim, and trembling from her distress, had stirred emotions in him that he had never experienced before. A bewildering array of sensations had swept over him. Foremost had been the yearning to comfort her, to wipe away her distress as easily as he smoothed back her hair and to make everything all right again. Following that, dawned the awareness of how beautiful and desirable she looked. And last came the realization of how wonderful and yet how natural it felt to hold her in his arms and how much more he wanted.

Thinking over it all, reliving every gesture, every sigh, he longed to hold her again. His arms ached to go around her, to comfort her, to protect her from the world in spite of her constantly and vociferously expressed wish to take care of herself. You must be in your dotage, Ned, old boy, he admonished himself. That's Cassie you're thinking of. She's practically your sister. People don't feel such things about their sisters. It's just the concern you have for her happiness that makes you respond this way. She is not the type of woman to appeal to you—too damnably sure of her own mind, too prickly in her independence, too caught up in her interests to relax and enjoy herself. You don't want or need someone like that when those are already your natural proclivities. You should have someone charming and sophisticated who can introduce you to the gaieties in life and help you indulge yourself. You might be able to tolerate a sister who tells you that you have nothing in your cock loft or that your opinion on some issue is bacon-brained, but it don't make for an amusing companion. So why do you want to waste your time on someone who would lead you on such a merry dance?

This last question was so unanswerable that he tossed off the last of the brandy and tumbled into bed, hoping that total oblivion would erase those tantalizing but disquieting memories of the evening and allow him to pursue the less taxing, more pleasurable society of people such as Arabella and Lady Jersey, who could be counted on to demand so much flattering attention from him that he could give himself up to the pursuit of agreeable sensations. He needed someone whose gaiety and coquettishness would counteract his naturally serious personality, not someone who would exacerbate it. Flirting with beautiful worldly women from India to the capitals of Europe had taught him that life could be pleasurable. He had learned to appreciate the beauty, wit, and the delights of civilized society. It had made him more aware of the social needs of others and of his own desire and capacity for taking pleasure in the more sensual aspects of life, including fine food, wine, music, and art, all of which, in his headlong pursuit of his studies, he had rejected as wastes of time. These discoveries had expanded his perspective, enhanced his faculty for enjoyment, and had made him a richer person emotionally.

Upon returning to London, he had resolved not to become like the old reclusive Ned, who had shut himself off from the rest of the world in devoting his attentions to his scholarly pursuits to the exclusion of all else. Along that path lay shallowmindedness and self-centeredness. Unlike Horace Wilbraham, he resolved to avoid those at all costs. Somewhat to his surprise, he had succeeded so well in this resolve that he had been avidly pursued by the *ton*. Courted at first because he was a novelty who exhibited those perennially popular attributes of bachelorhood and wealth, Ned eventually came to be sought out because he was good company.

Ned and Cassie were not the only ones subject to post-festivity reflections. Bertie Montgomery was also pondering the evening's events as he sat at his ease swathed in a gorgeous dressing gown and sipping brandy in front of a fire. For all his insouciance and his intense devotion to fashion, Bertie was a sensitive and perspicacious observer. After having delivered Cassie to Horace that evening, he had hovered protectively on the edge of the group, fearing that one of the participants at least was so caught up in the discussion that he might completely ignore his previous social commitments. Bertie's quick ear for the nuances of social discourse had, on hearing the Earl of Aberdeen's infelicitous remark, immediately noticed Cassie's shocked expression of disbelief, quickly banished though it was, and the stiffening of her spine, more eloquent of her displeasure than any possible facial expression could have been. Not wanting to break in on the conversation, he had left her with Horace, but had lingered long enough to witness her departure from the ballroom closely followed by Ned. His curiosity aroused, he had kept a close watch on the French windows long enough to witness their subsequent reappearance.

To any other observer, nothing would have appeared at all amiss, but to Bertie, who had watched Cassie metamorphose from an adventurous tomboy to a vivacious young woman, she had seemed unwontedly subdued the rest of the evening. Bertie Montgomery was not completely the amiable brainless fop that all of society believed him to be. Though quick to admit that he did not have as much in his upper story as his friend Lord Julian Mainwaring, he did maintain that he was not entirely cork-brained. In fact, he had more than once astounded that exacting peer with his incredible grasp of the art of antiquity. He had not, as he had responded in his own defense, wholly wasted his youth, and his friendship with the Cresswells had sprung up more because of a common interest in classical Greece than from physical proximity. Though his ancestral estate was not far from Cresswell, he had spent more time with them while they were in Athens than he had when they were in Hampshire. It was only after Lord and Lady Cresswell had died that he had become such a frequent visitor to their household as to seem to be another brother to Frances and uncle to the twins.

It was his familiarity with both classical scholarship and the mind of Lady Cassandra Cresswell that had led Bertie to hazard some very accurate guesses as to what had happened. As someone who shared a common interest in antiquity, Bertie had become acquainted with Horace Wilbraham, but finding him to be a less than original scholar with no appreciation whatsoever for aesthetics, he largely ignored him. In fact, Bertie had been astonished to find Horace under the Comte de Vaudron's aegis, for the comte was someone he profoundly respected both as a brilliant scholar and as a man of the world, but he had known the comte to be overworked and thus surmised that whatever Horace lacked in brilliance, he made up for in pedantry and could therefore be counted upon as an amanuensis. Bertie had been less surprised at Cassie's friendship with Horace, knowing her dislike of fashionable bucks and her often expressed wish to find a friend who could share her interest. There was no doubt that Horace Wilbraham was well connected and well enough to look at. Bertie had wondered how long it would be before Cassie discovered her infinite superiority to him both in education and intellect. If his guess were correct, she had discovered it that evening along with several other rather unpleasant truths. Though not inclined to become romantically involved himself—he shuddered at the thought of running the risk of messy entanglements which invariably made one lose all sense of social grace and propriety—Bertie had a tender heart. He sympathized with Cassie's disillusionment and unhappiness and resolved to do something to help her get over it. I shall take her for a ride in the park tomorrow, he decided. Having cleared his conscience in this manner, he swallowed the last drop of brandy and buried himself luxuriously in a mound of pillows.

CHAPTER *19*

Daylight did not bring further enlightenment to those who had fallen asleep the previous night mulling over the implications of the scenes at the ball. However, each one arose with a heightened awareness, looking forward to further revelations or understanding that the next day might bring. The only person who did not awake to a sense that somehow the world, or his perception of it, had altered was the precipitator of the entire thing—Horace Wilbraham.

Though intelligent enough, Horace had devoted himself to scholarly passions more because of his interest in classical antiquity and a concerted application of this interest than because of any high degree of brilliance, sensitivity, or natural aptitude. This singleness of purpose which had allowed him to progress as far as he had in his studies had also completely blinded him to the people and events around him. He moved through life in a state of unconsciousness that would have been fatal to anyone who did not have servants and a family, disgusted though they were by his chosen occupation, to look out for him. Thus he remained totally oblivious to the offense he had given his lady love. In fact, he had not even noticed that she had never danced the dance she had promised him. So it was in a state of happy insensibility that he presented himself at Grosvenor Square the next morning. At the ball the Earl of Aberdeen had graciously suggested that Horace and Cassie visit him to discuss their work, and never one to lose the slightest chance of advancing himself, Horace was quick to accept the invitation. He would have preferred calling on this learned peer alone, as lately the creeping suspicion that Cassie might be more accomplished than he in their field of endeavor had occasionally caused him some uneasiness. However, he had reassured himself with the excuse that in acquiring the expertise, Cassie had the advantage of having been immersed since infancy in the world of classical antiquity and had been constantly in the company of its brightest scholars. This had made him feel somewhat better, but he continued to find her natural quickness and brilliance of conversation rather unsettling, especially when other parties were present. However, the earl had spent time in Greece with the Cresswells and become a close friend of her parents, so there was no help for it but to include her.

Cassie, sitting in the library flanked by Ethelred, Nelson, and Wellington, was forewarned of Horace's approach by Teddy, who, on his way to claim his aunt's assistance in cricket practice, had seen Higgins greeting Horace in the front hall. In an effort to avoid condescending pats on the head and ponderous questions about the progress of his Latin, Teddy had beaten a hasty retreat, calling, "Cathie, Cathie, that man ith here, but you promithed me that you would help me with my batting today, remember?"

Fully aware of who "that man" was, Cassie frowned. Teddy, who ordinarily possessed the friendliest of natures, had so little regard for Horace Wilbraham that he could never remember his name and usually referred to him as "that man who took me to the park the day Wellington saved my boat." This had proven to be such a mouthful that it had eventually been shortened to "that man."

"Don't worry, dear," Cassie consoled him, touched by his confidence in her prowess and his crestfallen face. "He isn't going to be staying long. I shall be with you directly."

Teddy looked dubious. Horace was a frequent enough visitor at Grosvenor Square that every member of the household was fully aware of his tendency to hold forth at length and keep Cassie unavailable to the rest of Mainwaring House for hours.

" 'That man,' " Higgins often grumbled, adopting

Teddy's epithet as he complained to Cook. " 'That man' kept me holding the door for an age while he prosed on at Miss Cassie."

Or Freddie, in a fit of exasperation at having been made late once again to his appointment with Gentleman Jackson because Horace insisted on proving in minute detail the superiority of Chapman's *Iliad* to Pope's or some equally dull theory, would exclaim, "Lord, Cassie, ain't that fellow ever quiet?"

Even Lady Frances, the essence of graceful manners, had been unable to restrain herself from yawning in his company.

Nevertheless, all these people loved Cassie, and critical though they were of Horace's extended discussions, if they pleased her, well they were willing to put up with a good deal to make her happy. Teddy, subject to the unequivocal likes and dislikes of the very young, was the only exception.

Pleasure could not have been further from Cassie's voice and countenance now as she greeted Horace. Totally oblivious as usual, Horace ignored her rigid posture and frosty tone as he plunged into the reason for his visit. "Cassandra, the Earl of Aberdeen has been so kind as to invite me to call on him and he has most graciously asked you to accompany me."

Cassie's eyes darkened. "No doubt he wishes to learn more about your theories of the Panathenaic procession," she replied in a voice of dangerous calm.

"Why yes, I expect so," Horace responded, still unaware of the signs of Cassie's rising temper. Even Wellington and Nelson, blissfully asleep at the beginning of the encounter, and Ethelred, who had never seen Cassie angry before, recognized the danger signals and uneasily awaited further developments. Horace continued with becoming modesty, "He certainly appeared to be much struck with all my thoughts on the subject and desired to discuss them at greater length."

"Doing it much too brown aren't you, Horace?" Cassie inquired. If there had been any uncertainty as to Cassie's state of mind before, there was none now. She was coldly furious. "What a bacon-brain you must think me not to recognize my own ideas. And how you can appropriate them as your own so calmly without even acknowledging their origin, especially after you ridiculed them to the comte, is beyond comprehension!"

Horace looked to be genuinely surprised and hurt. "But Cassandra," he began in an aggrieved tone, "I did come to agree with you about the theory of the Panathenaic procession, you know. Besides, I thought we shared everything."

"That's precisely the point, Horace Wilbraham," she snapped. "You're not sharing the slightest thing, not even recognition for something that wasn't your idea in the first place."

"Cassandra, be reasonable," he begged. "Even if I were to acknowledge that you had some hand in it, no one would credit a woman, a mere girl moreover, with such ideas."

By now Cassie was so furious that she could hardly speak. Wellington, sensing this, was beginning to growl under his breath while Ethelred and Nelson had fixed Horace with baleful stares. "You seem to have completely forgotten that my mother was regarded as equally brilliant as my father whom you profess to hold in such deep respect and he always accorded *her* the acclaim due to her work."

Still ignorant of the danger he was in from all quarters, Horace went blithely on, "But that was because she had your father to guide her and she was able to be of use to him in his work."

Cassie looked murderous. Not too many years ago she would simply have planted Horace a facer as Freddie had taught her. But, she told herself, you're grown up now and you must not allow such a miserable excuse for a man make you lose your dignity. She straightened up, drew a breath, and adopting her most imperious voice and manner, she ordered, "Horace, I think you had better leave now."

"But Cassandra," he protested in bewilderment, "we're expected at the earl's."

"That is of little interest to me, Horace, as I don't wish

to see or be seen with you ever again," she replied haughtily.

"Cassandra, what maggot have you got in your brain?" Horace asked uneasily as he finally realized that she was truly upset.

"If you haven't fathomed it by now, you never shall, Horace," Cassie reponded. Her dignity began to disintegrate as he continued to stand there transfixed, staring at her stupidly. "Oh, *do* go away, Horace," she said crossly.

He might have remained that way forever had not Wellington, seeing that his mistress did not like "that man" and was having trouble getting rid of him, intervened. Looking significantly at Ethelred and Nelson, he growled viciously and, frowning ferociously, approached to snap at Horace's feet, closely followed by Nelson, who looked truly alarming with his ears back and teeth bared. Ethelred, unable to adopt such a dangerous mien, nevertheless managed to appear quite threatening. The fur-and-feather contingent succeeded where Cassie had failed, and Horace fled.

Though Horace was unaware of any witnesses to his ignominious rout, there had been two who had enjoyed it hugely and shared it with the other members of the household. Higgins had been across the hallway in the dining room buffing silver when the door had opened and Horace emerged, looking harassed. From behind him issued the sounds of growling, hissing, and a muffled quacking. Curious, the butler shot a quick look in the library as he went to open the door and caught a glimpse of the phalanx of vicious and victorious animal defenders. It was with some difficulty that he was able to preserve his countenance as he bid Horace good day and closed the door behind the unfortunate young man. As it was, the minute he pushed the door to, he broke into a grin.

"And that's the last we'll see of that young man, I'll be bound, Mrs. Wilkins," he confided to Cook. Once again, Higgins's devotion to the Cresswells and his recognition of a similar attitude on the part of the rest of the Mainwaring House staff, made him overcome his customary aloofness and sit down to dinner with them later in order to share the good news that, if he had interpreted the signs correctly, the Honorable Horace Wilbraham would no longer be calling at Grosvenor Square.

"I shall have to give Wellington and Nelson the remains of that joint I served last night," declared Cook. "And Ethelred shall have the rest of the poppyseed cake. Those good-for-nothings have certainly earned their keep this time."

"Ooooh, I *am* glad!" Rose exclaimed. "He wasn't up to snuff in the least. Miss Cassie deserves a real out-and-outer, she does." Rose, who had the most exacting standards for her mistress, had never been pleased with Horace, but familiar with Cassie's distaste for most of the young bucks, she had been grateful to him at least for escorting her mistress to the places where she might encounter gentlemen more her style. A high stickler where fashion was concerned, Rose had not appreciated Horace's influences on Cassie's toilette, as he encouraged her to wear the plainest of coiffeurs and the most drab colors, which contrived to make her look as dowdy as anything could make Cassandra Cresswell look. While Rose had not been privileged to observe her mistress in society, and therefore could not judge his influence on her character, she suspected that it was similar to his effect on her appearance, for it had seemed to her that since Cassie had met Horace she had been more quiet and serious and less vivacious than before.

"And good riddance to him," Rose concluded. But his departure did leave a gap and Cassie's maid was worried. "But *now* who will take her around?" she wondered aloud. "She's so particular about gentlemen and there are few who are fine enough for her."

Higgins smiled smugly. "I've a feeling that Master Ned will take care of Miss Cassie," he replied, nodding sagely.

Rose looked up in surprise. "But Miss Arabella," she began.

Adopting an even more astute expression, he elaborated,

"Miss Arabella has overstepped herself this time, mark my words. And Master Ned isn't one to live under that cat's foot."

Rose frowned doubtfully. She was agog to know where the butler had come by this notion, but it wasn't her position to question the oracle, so she let it pass, remarking merely that she would like it above everything if Miss Cassie were to find herself a nonpareil like Mr. Ned.

Another witness to the humiliating scene in the library was Teddy, who had been hanging around the door in hopes that his aunt would be true to her word and not spend too much time with "that man."

"You thould have theen it, Jim," he confided later to his bosom buddy in the stable. "Wellington wath a real Trojan. He'th a fearth one all right. Ethelred and Nelthon were right behind him. 'That man' wath scared out of hith witth. I always knew there wath thomething havey-cavey about him. What a chicken heart," he concluded scornfully.

Off in an other corner of the stable, John Coachman muttered to himself as he mended a harness. "Well rid of that one she is. He's cow-handed, I'll be bound, and our Miss Cassie would never be able to stand with that for long."

CHAPTER 20

While the various members of the household were rejoicing at Horace Wilbraham's decampment, each for his or her own particular reasons, Cassie remained in the library deep in thought. In fact, she wondered at herself. It seemed as though, given the attachment between Horace and her, and all that they had shared together, she should be feeling desolate. Instead, her chief emotions, as nearly as she could sort them out, appeared to be anger and . . . could it be relief? The more she considered it, the more she realized that relief was just what it was. Though Horace had provided her with a companion who had participated in her interests and had proven that she could be appreciated beyond the requirements set by the *ton,* she had been aware, unconscious though it may have been, of a niggling sense of doubt about their friendship. As she examined it, the reason for this unease became clearer. It had not, she decided, been a true friendship because, to Cassie at least, friendship meant something shared between equals. Though they had enjoyed common interests and were alike in their rejection of the purely fashionable life of the *ton* for more serious pursuits, they had not been an even match. Though Cassie had reveled in having an escort who, instead of dismissing her as a bluestocking, could, on the contrary, understand and appreciate her ideas and could converse knowledgeably about them, she realized now that Horace had never challenged or stimulated her. Rather, he had resembled a sponge—soaking up her knowledge and her vivacity without giving a great deal in return.

At first she had rejoiced in his admiration and appreciation of her, but lately this appreciation had come to pall on her to a certain degree, for it had begun to seem as though the attributes he admired in her somehow redounded to his credit. It had happened so slowly as to be unnoticeable at first, but now it dawned on her that gradually he had begun to irk her. She had refused to recognize this irritation, putting it down instead to the natural change in feelings that occurred as a result of increasing familiarity. Of course the excitement one felt upon first discovering someone who could partake of one's views of the world would decrease as one became accustomed to it and began to take it more for granted. And naturally the first unquestioning enthusiasm one felt for this person and this friendship would cool as one became better acquainted. Cassie realized now that it had not been the normal lessening of ardor as infatuation was replaced by the less exciting but more long-lived emotion of friendship, but that her irritation had been caused by her slow and virtually unconscious awakening to the fact that while Horace provided her with an escort who appreciated the same things, he gave her little else. Furthermore, as she had discovered at the ball, not only did he not provide her with much, he took from her.

As she reviewed all this in her mind, Cassie began to realize all the things she had been missing in their relationship. For all their similar interests, she had felt no sense of intimacy. She would have felt less inclined to confide in Horace than she would have in Freddie or even Rose. And though he could speak with more knowledge than most people on a very few isolated subjects, beyond those, Horace did not offer much in the way of conversation, and even less in the way of wit. As she considered it, Cassie concluded that he had no humor whatsoever. It was this lack of humor that led to a certain rigidity of mind that had made her uncomfortable. All in all, she was well out of it, and though the discovery that he and his friendship had failed to fulfill her initial hopes and expectations made her sad, she was glad that she had awakened to her delusion soon enough to avoid committing herself to him further. Still, it was a somewhat melancholy thought that perhaps there was no one out there who could offer her what Horace had appeared to offer.

That's enough moaning, my girl, she scolded herself. Falling into a fit of the dismals won't help you in the least, and it certainly won't help Teddy with his cricket. Giving herself an admonitory shake and calling to Wellington and the others, Cassie arose and went in search of her nephew.

Teddy was soon located in the garden aimlessly thwacking the ball around and whistling tunelessly. He broke into a grin the moment his aunt appeared. "Oh, famous! I knew you'd come!" he exclaimed happily. His face fell slightly when he saw her companions.

Recognizing his concern, Cassie reassured him, "Don't worry, they won't interfere. Let's make some wickets and set up a pitch. Once Wellington sees them, he will understand what we're about and will keep the others in line."

In this she was entirely correct. Once the sticks Teddy hunted up in the stable were in place, Wellington planted himself firmly on the sidelines. He ran a practiced eye over the proceedings and kept a stern watch on Ethelred and Nelson to make sure they didn't stray onto the pitch.

"That's the ticket, Wellington," Cassie approved, smiling at the little dog as she loosened up her bowling arm.

Teddy took up the bat and went to stand before the wicket. Cassie let fly the first ball and Teddy was so bemused by the sight of his studious aunt bowling with such speed and accuracy that he forgot even to lift the bat. The ball hit the ground and rebounded in an unexpected direction. A look of astonishment came over his face. "Aunt Cathie, you put a spin on it!" he declared indignantly.

"Well, of course I did, you gudgeon. It wouldn't be helping you to improve your batting much if I were to bowl directly to you, now would it?" she retorted.

Acknowledging the justice of this, Teddy gripped the bat firmly, planting his feet and awaiting Cassie's next pitch with a determined set to his jaw and his eyes squinting in concentration. It was a fast one, but he was able to connect with a satisfactory thwack, and Cassie, transforming herself in an instant from bowler to fielder, had to scramble to retrieve it.

Breathless from her exertions, she returned to her place to wind up for another bowl, panting, "It would be a good deal easier if we had someone to act as wicket keeper."

"And thus, your prayers are answered, fair maiden. Behold a willing and obedient wicket keeper," a deep voice spoke behind her.

Cassie whirled around. "Ned!" she exclaimed. "I'm that glad to see you. You're the very person!"

Ned winked at Teddy. "If there were more people, I should be flattered into thinking you wanted me for my cricketing prowess, but given the meagerness of your numbers, I suspect you'd be glad to see anyone who had more grasp of cricket than Ethelred," he said, laughing.

Surveying the small group of onlookers at the sidelines, Cassie's face brightened. "Of course, the very thing!" she cried. "Wellington can field for us!"

"Arf, arf," Wellington agreed enthusiastically.

"Still the same old Cassie who could never bear to see anyone sitting comfortably," Ned teased as he stripped off his coat and tossed it onto a bench. He strolled over to the wicket, remarking, "Very well. Your wish is my command, but see that you bowl so well that Wellington and I don't have to work too hard."

Cassie made a face. "And now who doesn't want whom to be comfortable?" she taunted. "Here, Wellington." She walked over to a spot and snapped her fingers. With a backward glance of triumph at his less skilled companions, Wellington proudly took up his place.

Cassie hurled the ball. There was another crack and Cassie yelled, "Fetch!"

Wellington jumped with alacrity, fielding the ball before it hit the ground.

"Aha, caught. Good job, Wellington," she cried as he raced to the wicket with the ball.

Teddy was disgusted. "You traitor, Wellington. Dithmissed on my second try," he grumbled.

Further commentary on his pet's loyalty was cut short by his mother, who called, "Teddy, Teddy, you must come do your history lesson now before I have to go out."

"Botheration," Teddy declared, hunching a mutinous shoulder. "Just when I was getting the hang of it!"

"Don't refine on it too much, Teddy," Cassie consoled him. "Wellington and I will be happy to practice with you whenever you like, and if we can prevail upon Cook to make her famous Dundee cake, I am certain that we can count on Ned as well. Run along, now. I promise you Ned and I will stop playing and talk of the dullest things imaginable so you won't be missing anything."

"Can we try tomorrow?" Teddy begged, knowing full well the vagaries of adult schedules.

"Certainly. I shall be happy to," Cassie responded, smiling reassuringly at the anxious face turned up to hers.

Teddy collected the ball and bat and scampered off. But just before disappearing into the house, he turned to call, "Thank you, Aunt Cathie and Ned. You're great guns, both of you."

"You couldn't hope to win higher praise from the most besotted of admirers," Ned rallied her.

"Of which I have countless numbers, naturally," Cassie replied, smiling impishly at him in such a way that he wondered why she didn't have hundreds of them haunting her doorstep.

He looked down at her, taking in every detail of the way the sun made the curls surrounding her flushed face glow like spun gold, how the thick dark lashes fringing her eyes made them look an even deeper blue. Even the smudge of dirt on her chin emphasized the smoothness and softness of her skin. He stood thus bemused until her expression changed and an inquiring look wrinkled her brow. Giving himself a mental shake, he apologized. "I am sorry. My wits have gone begging. I hadn't thought to be pressed into service so quickly and I clean forgot why I came, which is to bring you this." He pulled a small bundle out from under his coat as he spoke.

"Why Ned, a present . . . for me." Cassie looked so eager in her anticipation that he was touched. Ned had presented far more expensive-looking boxes embossed with the names of famous jewelers to far less effect than this simple packet done up in plain brown paper and string.

"Well, I just saw it and thought you might find it inspiring," he replied offhandedly.

She tore off the paper to reveal the works of Epictetus translated by Elizabeth Carter.

"Do not for a moment think that I doubt your ability in the least to read it in the original, Cassie. I just thought you would like to see that women such as you *are* taken seriously and that they *can* succeed at their endeavors. And I believe that this represents the second printing."

Cassie was greatly touched. "Ned, how very kind you are. I can't wait to read it. And thank you for, for . . ." She fumbled for the words to express how much it meant to her for someone to have faith in her abilities and to treat her as one would treat any scholar with aspirations.

Living as she had in such a talented household, Cassie had never been fully aware how little respect she could command outside it—even from those who comprehended and applauded her interests—simply because she was a woman. She had resigned herself to being misunderstood and labeled "blue" by the rest of the world, but having no social aspirations, she had not been bothered greatly by it. She had, however, expected to be taken seriously by those who could appreciate her scholarship. Horace's attitude had dealt her a severe blow and she was just now realizing how much it had hurt her. This demonstration of support expressed by such an appropriate gesture and from someone who was truly capable of appreciating and judging her abilities meant more to Cassie than she was able to express. She blinked rapidly as she extended her hand, trying to find some way to articulate her gratitude. "I wish, I wish you could know how much this means to me, but . . ." Her voice cracked and she found she could not go on.

Ned raised a mobile eyebrow. "What? Cassandra

Cresswell at a loss for words? Things *have* come to a pretty pass,'' he teased. "Don't refine on it too much. I just thought you could use an example of feminine scholarship right now. But that's not the entire purpose of my visit. I also came to inform you that there is to be a balloon ascension next Tuesday and I thought you, Teddy, Freddie, and I might enjoy going. If it's a very fine day, we could make a picnic of it.''

"What a lark! I should like it of all things and so would Teddy!'' Cassie exclaimed. "He's been teasing Freddie and me to take him ever since Freddie read the announcement of the ascension and the exhibition in the *Times*. I've only been to one balloon ascension when I was quite small and couldn't see a thing because the crowd kept pushing so. A nice man put Freddie up on his shoulders so he was able to describe it to me, but that's not the same thing at all.''

"That's set, then. You ask the others and we'll hope for a good weather. Now, I must be on my way as Canning has asked me to call on him.'' Ned added this last bit in as offhand a manner as possible, but it was with great difficulty that he kept the pride out of his voice.

Cassie lit up immediately. "Oh Ned, how perfectly splendid!'' she cried. "However did that come about? I *am* so proud of you.''

Ned recounted his discussion with Lord Charlton at Brooks's. Good as his word, Lord Charlton had spoken to Canning about Ned. The statesman had been intrigued by Ned's background and experiences and had very graciously invited him to call on him.

"That's wonderful beyond anything! You are certain to impress him with your views on conditions in India. Not only have you been there and worked with the system, such as it is, but you have reflected seriously on it and have devised your own particular plan for what should be done to improve things. Everyone declares him to be rather temperamental, but I believe that it's because he refuses to suffer fools gladly. You are quick and clever and, I should think, would be just the sort to appeal to him. I heard him speak in Parliament and I must say that I thought him brilliant, though his sarcasm, amusing though it is, must make him many enemies. Do please come tell me everything afterward.''

Ned smiled at her exuberance, as he demurred modestly. "You are prejudiced in my favor. I should take you along as my advocate. How could he fail to think I am a coming man after hearing you on the subject? However, with you espousing me, I shouldn't be able to get a word in edgewise.'' His tone was teasing, but secretly he was pleased and touched by her support and her unbounded faith in his abilities. Cassie better than anyone comprehended his ideas and understood his political aspirations. Her opinion was more important to him than anyone else's, as she could best appreciate what it meant to him to have these ideas recognized by such men as Lord Charlton and his peers.

Cassie's enthusiastic reaction, her happiness at his recognition, and her passionate support were all he had hoped for and he headed off to Canning's chambers in Stanhope Street buoyed up by the knowledge that she would be thinking of him.

CHAPTER 21

Ned was not able to share the details of his visit to the foreign secretary until the next evening when he joined Cassie, Frances, and Julian in the Mainwarings' box at the opera. Frances had for some time expressed a wish to see Rossini's *Otello*, particularly as the composer was conducting his own work. Her husband had ruthlessly turned down several important invitations from his political cronies in order to spend a peaceful, enjoyable evening in the company of his family and free from the brilliant government circles in which they ordinarily moved. Knowing that Ned was also very fond of Rossini, Frances had urged him to join them.

Her motives were not entirely unselfish. Ever since the ball she had noticed a change in her sister. Cassie seemed restless and disinclined to fix her interest on anything for any length of time—an unusual state of affairs for one who often had to be pried loose from the library to attend meals. At the same time Frances was aware that Cassie had ceased her regular visits to Hanover Square. This unusual circumstance coupled with the notable absence of Horace Wilbraham led her to suspect that the friendship had ended, but being the good sister that she was, Frances would have died rather than mention this state of affairs to her sister.

She was indebted at last to her maid Daisy, Rose's eldest sister, for her enlightenment. Daisy, having been with Frances since both were barely more than twelve, was not one to stand on ceremony. "And though I am sad to see Miss Cassie lose any admirer, mark my words, she's better off without that Horace Wilbraham. Can't hold a candle to her,

153

he can't, and he's always bragging about his learning. Pooh! Why Miss Cassie could run circles around him. Learning! That's his excuse for being such a dead bore. Miss Cassie's well rid of him, I say. Why he was such a dullard he was making Miss Cassie into one, too. Not many a man could bear to have a companion who is gayer and wittier than he is. For all his mealymouthed ways he's as selfish as he can stare. Anyone can see he must always have the first consideration. As I see it, Miss Cassie needs someone who can keep up with her, someone who is a true out-and-outer.''

Aware that Daisy's sources of information were impeccable, Frances didn't question her knowledge but acted accordingly to ensure that Cassie would have some sort of escort even if it were a person she'd known since she'd been in pinafores.

There had been no time for discussion before the opera, but at the close of the first act Cassie turned to Ned. ''Do tell me what transpired with Canning, I've been bursting to know. What did you talk about? Were you able to tell him any of your notions for improving trade?''

Ned held up a well-shaped hand to stem this impetuous outburst. ''Hold on, my girl. One question at a time. Yes, we did discuss my ideas. And I must say we dealt excellently with each other. We both agree that we must work to improve our colonial trade and direct our policies toward strengthening the Colonies, even if that means modifying our Navigation Acts and freeing England from the Holy Alliance. We have involved ourselves too long in the affairs of Europe to the detriment of our mercantile interests in other corners of the globe, and now something must be done about it.''

Cassie nodded. ''And what with Napoleon no longer on the Continent to cause wars and require armies and supplies, we need other markets for our merchants to supply.''

''Just so,'' Ned replied, reflecting on what a refreshing change it was to be able to relate his ideas to someone who grasped them and responded, instead of treating him to a bored pout or changing the subject immediately to something that forced his attention to revert solely to his charming companion.

Suddenly he was forced to do just that as Frances interrupted to point out that his attention was being demanded by just such a charmer. "Isn't that Arabella beckoning to you?"

Sighing inwardly, Ned glanced over to the box opposite, where Arabella, resplendent in diamonds and a revealing décolletage, was beckoning purposefully to him. Her attire was in fact a trifle daring for a young unmarried woman, but Arabella, who had detected a lessening in Ned's attentiveness, had not cared. Inquiries from her maid, who had grown up with Rose and continued the friendship in Town, had revealed that the Mainwarings were planning to attend the opera that evening, and the beauty had bullied her parents, neither of whom could bear opera, into taking her. She was confident that her bright poppy-colored muslin gown with sprigs of gold and ornamented with gold lace was certain to make anything Cassie wore seem pale and insipid by comparison. She was also certain that no young woman in her first Season would dare expose such a creamy expanse of beautifully rounded bosom and shoulders as she was now displaying to the delight of the besotted young men who hovered around her. Secure in the knowledge that she was in her best looks and drawing appreciative stares from all over the theater, she positively glowed.

- Attired perfectly correctly in a white *gros de Naples* round dress which was becoming enough but certainly not distinctive, Cassie breathed a wistful sigh. As long as she was well groomed and wearing something that was not noticeably out of fashion, she ordinarily discounted her appearance as unimportant, but for once she longed to be more than acceptable; she wished she was dazzling. Not that she wouldn't have been heartily bored by the insipid conversation of men such as those surrounding Arabella, but she did for a moment wonder what it would be like to be so fatally attractive, so confident of one's beauty and power to be admired for it. She had been acquainted with Arabella all her life and knew that her intellect was not strong, nor was her conversation particularly witty and charming. It seemed dreadfully unfair that something as simple as big dark eyes, dimples, dusky curls, and a voluptuous figure could command the total attention of so very many gentlemen. And just once she wished she could change places with her. But only for a moment, she said to herself. I should be bored silly within the hour.

Ned, who had responded to Arabella's summons with a slight nod and was debating whether or not he could ignore her obvious wish for him to join the devoted little group of admirers, caught Cassie looking at her. Her expressive face revealed a good deal of what was going on in her mind, and Ned was both amused and touched by it—amused that his feisty little playmate, who had never spoken of fashionable women who devoted themselves to their appearances except in tones of deepest scorn, should now look so thoughtful at the sight of someone who thought of nothing else, and touched by the wistfulness of that look. The irony of it was that though Arabella cultivated every art to attract while Cassie remained largely oblivious to such guile, Cassie's natural liveliness, her genuine interest in those to whom she was speaking, combined with the wit and intelligence of her conversation made her far more appealing to all but the most superficial of the *ton*.

An urgent desire to rally to Cassie's defense and honor her qualities made him decide to ignore Arabella's summons. He turned instead to his companion, inquiring, "Did you read the account of the subscription to help the Greeks in the *Times* last week?"

Cassie's eyes sparkled. "Yes, I did. And I'm glad that someone is at last doing something for those poor people. How anyone can say that they are as barbaric as the Turks I simply cannot comprehend. What could be more uncivilized than storing ammunition in one of the greatest artistic feats of mankind? I only thank heaven that Lord Elgin, Papa and Mama, and the Comte de Vaudron were able to save as much of the Parthenon as they did. It's a dreadful shame that the marbles had to be taken from their proper place and the nation that created them, but if it inspires people who would otherwise never have the opportunity to see and appreciate the monuments from classical antiquity, then I am all for it. And you must admit that the decorative arts in general have improved because of this very appreciation.''

"Gently, my girl," Ned teased. "Don't get on your high ropes with me. I am as devoted as anyone to the Greeks, past and present. I was merely curious to know if you were aware that at long last a movement is afoot to—''

But whatever the movement was to accomplish was lost as the door to the box opened. There was a rustle of skirts, a breath of seductive perfume, and then Arabella broke in gaily, "How delightful to see you!" Her dazzling, but perfunctory smile included the entire company; however, the languorous look accompanying it was directed to Ned alone. Unwilling to brook Ned's ignoring of her invitation, Arabella had been overjoyed when Sir Brian Brandon had appeared in her box, for she could hardly visit the Mainwarings' box alone and Sir Brian was the perfect escort to rouse envy in the breast of any female and dismay in any male's. Let Ned see that she was sought after by the very pinks of the *ton*. That would put him on his mettle!

Smothering his annoyance as best he could, Ned inclined his dark head as he acknowledged them. "Arabella, Sir Brian, good evening. And how do you find the opera? Cassie, here, is a severe critic, you know. She has been telling me that while she admires Rossini and finds *Otello* particularly delightful, she does not find the performers equal to the music—a sad state of affairs, don't you agree?''

Cassie's jaw dropped as she had said no such thing, nor could she have the least idea why Ned would let fall such a plumper, but a conspiratorial wink brought her to her senses. Trying to sound as world-weary and sophisticated as possible, she sighed. "Yes, I find it quite upsetting when the singers cannot do justice to the work. If the corps de ballet is as uninspired in the dance to follow, I am sure I shall be

frightfully *ennuyée*. And I most certainly object to the
tampering with Shakespeare's masterpiece. The happy ending
is beyond all things absurd.''

She was rewarded by another wink and a lopsided grin.
Unaware of this private interchange, Arabella struggled to
regain control of the scene that Ned had so successfully stolen
from her. He had succeeded far beyond his wildest hopes,
which had merely been to rob Arabella of some of her
infernal confidence in her ability to dominate the center of
every stage, because upon hearing Cassie's remark, Sir
Brian, whose gaze had been slowly sweeping the theater,
now fixed upon her with some interest.

''Are you a devotee of opera, Lady Cassandra, or merely
of Rossini?'' he asked, moving closer to her chair as she
spoke.

Cassie smiled. ''Oh opera, certainly,'' she replied. Then,
lowering her voice conspiratorially, she added, ''I know that
one shouldn't admit to such a thing when Italian opera is all
the rage, but I find that Mozart appeals more to my tastes.''

He nodded sagely. ''I should have known.''

''Oh dear,'' Cassie sounded rueful. ''Do I look so
démodée? My entire family is hoping I shall acquire some
town bronze and I shouldn't want to disappoint them. It's
not for myself that I care about being au courant, you understand,'' she concluded somewhat defiantly.

''Not in the least.'' Sir Brian was amused. ''I had expected
that a composer as refined and subtle as Mozart would be
more appealing to someone who has such an elegant mind.''

''But you have no notion of my mind,'' she protested.

His brown eyes dwelt on her appreciatively as he
responded. ''On the contrary, the clothes you wear, the way
you carry yourself, your voice are all very elegant. How
could your mind fail to be so?''

Cassie's eyes opened wide as she exclaimed, ''I, elegant!''

''Don't let it go to your head, Cassie,'' Ned teased. ''There
are those of us who remember you with mud on your nose
and grass stains on your pinafore. Be aware, Sir Brian, that
underneath that elegant exterior you describe, there lurks the

best tree climber and one of the most bruising riders in all of Hampshire.''

If they had not been in polite company, Cassie would have stuck her tongue out at Ned, but she contented herself with shaking an admonitory finger at him. ''Have care, Ned. As the Marriage Mart's biggest catch, you have a greater reputation to be ruined by childhood reminiscences than I do. And if you can dredge up my past, I can certainly recall some inglorious moments in yours.''

He grinned appreciatively. ''Wretch!'' he responded, laughing.

Arabella, who had been forced, and with very poor grace at that, to maintain a desultory conversation with Lady Mainwaring and the marquess, could bear it no longer. Laying a possessive hand on Sir Brian's sleeve, she cooed, ''Come. We must be going or we shall miss the next act.'' Then, bending toward Ned and treating him to the full benefit of her décolletage, she whispered intimately, ''I hope to see you at Lady Portman's masquerade.''

''I expect so. I shall be there, I suppose,'' he replied carelessly as he quickly turned his attention to the stage. Left with nothing to do, Arabella swept out as grandly as possible, clinging seductively to her escort.

CHAPTER 22

The projected outing to the balloon ascension had met with
Theodore's instant and enthusiastic approval. "What a bang-
up plan!" he exclaimed when Cassie relayed Ned's invitation
to him. He looked up at her, adding shyly, "I like Ned. He's
a regular Trojan, isn't he?"

Cassie smiled fondly at him. "Yes, he certainly is." The
warmth in her smile was as much for the man who had made
the boy so happy as for the eager boy himself. Dear Ned,
he always was there offering advice, distraction, support,
whatever she needed and whenever she needed it most. Few
people could count themselves as fortunate as she in having
a friend like him. She thought of how consoled she had been
by his quick understanding and sympathy, how comforting
and secure it had felt to be in his arms, and her smile became
even more tender.

Her reverie was interrupted by a grubby hand tugging at
her sleeve. "Aunt Cathie, I thay, Aunt Cathie."

She came to with a start. "Yes, Teddy?"

"Will we be able to get clothe to the balloon? I would so
like to thee what ith like."

Cassie looked uncertain. "I don't know, dear. It may be
a sad crush, but we shall certainly try."

The day of the balloon ascension dawned clear and warm.
Ned had borrowed his sister's barouche and also availed
himself of her cook, who had packed a tremendous hamper
of game pies, cold chicken, and cheese, as well as tarts and
cakes of every description. Teddy's eyes bulged at the sight

of it as he climbed in the carriage and settled himself in anticipation of a day of unprecedented delights.

Wellington sat happily on the box by the coachman. Ned was an old crony of his, and when the little dog had seen his best friends about to depart in a carriage without him, he had looked so miserable that Ned had relented. "Very well then, Wellington, but you must stay on the box because we wouldn't want to lose you in all the crush. Hackney is not the genteel area of London that Mayfair is. No telling what mongrels will be abroad."

"Arf," Wellington barked obediently. He had no intention of leaving his seat, not because he was afraid of even the fiercest canine, but because he did not want to miss the slightest detail of the ascent. Besides, fancying himself an equestrian sort of dog, he was never happier than when he was seated on the box next to the coachman.

Ned had drawn the line at Nelson and Ethelred, however. Nelson had not really wanted to go, as the idea of sunning himself on the front steps was infinitely more appealing than perching way up in a swaying open carriage amid throngs of people, but it would never have done to let on to Wellington. Ethelred really did not care one way or another, but not liking to be separated from his hero, he looked mutinous at Ned's decision.

"I'm not certain they would understand about ducks as pets in Hackney," Ned explained. "And you would undoubtedly prefer to remain here than end up in someone's stew pot."

"Arf," Wellington agreed, settling the matter, and Ethelred, sighing sadly, waddled off to join Nelson on the steps.

A silent observer of Ned's kindness and understanding toward the trio, Cassie couldn't help comparing him to Horace, who had ordinarily been rendered acutely uncomfortable by the menagerie. He had always trodden awkwardly and uneasily when they were around and more than once had remarked in exasperation, "Really, Cassandra,

I don't understand why they are allowed the run of the house.
Animals in a drawing room are absurd, not to mention most
improper.'' Well aware of his unpropitious attitude, and
hoping to discourage such a caller, the three had invariably
made it a point to hover around his feet when he called, and
they had been as relieved as everyone else that Horace's visits
to their mistress had ceased.

The party arrived in the Mermaid Tavern, Hackney, in
time to view the balloon and equipment which was on exhibit
to the public in the assembly room. As they walked around
inspecting it, Ned explained the principles of ballooning to
an enrapt Theodore. ''And we are fortunate to be able to
see such a noted balloonist as Mr. Green. He has made
several innovations in ballooning, inventing the drag rope
go make the descent slower and smoother and using coal gas
instead of hydrogen. Though it's much more likely to catch
fire, it's a great deal cheaper.''

Pleased by the rare occasion of having a truly knowledgeable spectator and one who was a nonpareil, by the look of
him, Mr. Green himself came over to explain the science
of ballooning to the little party. Teddy was thrilled by his
description of his more daring exploits and was so excited
by the outing and the opportunity to meet the famous
balloonist that he hardly touched the picnic which had
captured his eye when they first set out.

''What a knowing one you are, Ned, old boy. Never knew
you was so into the scientific stuff as well as the classics,''
Freddie commented through a mouthful of game pie.

''I'm not, but I've always been intrigued by the idea of
being able to fly. The idea of gliding peacefully along over
the countryside above all the hustle and bustle and the horrors
of country lanes appeals to me mightily,'' Ned averred.

They were interrupted by a gasp from the crowd as Mr.
Green and his assistant pulled in the anchors and the gaily
striped equipage rose slowly and majestically above them.
Wellington let out a startled ''woof'' while the rest of them
sat silent gazing at the magnificent sight.

"Oh, how I should love to ride in one!" Cassie exclaimed. "How wonderful it would be to look down on everything while sailing along free as a bird."

Ned smiled fondly at her. With her face alight with enthusiasm and the stray golden curls catching the sunlight as the wind gently blew them, she looked more like the Cassie he used to know—passionate, vital, and adventurous—than the serious and proper person who had lately been appearing at all the fashionable haunts of the *ton*. It was as though her true spirit had broken through some restraint and was reasserting itself. Ned was glad to see that it was still there and hoped that somehow he had been instrumental in bringing about the transformation.

He felt a great rush of tenderness toward his old playmate as she sat there rapt in the excitement of the event. You're too young to be getting nostalgic, Ned, my boy, he admonished himself. You've only just kicked off the dust of the schoolroom yourself not so many years ago and have all those fascinating women out there to amuse you. You must be all about in the head to be so happy at the thought of being with someone you spent your boyhood rescuing from one scrape after another. She has no more idea of how to go on in the world than she did when she was falling out of trees. But he couldn't help remembering how she had looked at him the night of Horace's betrayal, and how comfortable she had felt in his arms. He gave a snort of disgust at his sentimentality over a childhood companion.

Cassie was enjoying herself too thoroughly to be paying much attention in return to this particular childhood companion, but on the drive home she was strangely silent. While Ned and Freddie hotly debated the relative merits of the matched bays Sir Charles Pierrepont had just purchased, she sat quietly reflecting on the day's outing.

She realized that it had been an age since she had felt as comfortable and at ease in a group of people as she had felt today. With Horace she had enjoyed the conversation, but had always been conscious of some constraint, knowing how high-minded his principles were, lest she say something that offended his sensibilities. Often she had caught a look of disapproval in his eyes as she had waxed enthusiastic over something. And frequently he had made her feel as though her love for adventure was, if not improper, certainly hoydenish and unattractive. The consequence had been that she had always held back and examined every thought before expressing it. Ned, on the contrary, not only did not act disapproving, but he encouraged her to express herself and explore her interests no matter how unusual.

"I'm delighted that you enjoyed yourself, Teddy," Ned's voice broke into her thoughts. "We shall have to plan another outing in the near future before your aunt can acquire too much town bronze to enjoy such things." He turned and winked at Cassie, amending, "Not that she is in much danger of preferring a ballroom to a chance for adventure."

Cassie grinned at him and he thought how wonderful it was to have the impishness back again breaking through the air of reserve she had worn since he had been in London. "What do you say to an excursion to the Egyptian hall to see the reindeer and the wapiti on exhibit there? I have read that the horns of the wapiti are very curious."

Teddy could hardly breathe in his excitement at the thought of another such outing. He was in seventh heaven sitting alongside Ned conversing with him as though he were a true grown-up. Aunt Cassie and his mother were great guns, but though they knew their history backward and forward and were practically on speaking terms with all those Greek fellows, they did show a sad lack of interest in things scientific and mechanical, any detail of which was of passionate interest to the little boy. Uncle Freddie was a trump and could be counted on for his knowledge of any type of sporting endeavor, but if Teddy were to ask him about some point of science such as why stars twinkled, or how water became steam, Freddie would look rueful and reply apologetically, "You know, Teddy, you'd better ask your father. I haven't got all that much in my brain box, my lad."

Lord Mainwaring, when he could be found, could be counted on to supply satisfactory answers, but he was often away or busy, and besides, he was his father. It was so much nicer to have a friend with whom you could discuss things.

Seeing the worshipful light in Teddy's eyes, Ned was touched. He remembered his own admiration of Lord Mainwaring, who had proven to be a similar friend and mentor for a bright inquiring boy raised in a household of kind but unintellectual women, and he resolved to spend more time with the lad. There was another aspect about Teddy's eager expression that moved him. It reminded him strongly of the look Cassie wore when some question or some new thought had struck her. That constant desire to learn and to discover new things or new ways of thinking about things was what he loved most about her.

At this thought Ned stopped dead. How long had he loved her? Consciously he had always been inordinately fond of Cassie. She had been his best friend and playmate for almost as long as he could remember. His life before her was a jumble of small insignificant memories, but after he became her friend, it had taken more shape and purpose. Knowing her had made him more aware of his interests and propensities, so that he was better able to pursue and develop them. But when had this sense of companionship changed to something deeper? He supposed it had come about quite gradually as he moved about in society flirting and enjoying liaisons with the sophisticated women of the *ton*. They had been amusing and seductive and he had been attracted to them in a way that had gratified his senses, but he had never felt the least concern for their happiness, had never wished so desperately to protect them from hurt, had never wanted to help them grow and flourish the way he wanted to take care of Cassie. Though these entertaining coquettes of the fashionable world had stimulated the sensual side of his nature, not even the most charming and accomplished of them had challenged his mind or inspired such a feeling of tenderness in him as she did.

As he watched her entering into the discussion of Pierrepont's bays, it suddenly came to him that he had never been so at ease with anyone as he was with her.

"They may be sweet goers, Freddie, but they haven't enough wind. They won't last. You and Ned may think he got a bargain, but the two of you are forever being taken in by these showy high-spirited bits of blood that have no strength," Cassie maintained, glancing impishly at Ned, daring him to contradict her.

Recognizing that challenging glint in her eye, Ned realized that of all the women he had ever known, Cassie was the only one whose interest in him was so purely friendly and so utterly disinterested that she could tease him. He felt strangely gratified by this proof that she paid attention to him for himself and not for the social cachet his companionship could bring her. Other women to whom he was important because of his wealth or his status as an eligible bachelor and nonpareil could never risk giving offense by laughing at him or mocking him. In fact, most of the time, though he had enjoyed his flirtations immensely, he had felt as though he were a mere actor in a carefully orchestrated play where anyone else of equal economic or social status would have been equally acceptable in the leading male role. With Cassie, it was different. She reacted to him as Ned Mainwaring and liked him for all his own particular interests and accomplishments, not for his social position.

These revelations, while they brought a wonderful sense of discovery and excitement, were also somewhat disturbing because he was not altogether certain of Cassie's state of mind. Could she possibly feel that same special way toward him or was he nothing more to her than a family member, someone like Freddie, who was loved because he had been a part of her life for as long as she could remember? Was she comfortable and natural with him because she liked and trusted him for himself or because he was like her favorite chair in the library at Cresswell, something that she had become so accustomed to having around that she was unaware of it in itself? This was such an upsetting notion that he was glad it was time to leave so that he could be alone with his thoughts and the turmoil of emotions they had aroused.

CHAPTER 23

Lady Portman's annual masquerade could always be counted upon to be one of the highlights of the Season. Anybody among the Upper Ten Thousand who had the least claim to fashion could be counted upon to be there. For weeks before the big event seamstresses and Bond Street modistes cast aside pictures from *La Belle Assemblée* and worked on costuming multiple Mary Queen of Scots, Queen Elizabeths, shepherdesses, and Titanias. Conversations over teacups in drawing rooms from Brook Street to Hanover Square centered around which member of the *ton* was going to appear as what fictional or historical figure that year.

Weary of all the thought of the upcoming masquerade and of how she had already been forced to dress this Season, Cassie seized this opportunity to select a character whose attire would be simple and comfortable, and she directed Madame Regnery in the creation of a costume of the Greek goddess, Diana. Madame, an old friend of the comte's from prerevolution days, had been dressmaker to the Cresswells since she had so successfully created the gowns which had helped Lady Frances establish her own special style the year she became Marchioness of Camberly. Madame, who had understood and sympathized with Cassie's reluctance to become just another fashionable young woman dividing her time between preparing her toilette and then parading it at social functions, had done her best to ensure that the creation of Cassie's wardrobe was a process that was as simple and swift as possible, with the result that Cassie liked her and trusted her judgment implicitly. At last, she and Madame could enter into a project for which Cassie could evince some degree of interest and she and Madame spent several happy hours at Madame's shop in South Moulton Street going over the details of the costume.

Madame was delighted to see Mademoiselle Cassie entering into its creation with such enthusiasm and was suitably impressed with her knowledge of Greek culture and mythology. "Mademoiselle has chosen well. Such a simple style and the gracefulness of the drapery will show off her *taille élégante* to perfection. There are not many young ladies who could wear such things without looking like a pudding bag tied in the middle," she remarked with satisfaction. The classical elegance of the Cresswell ladies' figures was always a great source of gratification to her, for it did justice to her creations. She felt fortunate to be free to design instead of having to struggle to cover her patrons' deficiencies as so many other modistes were forced to do.

Madame was entirely correct in her opinion. The chaste pleated white silk tunic secured with gold cords emphasized Cassie's slender figure while the flow of the drapery called attention to the gracefulness of her movements. As she stood in the archway of Lady Portman's ballroom clutching a golden bow, the light from the chandeliers catching the glow of the golden crescent moons in her fair hair, she did look as ethereal as if she had just stepped down from Mount Olympus. She was accompanied by her sister and brother-in-law, who, attired as Helen and Paris, made a fitting backdrop. The trio had dressed with classical simplicity that only called attention to their elegant bearing and they presented a marked contrast to the fantastic multicolored assemblage before them.

Standing off in one corner with her parents, Arabella felt a pang of envy. No, it couldn't have been envy for someone like Cassie Cresswell, still a scrubby schoolgirl despite her presence in Town this Season. It was certainly not envy, but all of a sudden Arabella, who had been confident of her capturing all eyes dressed as a shepherdess in a costume that contrived to look demure while revealing as much of her

charms as possible, felt less certain of these charms.
Compared to Cassie's, her costume seemed fussy and overly
elaborate, the décolletage obvious and slightly tawdry when
put beside the subtle charm of Cassie's draperies, which only
hinted at instead of blatantly revealing the beautiful figure
beneath them. It didn't help matters in the least when her
roving eye discerned Ned Mainwaring off in another corner
of the ballroom flirting with Lady Jersey, for Ned, clad in
a tunic which only served to emphasize his height and athletic
physique, a lion skin draped over his broad shoulders, was
dressed as Hercules—the perfect foil for Diana and a
ridiculous partner for a shepherdess.

Ned's abrupt departure from Lady Jersey when he
recognized the party from Mainwaring House did nothing
to improve Arabella's temper, and she watched, seething,
as she bent first over Lady Mainwaring's and then Cassie's
hand. To one whose existence was defined by the least little
nuance in any social gesture, it seemed that he clasped more
of Cassie's hand than the requisite few inches of finger and
held it for longer than politeness dictated. Arabella, who had
for years taken his admiring glances for granted and had only
this Season come to recognize and value them as something
to be envied by other women, was now truly annoyed to see
the warmth in the look he directed at Cassie and the intimacy
of his smile as he teased her about something. Such a situation
would never do! No one must be allowed to outshine such
a diamond as Arabella Taylor, much less supersede her in
someone's attentions, especially not an unfashionable
bluestocking like Cassie Cresswell. Marshaling her considerable powers of seduction, Arabella prepared to do battle.

Pinning a charming, if totally false smile on her face, she
glided over to the little group, exclaiming, "Oh, I am so
glad that I did not come as Aphrodite after all because it
would have been quite dreadful if there were two of us."

Catching the amused glint in Ned's eye at Arabella's
misreading of her costume, Cassie found it difficult not to
laugh, but managed to respond without a quaver, "What a

fortunate circumstance. To have been caught in similar attire would certainly have been a social disaster.''

"Yes, I'm so thankful that I realized that people might think me shockingly blue if I were to appear as a character from Greek mythology," Arabella replied with a triumphant smile.

Cassie's eyes danced. "That would never do, certainly," she agreed seriously. "How perfectly dreadful to be mistaken for a person of culture."

Even Arabella had the grace to blush as she recognized the full import of her words. "But Cassie," she protested, "you don't understand. I have my reputation to consider. The whole of the *ton* knows you to be a bluestocking, so what can it signify what you wear? Whereas I am reckoned someone of taste and fashion among my acquaintances. One should never appear too serious, you know," she added in a confidential tone. Then, warming to her favorite theme, she continued a trifle defiantly, "Sir Brian Brandon, whose knowledge and experience in these matters I rely upon entirely, has even said he considers me to be an incomparable.''

Here, Freddie, as he had done since they were children, stepped in and thwarted Arabella's plans. "I say, Arabella, you and I don't fit in with all these lofty Greeks. Why don't we leave them to their own intellectual devices and join the set that's forming for the quadrille. Nothing could show off your costume to better advantage than being a partner to a pirate." And it was certainly true that Freddie, who had utterly refused to wear a namby-pamby tunic like the rest of his family, did make a most fearsome pirate indeed, complete with cutlass and a wicked-looking scar that Cook had helped him concoct with flour and water.

Poor Arabella could do nothing but thank him prettily and allow herself to be led onto the floor, though her eyes continued to follow Ned and Cassie as they chatted and laughed with Lady Frances and Lord Julian.

Arabella's ill humor was considerably mollified when Sir

Brian Brandon, gorgeous to behold as Apollo, solicited her hand for the waltz, but the pleasure of being seen to captivate such a leader of fashion was soon spoiled when she saw Ned take Cassie's hand and lead her into the waltz as well. The fact that they perfectly complimented each other—he, tall and dark, she fair and slender, wearing costumes that showed their figures to the best advantage, and were so perfectly suited to each other—did nothing to improve her mood. Nor did the graceful way they moved together, oblivious to everyone but each other, improve the situation.

Cassie herself was commenting on this. "I had no idea you waltzed so well, Ned Mainwaring. If you don't make a go of politics, you could be a first-rate caper merchant," she teased.

Ned grinned. "You have no notion of the skills I've acquired in my travels," he replied airily.

"Oh"—she laughed—"Freddie has been hinting darkly at beautiful Italian contessas, Austrian baronesses, and Spanish marquesas, but I thought it was all a hum because the Ned I knew would have been off buried in some library or seeking out some desiccated scholar in all of those places."

One mobile eyebrow shot up as he looked down at her, smiling in such a way that her heart began to beat quite fast and it suddenly became difficult to catch her breath. "Not all scholars are desiccated, you know," he said. His gaze became more intent as he added softly, "In fact, some of them are quite charming and *very* beautiful. Those are the ones I waltz with." Observing the blush that rose in her cheeks, Ned decided that there were few, if any, times when he could remember Cassie disconcerted and he found it adorable.

Even more enchanting was the delighted surprise in her eyes as she raised them shyly to his, whispering, "Why, Ned, how kind of you. Thank you."

Her innocent astonishment at his remark brought to mind so many others who, with far less reason, took such compliments for granted. In fact, they often pouted if such pretty sayings were not regularly forthcoming, and he thought again what a rare unspoiled creature Cassandra Cresswell was and how infinitely dear to him. Recalled from his reverie by the other couples leaving the floor, Ned smiled fondly at Cassie and led her back to Frances and Julian, who had been joined by a monk so large that it could be no one but Nigel Streatham.

After her dance with Freddie, Arabella had stuck like a limpet to the Mainwarings, and the moment Ned returned, she pounced. "Ned, I hear you were at a balloon ascension of all things. What a charming notion! One does become so very tired of the constant social whirl and long for a divertissement to relieve one's boredom. But I fear that I should become quite dizzy watching such a thing," she protested, contriving to look interested but fragile all at the same time.

"Then it's most fortunate I didn't invite you," Ned responded equably.

Rapping him across the knuckles with her fan, she laughed playfully. "You're a dreadful wretch, Ned Mainwaring, and you must make up to me by dancing this next with me or I shall never speak to you again."

Fairly caught, Ned bowed and led her out onto the floor, though his eye followed Cassie as she laughed merrily at some disparaging remark her twin had made. Soon she, too, was on the floor, following the inexpert lead of Nigel, who had desperately sought her aid.

"Dance with me, please, Cass," he had begged. "M'mother's looking daggers at me, and if she don't see me on the floor with someone soon, she'll carry on dreadfully. It's not that I don't like dancing, but I feel like a regular chawbacon in this toggery. And it's not that I don't like women exactly, but why must they giggle so? I know I ain't a great wit, but my cock loft ain't completely empty, and no matter what I say to these young girls, they just look at me and simper. I've chosen the most unexceptional subjects of conversation, too," he complained. "I tell you"—he lowered his voice confidentially—"it's enough to turn a fellow off women completely. Why can't they be regular fellows like you and talk about something sensible like horses? Speaking of which, I've been meaning to ask you what you think of Bedford's hunter. I've been needing a hunter and I saw his at Tatt's the other day and I tell you, it was as pretty a piece of horseflesh as one could hope to see." Warming to his favorite subject, he continued, enthusiastically cataloging every one of the horse's features in minutest detail.

Cassie listened and nodded at the appropriate moments, but she was only half attending. Her thoughts were all on Ned, her waltz with him, and the odd rush of feelings that had come over her when he had looked at her in that special way. She had never thought a great deal about her appearance one way or another so long as it was presentable, but now, having been told she was beautiful, all of a sudden she cared a great deal how she looked and she wanted desperately to be truly as beautiful as he might think her—as beautiful as anyone he knew.

This was such a novel thought that fond of Nigel though she was, Cassie was glad when the dance ended so she could seek the peace and quiet of the garden to be alone with these disturbing new thoughts.

She stepped through the doors out onto a gravel path, but the solitude she sought was not to be hers, as another couple, also in pursuit of privacy, had preceded her. As Cassie stood there wondering what to do, the woman leaned toward the man and he caught her in a close embrace. Embarrassed at her unwitting intrusion into such an intimate scene, Cassie turned to go, but her feet scrunched on the gravel.

Alerted by the sound that their privacy had been invaded, the man looked up, and in the split second as she turned and hurried to leave, Cassie recognized Ned. The image of the woman locked in his arms rose before her and she realized that it was Arabella. It had all happened so quickly that she was stumbling back into the ballroom only moments after she'd left it. But in that short space of time, Cassie's entire world had changed.

Unfortunately, she had not stayed long enough either to see Ned look up or to see him unwind Arabella's arms from around his neck. In fact, Ned had been almost as unwitting a participant in the scene as Cassie. Certainly, he was as much a victim of Arabella's machinations as Cassie, though when Arabella had plotted to lure him into the garden, she could not, even in her wildest imagination, have hoped to find a way to ensure that Cassie would witness the entire scene.

Once Arabella had maneuvered Ned into soliciting the dance, the rest had been quite simple. Ned had kept up only the most desultory of conversations, all his thoughts on Cassie, so she was able, by dint of holding her breath, to become charmingly, but alarmingly flushed. Once that was accomplished, she turned her big eyes imploringly up to his, begging breathlessly, "Oh, Ned, I do feel so giddy . . . the heat . . . the crowd. I vow I am quite overcome. Do take me to some fresh air or I shall surely faint."

Ever the gentleman, Ned had led her to the doors and out onto the path, making for a small stone bench at the end of the garden. But they had barely stepped outside before Arabella collapsed against him, gasping, "I'm quite unable to stand." What could even the most callous of escorts do but come to the aid of a stricken lady? So Ned had put a supporting arm around her. No sooner had he done this than she had thrown her arms around his neck, exclaiming gratefully, "Dear Ned, so kind, so strong. The constant demands of the Season have quite worn me to a thread. I am such a poor weak creature." Here she looked up at him in an adoring way that had been the undoing of everyone who had been the object of it.

But Ned had not flirted with the beautiful women in all the capitals of Europe for nothing, and he knew very well that far from exhausting her, the frantic social round of the *ton* was tonic to Arabella. Suspecting that he was being manipulated for some unknown purpose, he was about to extricate himself when he heard footsteps on the gravel and looked up to see Cassie framed in the light streaming from the ballroom. Before he could utter a syllable of her name, she had turned and vanished, but not before he had perceived the stricken look on her face.

Already annoyed at having been forced into an unwanted embrace, Ned was now furious at Arabella, and it was with some difficulty that he was able to address her with any civility at all. Frowning, he declared, "This is quite serious. I am persuaded you should return home and lie down. Come, let us find your mother." And without giving her time to protest, Ned took her arm and led her forcefully over to the pillared alcove where a portly Queen Elizabeth who was the image of Lady Taylor was comparing notes with Mary Queen of Scots, equally obviously Lady Billingsley, on their charitable activities in their respective parishes.

"Good evening, Lady Taylor. Arabella is feeling faint. She is quite done up by the hectic pace, so I've brought her to you so you may take her home," Ned remarked, bowing to Arabella's mother and her companion.

Lady Taylor immediately began to fuss over her daughter.

It was difficult for a lady seething with frustration to maintain the appropriate air of lassitude that would render her story convincing, but Arabella had been such a consummate participant in the social scene for so many years that she had become an extraordinarily convincing actress. She murmured faintly, but heroically, "You're too kind, Ned. I would feel dreadful if anyone were to leave on my account. If I may just make use of your vinaigrette, Mama."

These last remarks were addressed to Ned's retreating back, as once he had assured himself of Lady Taylor's attention, he had beat a hasty retreat and gone in search of Cassie.

She, however, really did feel faint and so alarmingly ill that Frances was all concern when she saw her sister. "Cassie, you look quite done up. Shall we go home?" she asked the instant her sister had rejoined their little group.

But all of a sudden, Cassie, who only minutes before had been wishing to do that very thing, took a deep breath, straightened her shoulders, and forced a glittering, if totally false smile on her lips, and replied, "No thank you, Frances. For a moment the closeness of the ballroom was too much, but I would not miss this for the world."

Something inside of Cassie had snapped at the sight of Arabella and Ned. The stamina and desire to prove herself that had kept her from shedding tears and had inspired her to get up and try again after falls from trees and tumbles from horses had promptly asserted itself. If someone as stupid and vain as Arabella Taylor can become an incomparable, there must be something wrong with you, Cassandra Cresswell, because you have twice the wit she does, Cassie scolded herself. There is not the slightest reason that she should have things entirely her way and capture all the attention for herself, she continued. It's not that you want that attention, mind, but it just doesn't seem fair that someone as selfish and undeserving as she should be allowed to dominate and win the admiration of everyone.

Cassie, despite this reflective mood, was not willing to admit even to herself that it was the admiration of a particular someone rather than the world at large that she begrudged Arabella.

In the grip of this salutary anger, Cassie was unaware that she was being watched by one of society's most inveterate and acute observers, Bertie Montgomery. He had seen her return from the garden followed closely by Ned and Arabella and thus had a fair estimation of what had occurred. Oddly enough, thoughts quite similar to those going through Cassie's mind were going through his, and with the vague notion that he could help put things to rights somehow, he sauntered over to the alcove where Cassie, Julian, and Frances were standing.

"Hallo, Julian, Frances," he said, acknowledging Cassie's companions before turning to her. "Cassie, I see you've had a chance to catch your breath after all your exercise on the floor. Would you care to stand up with me? I've endured several toe tramplings in my attempts to sponsor the success of Lady Warburton's and Lady Hathaway's youngest and therefore I richly deserve a partner who not only will do justice to my dancing ability, but will reply to any of my poor attempts at conversation with something more than a monosyllable.''

"Why, thank you, Bertie,'' Cassie accepted his invitation gratefully.

After some minutes of silence during which Cassie, busy with her thoughts, performed her steps abstractedly, Bertie interjected in an injured tone, "I say, Cass, at least those blushing damsels had a mumbled response to my sallies even if they confined it to a mere yes or no.''

Cassie looked up, conscience-stricken, "Oh, I am sorry, Bertie. I was not attending. What did you say?''

He looked amused. "Nothing as yet, but you were so deep in your thoughts I could see that anything I could say would be to no purpose.''

"Oh dear,'' she replied. Then, impelled by the look of sympathetic interest on his face, she plunged into a rather tangled speech. "Bertie, why is it that some people who have more hair than wit and aren't very nice besides can become all the rage? How can people like people who only have a pretty face and nothing else to recommend them when there are so many other people who are much nicer but seem to be less admired?''

Despite his amiable and open countenance, Bertie was no fool and he did not for one minute believe that Cassie's question sprang from a purely general and dispassionate curiosity concerning the workings of the *ton*. He reflected for a moment before answering, "Well, Cassie, I ain't a particularly clever fellow, but I think it has to do with interest.''

"Interest?'' Cassie looked blank.

"Yes, interest,'' he replied. Warming to his theme, he

continued, "Most people ain't all that sure of themselves, so they watch what everyone else is doing and then do that. That's called 'fashion.' " He beamed triumphantly at his own perspicacity. "Now someone who spends a great deal of time thinking about fashion is someone these people understand. Moreover, someone like, like . . . Arabella Taylor, for instance, knows that fashion comes from everyone's doing or liking the same thing, so she spends an enormous amount of time and effort working to win their approval and demonstrate how much she cares about what people think of her. Much of her day is devoted to choosing a toilette that will be universally pleasing, and she can always be seen in the most approved places. She does her best to converse only on topics that are of the most general concern. All this attention to the opinion of society flatters people, and because she makes them feel that she attaches great importance to their judgment, they decide that they like her. Then they tell their friends that Arabella Taylor is a nice gel, and before you can say jackstraws, she's all the rage." Here, proud of this unusually long speech, Bertie stopped to catch his breath.

"But what a two-faced thing to do!" Cassie protested.

"It ain't two-faced. She truly is interested in those things and she truly is interested in people, in her own way of course. Now someone, say like you, enjoys many things and your whole existence don't begin and end with others' opinions of you. People know that being liked and admired by them ain't the most important thing in your life. They're never certain of what you're thinking. Makes 'em uncomfortable."

"Do you mean to say that someone like me could become all the rage if she cared to do so?" Cassie demanded in disbelief.

"Might do." Bertie looked thoughtful.

Cassie was silent for a while and then, glancing shyly up at him, asked, "If I were interested in cutting a dash, do you think you could help me, I mean show me how to go on?"

"Happy to," Bertie beamed at her.

"Could . . . could we start tomorrow, do you think?" she wondered.

"No time like the present," he declared stoutly. "I'll call for you tomorrow morning and we can begin with a drive in the park."

"Oh, thank you, Bertie. You're the kindest friend in the world," Cassie breathed.

He blushed, disclaiming, "It's nothing. Happy to do anything to be of service to you and the family."

Bertie led Cassie back to the alcove where Sir Brian Brandon had now joined Frances, Julian. and Freddie. Sir Brian claimed Cassie's hand, closely followed by her brother-in-law and her twin, so that Ned, try though he might, was unable to get near her for the rest of the evening.

CHAPTER 24

The next day found Ned riding north with Lord Charlton to visit Lord Haslemere, an aged peer who, though now retired in the country, nevertheless retained powerful political connections and was in many ways more aware of what was occurring on the political scene than those participating in it. They left so early that Ned was unable to call at Grosvenor Square and was thus forced to wait with as much patience as he could muster to offer his explanation to Cassie.

As he rode, he reflected on this odd state of things. Accustomed to living his own life and pursuing his own interests wherever they led him, he was one who highly prized his freedom and resented the slightest interference in his affairs. Previously he had conducted all his liaisons with women who had understood and completely respected his dislike of feeling obligated or having to answer to anyone. There had been one person who had inspired him to give up his freedom, one person he had spent his life dreaming of. Now, not only was he irked at her proprietary attitude, he was wishing desperately that a childhood playmate he had laughed at, teased, and argued with would demonstrate just such an interest in him. More than anything he wanted to wrap his arms around Cassie as tightly as Arabella had clung to him and reassure her concerning the scene she had witnessed in the garden. He sighed.

When he had first learned of Lord Haslemere's wish to meet him, he had been overjoyed at the opportunity. As Lord Charlton had said, "Any man who has Haslemere's stamp of approval will go far, no matter what his political party."

Now Ned was longing to be back in London, all because he
wanted to explain himself to someone he'd known since
childhood, someone who, for all he knew, may not have
cared whether or not he reassured her. I must be in my
dotage, he thought. Why am I worrying about her feelings
when in all probability she hasn't given a second thought
to seeing Arabella and me, or if she has, she is, if anything,
amused?

Here he was entirely wrong. Not only had Cassie given
second thoughts to the intimate moment she had intruded on,
she could not get the tableau of Arabella wrapped in Ned's
arms out of her mind. She was still too upset to realize that
it was Ned who had been wrapped in Arabella's arms despite
his heroic efforts to extricate himself gracefully. At this
moment, Cassie's valiant efforts to erase the memory and
direct her energies into more productive channels were taking
the form of a ride in the park in Bertie's new phaeton.

Even the friends who had known Bertie since schooldays
were constantly amazed that a man who spent so much time
on his wardrobe and seeking out and repeating fashionable
on-dits in London's most select drawing rooms, all the while
completely ignoring such male haunts as Manton's and
Gentleman Jackson's, could be such a notable whip. It
seemed incongruous that the languid and willowy Bertie
could possibly have the strength to keep a spirited pair in
control. Yet somehow, without disarranging his exquisite
attire or overcoming his loathing for any sort of exertion,
he managed not only to handle the most restive of high-
spirited teams, but drove with all the finesse of the most noted
member of the Four Horse Club. He had recently purchased
a beautiful pair and a new phaeton with yellow wheels, a
combination destined to cause a stir in the park and arouse
envy in the breast of every admirer of fine horseflesh.

Certainly his equipage had caused a favorable sensation
at Mainwaring House. Teddy and Freddie had agreed that
the turnout was slap up to the echo. Bertie and Cassie could
have waited forever for them to finish examining and
enumerating the fine points of the entire rig, if both Teddy

and his uncle had not had too much respect for such a mettle-some pair to keep them standing.

Even Cassie forgot her unpleasant thoughts long enough to exclaim over them as they bowled along. Excellent horse-woman that she was, she kept silent while Bertie maneuvered through the streets, and refrained from commenting on the smooth gait and the well-sprung ride until they reached the park. "You do drive to an inch, Bertie," she commented admiringly as he skillfully negotiated his way between two wagons and through the gate.

"Thank you, Cassie." Bertie, knowing that Cassie's own driving skills were something beyond the ordinary, looked gratified. "But," he began as purposefully as Bertie Montgomery did anything, "we ain't here to pass judgment on my driving. We're here to help take your rightful place in the *ton*."

Cassie looked dubious. During her sleepless night she had thought about her expressed wish to become all the rage with some misgiving. She now gave voice to these reservations. "I'm not at all certain that I can simper, smile, and act bird-witted as though I am in the greatest need of someone who can tell me how to go on and explain everything to me. Nor can I admire some overeager buck that I don't care a rap for."

"Whoa, Cassie. I ain't saying you have to do any of those things. You don't have to bamboozle anyone. Just enjoy yourself. If you're dancing with some blade who can only talk about the way he ties his cravats, it's Lombard Street to a China orange he has taste and can dance well, so you should take pleasure in the graceful way he executes his steps and appreciate the care he has taken with his toilette the way you would appreciate the skill of any other artist. If you're stuck with some beefy-faced squire who can speak of nothing but horses, why you can enjoy yourself discussing that without thinking that you would die of bordeom if you were condemned to spend your entire life with him. People don't want flummery. They just want someone who is interested in their particular passions and can share these, as well as someone who knows how to converse with them on their favorite subjects.''

Cassie was quiet. The more she thought about it, the more she realized that this was exactly what Bertie did. Every member of the *ton* liked him and sought out his company, not for his brilliant wit or overwhelming charm, but because of his amiable adaptability and the ease with which he could enter into any discussion. ''That's all very well, but to be a diamond or a nonpareil one must be well looking and have an air of fashion,'' she objected.

''Well, one certainly can't be an antidote,'' he conceded. ''But again, it's enjoying oneself that is important. Whatever rig one chooses, one should look upon selecting it as an artistic experience and take pleasure in using it as a way to express oneself.''

Cassie looked puzzled.

''Take you, for instance. You wear your clothes as though choosing them were a duty. You always look elegant, but you don't appear as though you relished preparing your toilette. In point of fact, you take this all too seriously. You look at it the way you would some task of Greek translation, as though it has some underlying significance. You don't need to know the meaning of everything to take pleasure in it. You like beautiful things, don't you—paintings, sculpture, music?''

Cassie nodded.

''Then why not enjoy wearing beautiful things and using them to make yourself feel and look beautiful?''

Cassie sat silently as they rolled along, nodding mechanically to familiar faces here and there. She realized that Bertie was echoing a criticism, once voiced by Ned, that she considered everything too seriously. She sighed. It was all so very confusing and difficult to think about. Had she been wrong in the way she looked at things for so many years?

They had completed the circuit before Bertie interrupted these rather melancholy reflections. ''Cassie, you mustn't look so blue-deviled. We'll take you to Madame Regnery, choose some new togs for you, and you're bound to feel much more the thing. You must begin with a riding habit.''

"A riding habit?" Cassie echoed blankly. "But I have a perfectly—"

"I've seen it and it's all that's suitable, but that ain't enough," Bertie interjected firmly. "You have the best seat of anyone I know, man or woman. You should wear something that calls attention to you in a situation where you show to advantage and most females don't—Arabella Taylor for one. She'd be terrified of a cart horse while you can manage a prime bit of blood with ease. It's time the *ton* was aware of that.''

Cassie, much struck by this idea, meekly allowed herself to be deposited at Madame Regnery's while Bertie found a boy to take care of the horses.

The next few hours flew by in a blur as Bertie, conversant with feminine fashion down to the last furbelow, ordered up gowns that would be an accurate reflection of the true spirit of Lady Cassandra Cresswell.

"And that hair," he concluded severely, subjecting her modest style to a critical examination, "positively must go.''

"What's wrong with it?" Cassie demanded a trifle rebelliously. She had submitted with tolerable good grace to being pushed and pulled, fitted, evaluated, discussed, and gone over as though she were a prime piece of horseflesh, but she was now beginning to feel rather tired of being treated as though she didn't exist.

"It makes you look like an ape-leader," Bertie responded with unusually brutal frankness.

"It does no such thing! Besides, it's dignified. I detest the odiously fussy way everyone is wearing theirs now," Cassie objected mutinously.

Ignoring her completely, Bertie waved to Monsier Ducros, Lady Frances's hairdresser, who had been hovering unobtrusively in the background. "You see what I mean?" he inquired despairingly.

"*Mais oui*, Monsieur is entirely correct. Mademoiselle looks *un peu sévère,*" he agreed. "*Oui, c'est trop sévère.* Mademoiselle must be *moins sérieuse, je pense.*"

Cassie sighed and gave herself up to the ministrations of Monsieur. When he was finished, she was forced to admit that Bertie and Monsieur Ducros were entirely correct. Her previous coiffeur had been too severe. With her hair cut shorter, her curls were freed to fame her face, adding piquancy to her expression, emphasizing the large blue eyes, the generous mouth, and the delicately but firmly molded chin. It felt lighter, freer, and made her feel just that much lighter and gayer herself.

Bertie nodded sagely as she pirouetted in front of the mirror. "What did I tell you?" he asked, unable to keep a trace of smugness from showing. "Put on that new walking dress and you'll feel a different person. No one should underestimate the importance of becoming clothes and coiffeur to one's sense of well-being. Anyone who tells you differently is a slowtop." He then directed Madame's assistance to help Cassie into the most dashing of the walking dresses and to wrap up the sober carriage dress she had been wearing. The cerulean blue spencer cut tight to the shape revealed Cassie's graceful figure and the matching gauze lining the very fashionable watered *gros de Naples* bonnet brought out the intense blue of her eyes.

As they strolled along to the carriage and Cassie caught sight of herself in shop windows she reveled in the moment of startled recognition when she realized that she belonged to that exquisitely fashionable reflection. This in turn made her conversation and expression more animated and sparkling. The air of gaiety and confidence, as much as her very real beauty, caused several passersby to stop and take a second look at the lovely young woman with Bertie Montgomery—a circumstance he was very careful to point out to her. This admiration increased Cassie's sense of well-being, so that she positively glowed with her enjoyment of the fineness of the day, her companion, and herself.

It was not only those on the street who were struck by

Cassie's newfound *éclat*. Freddie and Nigel, strolling along after an agreeable sojourn at Tattersall's, halted in their discussion of the auction taking place there. "I say, that's a dashed pretty girl," Freddie remarked.

At which Nigel, who had observed more carefully than his companion, nearly doubled over with mirth. "Freddie, you cawker! That's your sister!" he bellowed.

"Why, so it is," Freddie agreed in mild surprise. "Hallo, Cass. What have you been doing to yourself? You look fine as fivepence."

"Why, thank you, Freddie." Cassie turned quite pink with pleasure. Freddie, the best of brothers a girl could wish for and unfailingly kind about including his twin in every kind of lark, was totally oblivious to the niceties of feminine fashion. To have her toilette penetrate his consciousness was a coup indeed! Even Nigel, who had been as unconscious as Freddie until his service with brother Guardsmen inclined to ogle any woman between the ages of sixteen and thirty had taught him the niceties of feminine fashion, was looking at her admiringly. Bertie is in the right of it, she thought to herself as she promenaded along surrounded by these escorts, wearing fashionable clothes does affect one's frame of mind.

CHAPTER 25

It would have been too much to say that the transformation Bertie had effected in Cassie stunned the fashionable world, but the members of the *ton* were more aware of her presence. Captain Walworth, upon seeing her in the park mounted on Chiron and wearing a close-fitting lavender riding habit with its dashing hat, remarked to Major Dowling that Lady Cassandra Cresswell was a remarkably pretty girl. "Excellent seat, too," he observed, watching her with a critical but admiring eye.

Major Dowling repeated this to his bosom companion Henry Ffolke-Smythe, a noted clubman, who of course shared it with his fellows, and slowly Cassie found herself beginning to be scrutinized with a deal of interest and approval.

Taking Bertie's advice to heart, she relaxed and began to interest herself in the particular attributes and passions that each new admirer had to offer. Somewhat to her surprise, she truly began to enjoy herself in a way that she hadn't for a long time. She learned a great deal as well. As she sat next to him at Lady Waverly's musicale, instead of scorning the Honorable Winston Denham's obsession with his tailor, Cassie listened to his catalog of the agonies suffered over the perfect fitting of his coat and the creation of a new style of tying his cravat. She gained a new appreciation for the creativity that inspired this particular passion. Not that she could ever become the greatest of friends with someone who spent such an inordinate amount of time selecting just the right waistcoat and snuffbox to match his attire, but instead of discounting such attention to toilette entirely, she began to perceive it as a mode of self-expression and to have more sympathy toward him. This sympathy communicated itself to the Honorable Winston, who relaxed in its warmth and found himself opening up and speaking far more naturally and freely than he ordinarily did. In fact, he couldn't think when he last had a more delightful conversation. Later, recapping the evening to some of his closest friends, he pronounced Lady Cassandra Cresswell to be simply charming.

As Cassie pursued this new program she discovered that it put people more at their ease with her, and feeling comfortable, they were less likely to converse on the safe and boring subjects of the weather, the latest *on-dit,* or their health. Instead they began to share more topics that were their own particular concern, and this all made for much more enlightening and intriguing discussions. Cassie even began to look forward to some of the festivities of the Season and to take pleasure in social encounters. This new attitude expressed itself through the sparkle in her eyes and the vivacity of her expression. Those around her, attracted by this vitality, gravitated toward her naturally. The change was a gradual one, but it was distinct, nevertheless, and those near and dear to her remarked on it with pleasure.

"Is that knocker never silent, Mr. Higgins?" Cook demanded as she served the butler his supper one evening.

"Hardly. There is a constant succession of bouquets and eager young bucks, top-of-the-trees, some of them. At last Miss Cassie seems to have taken the *ton* by storm, though it was a long time coming. I began to wonder if they had eyes in their heads." If Higgins had not heard from Lady Kitty Willoughby's butler that the lady's brother was in the country, he would have been concerned over Ned's conspicuous absence as he still firmly maintained that of all Miss Cassie's London beaux, Master Ned was the only one capable of handling her. "She's a rare handful," he remarked reminiscently to Mrs. Wilkins. "There are very few with the wit and spirit to keep up with her. Mark my words,

Master Ned is the one for her. He's one of the few people she has ever listened to."

Rose, though less vocal in the servants' hall than her superior, was also relishing her mistress's new attitude, perhaps more than anyone else. Born with a strong creative streak, the young maid had always been sorry that her mistress, dearly as she loved her, did not care enough about her toilette to utilize Rose's talents to their fullest degree. Now, however, instead of looking askance at her hair when Rose had finished and asking hesitantly if she could make it a trifle smoother and less frivolous, Cassie would glance appreciatively in the glass at her maid's artistry, remarking, "You are as much a genius as Monsieur Ducros, Rose. I am indeed fortunate to have you to take care of me."

Rose would smile secretly to herself, but could not refrain from remarking, "It's that glad I am to see you enjoying yourself as you should do, Miss Cassie. It's good to see you at your old ways again."

"My old ways?" Cassie asked curiously.

"Why yes, miss. Ever since Master Freddie and Master Ned left you've been so very serious. When they came back, we all thought you would be your old gay self, but you weren't. I suppose it was that you spent so much time with that Horace Wilbraham, who always wore such a Friday face and filled your head with all those Greeks, so it was not to be wondered at that you didn't enjoy yourself."

Goodness, Cassie thought to herself, Bertie rescued me just in time. It seems as though I was on my way to become the deadest of dead bores.

That evening she threw herself with such renewed effort into the gaiety that people, seeing her vivacity, wondered if there was to be some special forthcoming announcement that would account for it.

In the meantime, far removed from the frivolity of the capital, Ned had ample time on his own to reflect. Lord Haslemere, never the most sociable of men even when young, now retired very early in the evening, "to save what little strength I have in this desiccated frame,'' he explained. "Never get old, lad. Being treated as an oracle isn't worth the cost in the aches and pains of growing old and wise.''

So Ned was left to his own devices and he spent a great deal of time sitting in front of the fire, a glass of brandy in hand, thinking of Cassie. He always began by wishing she were there so he could recount the day's discussion and hear her views. As he warmed to his topic he would envision her sitting with the firelight catching the golden highlights in her hair, her head tilted to one side, her forehead slightly wrinkled in concentration, and he would long for nothing so much as to have her in his arms.

He would imagine so vividly how it would feel to hold her against him, her head resting on his shoulder, that he could practically smell the rosewater in her hair. But then the image of her face as she saw him with Arabella would always intrude and shatter the delightful vision.

"Damn and blast! I must get back to Town!'' he would fume in frustration. But there was no help for it. He couldn't leave such a golden opportunity to absorb political wisdom from ''the oracle,'' as Lord Haslemere so ironically dubbed himself, so he remained in the country with as good grace as he could muster, learning all Lord Haslemere had to offer and advancing his own ideas for criticism and discussion. Warmed by the approbation he heard in his mentor's voice and stimulated by the day's conversation, he would retire at night to be tortured anew by the sequence of events which kept him away from Cassie and this strange new longing to be with her, to hold her and feel her close to him.

Cassie, on the other hand, was keeping herself far too busy to be suffering such agonies. At the back of her mind was a part of her that looked for Ned as she entered every ballroom or stepped into the box at the theater or the opera, but such unwelcome thoughts were speedily banished by recalling the scene with Arabella. If Cassie missed having her best friend to share things and laugh with, she soon overcame that with the thought that no one who lived in Arabella Taylor's pocket could have the discrimination and sensitivity to be dubbed her closest friend.

Still, amidst all the gaiety and the bevy of young men soliciting her company for every sort of entertainment, she felt a small empty space and knew that something was missing to keep her happiness from being complete. It was not a big enough hole that she was constantly aware of it, but in the quietness of the carriage returning to Mainwaring House from some brilliant soirée, or as Rose was helping her to undress, the little feeling of incompleteness would insist on intruding. Cassie would quickly shake her head, telling herself that she was just tired, but as she drifted off to sleep, her mind wandering aimlessly, she would admit to herself that it wasn't exhaustion but the wish to have, if not Ned, someone who could be exactly as he had been for her before Arabella had taken him over.

Ned and Cassie were not the only ones suffering disturbing thoughts. Arabella, though she did her utmost to avoid serious reflections of any sort, was undergoing some unpleasant revelations of her own. These had been prompted by the reactions of a dancing partner, a callow youth that she only suffered to lead her on the dance floor because he was the youngest brother of a highly eligible marquess who, in Arabella's opinion, had remained unattached or even unattracted to any single woman for far too many Seasons. As they went through their figures she noticed his attention wandering. Accustomed to being the sole focus of anyone's interest, the beauty was considerably miffed and followed his gaze, which seemed to be fixed on a group of young blades at the other end of the ballroom. Realizing that Arabella was aware of his distraction, her partner looked somewhat uncomfortable but asked eagerly, ''Who is she? I know you know everyone who is anyone so you must know her, but I don't ever recall seeing her.''

Neither did Arabella recognize the particular slender vivacious blond girl with a decided air of fashion about her who somehow seemed vaguely familiar. She looked again more closely only to discover that not only was she acquainted with what appeared to be society's newest interest, but she had known her since they had been in pinafores instead of ball gowns. Trying to keep herself from audibly grinding her teeth, Arabella responded with an air of sweet condescension. "Why that's little Cassie Cresswell. It must be her first Season. How time flies! It seems no time at all since she was the biggest tomboy for miles around."

And that was not to be the last of it. The next day a tactless young gallant whose protestations of undying affection had become something of a bore because his constant hounding of Arabella had begun to discourage more sophisticated and more eligible admirers, further annoyed her by remarking to her that the Hampshire air must be extraordinarily salubrious as it had produced two of the Season's reigning beauties: Arabella Taylor and Lady Cassandra Cresswell. Seeing the frown settling on his deity's brow, he had hastily added that of course everyone knew brunettes were all the fashion and that he himself found blondes a trifle insipid for his taste. But it was too late. The damage had been done and Arabella was now were aware that that upstart Cassandra Cresswell, who was a tomboy and a bluestocking besides, had become a force to be reckoned with. She retired to plot her course of action, for it would never do to have the *ton* linking their names just because they happened to have the misfortune of having grown up together.

CHAPTER 26

At last Ned was able to break away from Lord Haslemere's most flattering hospitality and return to London, where it was not very long before it was borne in upon him that some changes had transpired during his absence from the capital. He had barely changed clothes and washed the dust of travel from his person before he presented himself in Grosvenor Square, requesting to see Miss Cassie.

Now Higgins, wise in the ways of the world and the Cresswells in particular, though he had long ago decided that Master Ned was just the person to keep his mistress in line, had also decided that it would never do for Master Ned to take her for granted. He was pleased, therefore, upon hearing the object of Ned's visit, to inform him that this object had just departed in Sir Brian Brandon's elegant curricle.

Ned was forced to cool his heels with ill-disguised impatience, which only increased when his valet reminded him that he was promised to his sister for her card party that evening. Knowing that the group from Mainwaring House was far too dashing to frequent card parties and were far more likely, it being a Wednesday night, to be gracing Almack's select assemblage, he was forced to contain his frustration until the next day.

Having been beaten out the first time, Ned was careful to present himself at Mainwaring House at an early hour the following morning. Hearing the slightly anxious note in his voice when he asked again for Miss Cassie, Higgins was happy to inform him that she had just left for the park mounted on Chiron and accompanied by Nigel Streatham and his fellow Guardsmen. Concerned lest such an old friend as Miss Cassie be unappreciated because her familiarity and eager for her claims to fashion and popular acclaim to be recognized and properly respected, Higgins was delighted to note Master Ned's reaction upon receiving this news with no little satisfaction. His jaws tightened, his shoulders tensed, and his blue eyes darkened—all very propitious signs to one who wished him to wake up to the fact that his Miss Cassie was crucial to his happiness and that her presence was not necessarily to be taken for granted. He's the one for her, all right, the butler chuckled to himself. But our Miss Cassie will give him a run for his money and that's no bad thing for someone who has had women shamelessly pursuing him, if the tales Master Freddie tells are to be believed.

Not having anything better to do, Ned decided to go to the park anyway by himself. He had no very clear-cut plan in mind beyond the wish of at least seeing Cassie even if he couldn't talk to her—a wish that had grown stronger with every obstacle put in his way. Hoping to accomplish this, he rode off toward Stanhope Gate and began a slow circuit of the park. It was a fine day and the place was crowded with beautiful women in elegant equipages and bucks of the first stare mounted on the finest bits of blood England had to offer.

At long last, after much fruitless searching, he located Cassie, the center of a group of Guardsmen who seemed to be enjoying themselves hugely, if their guffaws of laughter were any indication. However, there was a press of horsemen and carriages surrounding him and his progress toward her was slowed considerably. Controlling his mounting irritation, Ned resigned himself to observing the crowd around him and sizing up their mounts. He had just finished mentally going over the points of the handsome bay in front of him when its rider leaned over to address his companion. "I say, who is the Aphrodite on that great black horse?"

The companion looked at him in some surprise as he replied, "Where have you been, old fellow? She's the latest sensation. That's Lady Cassandra Cresswell, Freddie's sister, and, if Nigel Streatham is to be believed, it's the greatest shame that the rest of us are only privileged to see her trotting sedately along in the park. Says she's a bruising rider. Got the best seat he's ever seen in a woman and what she don't know about horses wouldn't fill a thimble.''

Ned's ears had pricked up at the mention of Cassie's name and he urged his horse forward so he could hear better.

"By God, she's magnificent!" the first rider exclaimed.

"It won't do any good, Ferdie," his friend warned him. "She has scores of men dangling after her. Small wonder, she's the most taking thing. Arabella Taylor grew up with her and declares her to be shockingly blue, but she ain't a bit high in the instep and makes anyone feel comfortable. She talks to a fellow as though she were his brother—none of the mealymouthed flirting and simpering that so many girls seem to have to do. I've never heard Fortescue speak so many words at one time to a female in his life, but not only did he converse with her, he even stood up with her at Almack's the other night—enjoyed himself, too. Says he's never met a woman before who had anything to the point to say about horses. And young Buckingham's besotted. He can talk of nothing else. Making a cake of himself, I can tell you. If I have to hear him describe her dimples when she smiles once more, I shall do violence to him, I assure you. But there's something special about her, make no mistake. Tell you what is—she's kind. Got a sense of humor, but she laughs with you, not at you. You don't ever get the feeling she's passing judgment on you or seeing if you measure up to some standard.''

The rest of the conversation was obliterated as another group of Guardsmen went clattering past, hallooing to those in the group surrounding Cassie. Suddenly Ned had lost all enthusiasm for a ride in the park and the day which had seemed to promising felt quite flat. He decided to head off to Brooks's in search of distraction and more serious conversation. Once there, he made a praiseworthy attempt to immerse himself in deep political discussions, but he could not get his mind off the scene in the park. He told himself that he was delighted to find that Cassie was at last being recognized. In fact, she appeared to be all the rage, and who could be more deserving of praise and admiration? But it had shaken him to hear her, his Cassie, being spoken of so familiarly.

Hitherto, Ned had felt somewhat proprietary about her because he alone had known how unique she was. He alone had made her relaxed and comfortable enough that she revealed her wit and charm. Now, apparently, she was sharing them with the entire *ton,* and Ned was not best pleased about it. Don't be a dog in the manger, he admonished himself. Isn't that the very reason you paid such attention to her? You wanted to help bring her to the notice of society so she would be given the admiration and acclaim that was her due.

As he examined his motives and the turmoil of emotions he was now experiencing, Ned realized that he had been acting in his own interests all along. Face it, you've been in love with her since you were in short coats, you fool, he told himself. Arabella was the merest of infatuations and only now when you're at a standstill do you recognize all this. You're a nodcock, Ned Mainwaring, and now you must do your best to retrieve your position with Cassie and set about the task of convincing her of all this. He sighed. Complicated as this process of discovery had been, it was nothing compared to the task he was now setting for himself. It was extremely difficult to know how to proceed, especially when he could barely get near her, constantly surrounded as she was by a crowd of beaux.

Ned knew that Cassie was likely to be at the ball at Rutland House that evening, and since it behooved him to act as quickly as possible before she was more distracted by the attentions of other admirers, he resolved to try to approach her there in the hopes of explaining himself.

He dressed with uncommon care, taking more time than customary on his cravat and assuring himself several times that his coat fit without a wrinkle. Observing these preparations, his valet, a taciturn individual who had long ago realized that his master's interest in clothes was, at best, limited, knew that something of importance was in the wind. But, having been hired just because he catered to Ned's preference for silence and solitude, he refrained from revealing by the slightest gesture that he was aware of anything at all unusual in his master's conduct.

The extra care taken in Ned's accouterment had its effect, and more than one head turned as he entered the ballroom. Many hearts fluttered at the sight of his tall, well-knit form, the breadth of his shoulders, and the strength of his arms and chest, all heightened by the severe elegance of his attire. More than one woman sighed at the firm jawline and the dark blue eyes set deep under black brows in a countenance rendered more attractive but more forbidding by the contrast between the snowy whiteness of the cravat and the dark coat.

Unaware of the admiring glances he was attracting, his eyes swept the room, anxiously looking for the gleam of candlelight on gold curls. At last he found Cassie, an ethereal yet provocative presence in silver net over a white satin slip, her delicate grace emphasized by the somber lines of the costumes of the men surrounding her. As Ned watched she laughingly disengaged herself from the cluster around her and headed toward an alcove whose gently billowing curtains suggested an open window or balcony beyond them.

So intent was Cassie on gaining the sanctuary of the alcove that she did not notice that she was being followed by young Buckingham, whose besotted expression showed him to be as unconscious of the rest of the occupants of the ballroom as she was.

That puppy! Ned ground his teeth, as much annoyed by Buckingham's obliviousness to everything but Cassie as he was by the fact that the enamored swain was going to intrude on the moment of respite she was so obviously seeking. With no very clear idea of why he was doing so, except to keep Cassie's chance for a minute of peace and solitude from being ruined by an overeager young buck, Ned started toward the alcove himself.

Unfortunately, his progress was impeded by several friends who insisted upon learning the consequences of his sojourn in the country, so it was some time before Ned succeeded in gaining his objective. By the time he arrived, there was no sight of either Cassie or her follower. Deciding that it must be a balcony rather than an open window that was responsible for the breeze, he pushed the curtains aside and stepped out, only to have his gaze met by a scene straight from the most romantic of novels to be obtained from the circulating libraries.

Cassie stood, one hand on the railing, her slender form outlined in the moonlight. Directly in front of her, young Buckingham was smothering her hand with kisses and endeavoring to pull her into his arms.

Ned, normally a coolheaded man of sanguine temperament and a peace-loving nature, was suddenly seized by a murderous rage. The scene was blurred by a red mist of anger that rose before his eyes and his hands clenched at his sides as he accused her furiously, "So, not content with being the Season's latest sensation, you are now trying for the title of the biggest flirt in all of London!"

Cassie snatched her hand away and turned toward him, her eyes blazing with indignation. "I am *not* a flirt, Ned Mainwaring. And if I were, I don't see that it's the slightest concern of yours," she responded, her voice trembling with anger.

"And you, my lad, you ought to be ashamed of yourself, intruding upon a lady's solitude like that." Ned grasped the now quaking Buckingham by the cravat.

"Yes sir, of course, sir," the youth quavered. Released abruptly as Ned turned back to Cassie, he fled as quickly and quietly as possible, only too glad to escape the unpleasant scene.

Looking at him, Cassie couldn't think when she had seen Ned more angry. His countenance was truly alarming: the blue eyes were dark in his white set face, the firm lips were compressed into a thin line, and his black brows were drawn together in a dreadful frown. All the frustrations of the past week overwhelmed him and Ned's control snapped. He grasped her shoulders roughly and pulled her to him, gasping in a curiously grating voice, "And you . . . if you are determined to be a coquette and steal kisses in the moonlight, you ought at least to do so with someone who knows what he is doing."

With that he pulled her to him and brought his lips down hard on hers. He was furiously angry and at first his kiss was brutal, punishing, but as he felt the softness of her lips underneath his and sensed the warmth of her body against him, caressed the silkiness of her skin beneath his hands, his fury drained away. His lips relaxed. He sighed and gathered her closer to him, kissing her lingeringly, caressingly, as he traced her jaw with his lips, moving them down the smooth column of her neck. Through half-closed eyes he saw the net of her corsage straining as she gasped for breath and he longed to tear it aside and cover her with kisses.

Too taken aback at first to do anything but respond to the anger in his attack, Cassie struggled to escape, but the more she strove to free herself, the more tightly Ned pulled her to him. Dimly she was aware of her surprise at the strength of his arms and the hardness of his chest. As his lips became gentler and more persuasive, a wave of warmth and languor swept over her. The rigidity seeped out of her body and she found it molding itself to his, her lips opening under his insistent pressure. A haze swam before her eyes and she felt dizzy and weak.

But just as her senses threatened to be overwhelmed by the intensity of these new and disturbing sensations, a warning flickered inside her head and the ever-present voice of reason asserted itself once again. What ever are you doing, Cassie Cresswell? It's Arabella he wants. You've only made him angry. It's just that he doesn't like the idea of an adoring playmate growing up and paying attention to someone else.

It's not that he wants you. He is angry at you, not attracted to you. Gathering the last reserves of strength and self-esteem, Cassie pulled herself away, gasping, "How could you, Ned! Oh how could you treat a friend so?" With a swirl of skirts she fled.

CHAPTER 27

Somehow Cassie gained the staircase without being seen and located a footman to go in search of the Mainwarings' carriage. John, who had not expected to be called for hours, had been dozing happily, and came grumbling at the footman's summons. Catching sight of Cassie's white face, he was immediately all concern and threw the reins to a link boy so he could hand her tenderly into the carriage himself. "There, there, Miss Cassie. We'll have you home in a pig's whisper," he reassured her gently as he helped her in and shut the door.

Tears strung her eyes at his solicitude and as she settled back against the squabs, they began to trickle slowly down her cheeks. Wiping them furiously away with her hand, she muttered to herself. This will never do. It's only Ned after all. You've been angry at each other before. You'll see. You'll both come 'round and be merry as grigs in no time. She sighed, knowing full well that this time it was different and the difference was in her reaction to him. It's not Ned that's upsetting you, my girl, she told herself. It's you. You know you wanted him to go on kissing you, to crave you as much as you longed to stay in his arms and feel him close to you and holding you. That's what's upsetting you. You're disturbed because your body recognized before your head did that you're in love with him. In love with him, she repeated softly to herself. Yes, I suppose that's it. And he's in love with Arabella.

The carriage halted. Sighing wearily, Cassie gathered her

skirts around her and descended slowly with none of her characteristic quickness.

Higgins, opening the door and observing her wilted form, was all concern, ushering her in and sending Rose scampering to her mistress with a cup of hot milk and a soothing touch as she helped her out of her clothes and brushed her hair.

"Something is dreadfully wrong with Miss Cassie. I've never seen her so quiet before. She's in a bad way," Rose confided to the worried little group clustered in the kitchen. "I wish I knew what to do." She sighed heavily. "But you know Miss Cassie, never one to share her troubles and always wanting to fix them herself."

While the discussion was going on belowstairs, Cassie lay in bed staring wide-eyed at the pattern in the bed hangings. I must get out of here, away from all of this, back to Cresswell where I can be myself again, she thought. But she knew that she would never quite be the old, saucy, independent Cassie again.

She traced her lips with the tip of her finger, feeling the tingling that still remained there from his kiss. How could I have been so blind? she wondered. Thinking over the empty way she had been feeling since Freddie and Ned had gone to India, she realized with a start that she'd been missing Ned. Why I've been in love with him for ages, I just never knew it, she marveled. But why did I discover this tonight?

As she considered it, she became aware that until he had kissed her, she had thought of Ned as a dear friend. He was someone whom she was fond of as she was of Freddie or Frances, someone she felt comfortable with, someone she could confide in. But tonight she had recognized that he was someone who aroused far deeper feelings than that. She desired him. She wanted to be close to him, to feel him against her. And she wanted him to desire her.

For a moment when he had looked at her with such intensity, she had thought perhaps he did, but she knew that was just an illusion. She was not the type of woman men desired. Despite Bertie's tutelage, she knew she wasn't at all seductive. She could not be like Arabella and tantalize men until they craved her above everything else. She was just Cassie Cresswell, someone people enjoyed because they felt comfortable with her. She could talk on any subject, share any interest, make people relax and confide anything to her, and amuse them with her unexpected comments. Until now, thta had been enough. She had been more than happy to be sought out and enjoyed because he was good company and everyone trusted her. Now she wanted more, and she wanted it from someone who longed for someone else just as she longed for him.

She tossed restlessly, thinking and thinking, revisiting the scene until her head ached, but she could come up with no solution other than escape. Yes, I shall go down to Cresswell and I shall begin my studies again. In time, if I'm not wildly happy, at least I shall be at peace and I shall be able to occupy my mind and my time with something useful. That settled, she fell into an uneasy sleep just before dawn.

Meanwhile, Cassie was not the only one for whom sleep was an impossibility. Ned had only remained on the balcony, staring aghast at the empty space she had just left, a few minutes longer than Cassie before he, too, left the ball. Hoping to clear his head, he had dismissed his carriage and walked home, cursing himself for a fool all the way. What a cow-handed gudgeon you are! Instead of telling her that you loved her, you raged at her like an idiot and then mauled her like some importunate youth. And now you've alienated her completely. If she used to hold you in mild affection, she certainly won't any longer.

He had been walking along at a brisk rate, suiting his steps to his thoughts, and he arrived home even before he was aware of having turned in to Brook Street. His valet was waiting for him, but after requesting him to bring up a bottle of brandy, Ned dismissed him and sat down, staring moodily into the fire.

Despite the blackness of his thoughts, he smiled tenderly

as he recalled the brief moment when he had felt Cassie relax in his arms and her lips open beneath his. He had wanted that feeling to go on forever. Over the years he had kissed countless women and had held and caressed scores of voluptuous bodies in all states of dress and undress, but when he had felt the quiver of response in Cassie as her body moved to fit itself to his, it was as though he had discovered love and all the wonder and delight of it for the first time. In truth he had. He had certainly been attracted to women before, had desired them, been aroused and stimulated by them, even fancied himself in love with them, but he had never before undergone the variety and intensity of emotions besieging him now. He wanted Cassie desperately. He wanted to talk to her, to tease her, to discover and learn things with her. All at the same time he wished to protect her, cherish her, seduce her, and ravish her until she ached with the same fire that was torturing him.

He laughed bitterly to himself as he emptied a second glass of brandy. For so long he had been her closest friend, and though he had considered her and their friendship special, he had taken it somewhat for granted. Now, just as he was discovering all that she meant to him, she had suddenly blossomed and become all that he had always known she could become. Now, just as he realized how much he wanted her and that she was the only one for him, he was faced with the very real possibility that she might choose to spend her life with one of her many other admirers. And the thought of this, of life without her, was unbearable.

"Hell and damnation!" he exclaimed aloud as he tossed down yet another brandy. "I'll go and see her tomorrow. I'll *make* her see me. I'll *make* her listen and understand that I must have her, that we belong together. I must . . ." He slumped down in his chair, overcome by the intensity of emotions and the unaccustomed amount of brandy.

CHAPTER 28

If the morning did not bring counsel, it did bring resolve. Cassie got out of bed at an early hour, determined to put London, the Season, and all thoughts of Ned Mainwaring behind her. Throwing on a wrapper, she hastened to her sister's dressing room, where she knew she would find her alone at her writing. Busy wife and mother that she was, the Marchioness of Camberly still found time to write the children's books that had been the cause of her visit to London years ago when she had accompanied Kitty Mainwaring for her come-out and fallen in love with her uncle. Now the only time she could be assured of the peace and quiet she needed was early in the morning before the rest of the household was awake and making demands on her time and attention. She was unvarying in her schedule. No matter how late she had been out the night before, Frances always arose at six o'clock or earlier and sat down at her desk.

Cassie rapped softly on the door.

"Come in, Cassie," he sister replied, recognizing her knock.

Frances had been aware that something was wrong the previous evening when one of the footmen had delivered the message to her that Cassie had returned home, but familiar with her sister's penchant for solitude, she had left her alone, knowing that when she was ready to talk, she would seek her out. Forewarned as she was, she was still unprepared for the white strained face that greeted hers as she opened the door.

"Come in, love, and have some chocolate," she invited,

leading Cassie to a chair by the fire. She handed her a cup of the morning chocolate that Daisy had brought her and waited patiently for her sister to initiate the conversation.

"Fanny, I . . ." Cassie began, and then stopped. Where should she start? Cassie's eyes filled with tears. She was so worn out with thinking that she could not put two words together much less explain the state of her feelings.

Frances remained silent, allowing Cassie to collect her thoughts.

At last, feeling the weight of the silence, Cassie looked up, and seeing such a wealth of understanding and sympathy in her sister's hazel eyes, she could not hold back the tears any longer. "Oh Fan, I'm so tired . . . I mean, I need to get away . . . I mean, I need to go to Cresswell," she sobbed.

Frances nodded. She had seen Cassie stumble into the ballroom, and not long after, she had caught a glimpse of Ned, his face white and set, coming from the same direction, and had put two and two together. Having suffered a smiliar disastrous encounter once herself, she understood completely her sister's need to be alone, to draw into herself to reassess her sense of who she was and rebuild her inner strength.

"Would you like to take Teddy? Nurse will see to it that he doesn't bother you and then we shall put it about that he was feeling poorly and you, knowing I couldn't leave Julian to face the tender mercies of our political hostesses alone right now, kindly offered to take him there for me." Frances offered this suggestion in the calmest of tones, but she was truly worried about her sister. She had seen Cassie upset before, but ordinarily her sunny and resilient nature managed to reassert itself within an hour or two. The dark circles under her eyes and the stunned expression on her face showed that she had been awake and in this state of distress most, if not all, of the night.

Cassie's tired eyes lit up and some of the strain disappeared at her sister's quick grasp of the situation and ready sympathy. "I should like that above all things, Fran. And could Wellington, Nelson, and Ethelred come, too?" she asked hopefully.

Frances smiled. "I expect you couldn't keep them from accompanying you even if you would. I shall have Nurse prepare Teddy and his things and ask Cook to pack a basket for you. Now you run along and have Rose get you ready. Just ring for Higgins on your way out, would you, so that I may ask him to inform John and Cook that they are to get the carriage and a hamper ready for the journey."

"Oh thank you, Fan," Cassie replied gratefully as she planted a kiss on her sister's cheek before running off to find Rose.

That devoted minion was more outspoken than her sister had been. "It's running away you are, Miss Cassie," she accused her mistress sternly. "It's not like you and it won't mend a thing, mind you. Now I've had my say and I won't carry on any further, but it's my belief you should stay and have it out. No problem was ever solved by pretending it wasn't there."

"I know, Rose, but I must have some time alone to think first," Cassie sighed.

Seeing the misery in her face, Rose relented. "There, there, Miss Cassie," she consoled her. "You just wait and see. He'll come 'round. Now I must go and ask James to bring down the trunks." The maid bustled out of the room, leaving her mistress to stare after her in astonishment, wondering how much the rest of the household had guessed the true state of affairs.

For such a large household, Mainwaring House was run with incredible smoothness, and the staff, always efficient, responded with alacrity to Cassie's wish to return to Cresswell. Unable to express their sympathy with her unhappiness, they rallied 'round and saw it in that "our Miss Cassie" was on the road to Cresswell as quickly and comfortably as possible.

"And, mark my words, some fresh air and long walks in the country are just what she needs," Cook remarked to Higgins as she put the finishing touches on the hamper and assured herself that she had included some of Cassie's favorite delicacies.

Teddy was beside himself with excitement. Though he had been entranced with all the wonders London had to offer, he missed the liberty that he enjoyed at Cresswell and he longed to explore the woods and fields again, free to become as grubby as he wished. He ran through the house, shouting, "Hooray! Wellington, where are you? We're going to Crethwell! Hooray!"

"Arf, arf!" Wellington responded, as delighted as his master at this prospect. He went off to round up Nelson and Ethelred and lead them to the stable yard, where they waited patiently until the last box had been strapped onto the back and they could climb in. Nelson and Ethelred, who were made slightly ill by the swaying of the carriage, found safe places wedged under the seats while Wellington sat happily aloft on the box next to John.

They were soon off, and by the time Ned, suffering from an aching head and dry mouth had doused himself in cold water, drunk several cups of strong black coffee, dressed, had his horse brought 'round, and ridden over to Grosvenor Square, they had been on the road the better part of an hour.

"What do you mean she's not here?" he demanded querulously of Higgins upon being informed of Cassie's absence. "It's not even noon yet and she was at a ball till all hours last night!" Ned was indignant. Even a constitution as strong as that of his intrepid Cassie would have been taxed by the events of the previous evening. But not only was she not relaxing at home in an effort to recover from them, she had been up betimes. To one who was himself exhausted by the emotional turmoil he had suffered in the past twelve hours and was seriously in need of recuperation, this energy and apparent unconcern was daunting in the extreme.

"Neverthelelss, she's up and gone, Master Ned," Higgins responded firmly. Having worried that much over Miss Cassandra's state of mind, he was secretly pleased to see Master Ned looking so haggard and blue-deviled this morning.

"Gone?" Ned repeated stupidly.

"Gone," Higgins reiterated patiently.

"But where?" Ned was beginning to sound worried.

"She's taken Master Teddy to Cresswell," Higgins replied. Before Ned could remark on this unusual state of affairs, he added, "He was feeling poorly, poor lad, and as it's difficult for Lady Frances to leave just now, Miss Cassie volunteered to take him."

Ned was too bemused by the turn of events for it to register that when he had last encountered Master Theodore not two days ago, he had been as healthy as a horse. There was nothing to do but ride off again, but he was at a loss as to how to proceed.

The more he thought about it, the more Ned began to realize that it might be Cassie and not Teddy who needed the restorative peace and quiet of the countryside. And how am I ever to explain everything to her if she is so intent on avoiding me that she flees to the country? he wondered in despair.

The rest of the day went by in a fog. He had an appointment with Lord Charlton, but he was so distracted that the eminent peer, looking at him with some concern, asked if he had been driving himself too hard. "It won't do to wear yourself to the bone, my lad. Why, we old men are counting on your youth and energy to give us all new life."

Ned smiled faintly, but he was barely attending. He couldn't keep his mind on any one thing for very long. No matter how he tried to concentrate on other matters, he kept going back to the moonlit scene on the balcony, remembering how wonderful it felt to hold Cassie in his arms, and hearing the anguish in her voice as she cried, "Oh, how could you treat a friend so?"

The more he thought about it, the more he longed to hold her and kiss her just once more, and the more he worried that in his anger he had ruined any chances he had of ever doing it again. At last he could stand the torture of uncertainty no longer and he resolved to go down to Cresswell immediately and force her to listen to his apology, prove to her that she belonged with him for the rest of their lives.

That settled, Ned tried to contain his impatience as best

he could. He managed to get through the rest of the day, but it was all he could do to make himself go to the opera. However, he had promised his sister weeks before that he would take her, as Lord Willoughby, devoted husband that he was, declared that there were limits to conjugal affection and the opera was one of them. Being a fond brother and one who shared his sister's love of opera, Ned had volunteered to take her. He couldn't back out now, but his heart wasn't in it.

They had not been there above half an hour before Arabella was waving at them from her box and beckoning to Ned. Though he was able to cope with escorting Kitty, Ned felt unable to face the cause of all his difficulties. Knowing that he would be far more uncivil if forced to speak to her, he turned his head and concentrated on discussing the performance with his sister, ignoring Arabella completely. Between acts he rushed out of the box in search of Lord Charlton, who, given the eagerness with which he had been sought out, was then somewhat mystified by the desultory nature of his companion's conversation. Again, he put this down to the strain caused by Ned's immersing himself so wholeheartedly in politics as well as attending to the demands society placed on such an eligible bachelor.

At the end of the last act, Ned hustled his sister to her carriage with such speed that she barely had time to wave to any of her friends. "Gracious, Ned, there's no need to get me home with quite so much dispatch," she protested. "John is at his club and won't be home for hours." Then, catching sight of Arabella, who was watching their departure intently through narrowed and speculative eyes, she subsided, smiling to herself as she divined the reason for their flight. That will teach her to think she can make him dance to his tune, Kitty remarked to herself with slightly malicious satisfaction.

Arabella was thinking along much the same lines as Kitty, though her thoughts were more in the form of questions. Why had Ned not called on her recently? Why had he been so elusive after having been so attentive? He had not even stood

up with her for a country dance at the Rutland House ball,
much less waltzed with her. Knowing herself to be all that
a man could desire and confident that infatuation with her
charms couldn't possibly lessen, Arabella cast about for some
other reason for this incomprehensible coldness on Ned's
part.

She revisited every social scene of the past week—the park,
the ball—and the more she thought about it, the more she
began to suspect that this change in attitude had something
to do with that odious Cassie Cresswell. That sly thing with
her cozening ways, Arabella fumed inwardly. Why, I'll make
such a May game of her she won't dare set her cap at anyone,
much less Ned Mainwaring.

Thus resolved, she began plotting her campaign, the first
move of which was to set her maid Susan to find out what
she could about the state of affairs at Mainwaring House.

It was some time before Susan could discover anything,
but when she did, it was discouraging. With her rival buried
in the country, it was somewhat difficult for Arabella to
compete with her by showing her up. The more she
considered it, though, the odder it seemed that Cassie should
interrupt her first Season all because of a nephew's illness.
Arabella knew Cassie to be less than devoted to the life of
the *ton,* but even someone as cavalier in her attitude toward
the fashionable world as Cassie was not so blind to its
importance as to leave it in the middle of her come-out.

As she thought about it, she arrived at the same conclusion
as Ned, that it must be Cassie and not Teddy who had needed
to return to Cresswell. A plan slowly began to take shape
in her brain. She smiled slyly to herself. We'll see who is
the smart one now, Cassie Cresswell, she vowed as she set
about laying her strategy.

It was not that Arabella had set her sights on Ned. While
he possessed an attractively large fortune, a handsome
countenance, and an air of elegance, he did not appear to
be committed to making the best use of these attributes to
win an important place for himself in the *ton.* Besides, he
didn't have an impressive title, and Arabella was not ready

settle for anything less than a marquess. No, she didn't really want Ned. He did have an annoying tendency to see right through one or to become serious over the most boring things. But she could not bear the thought of anyone else attracting someone who had been her most devoted admirer, especially if that someone were that impertinent little tomboy Cassie.

Arabella began to weave her plot. As her scheme depended on convincing her parents that exhausted by the rigors of the Season, she needed to return to a place that she had hitherto referred to in terms of deepest loathing, it took some doing. But Arabella had not been the toast of society without developing her dramatic capabilities to a high degree and she began to cultivate a charmingly languid air which threatened an immediate decline if the beauty were not removed to the restorative climate of the countryside.

Despite their wealth, Sir Lucius and Lady Taylor had never been particularly comfortable in the *ton,* conscious as they were that the fortune which had opened all the doors for them had come from trade on Lady Taylor's side. For them, the simple life of country landlords concerned with parish affairs and the pleasures of gardening and farming was far more attractive than the frenetic pace of the London Season. They would have been more than content to spend their lives without setting foot in Town if it had not been for the social aspirations of their beautiful daughter. Unable to deny her anything, they had put up with the dirt, the crowds, and the noise of the capital, taking pleasure in her happiness and pride in her success. Thus they were entirely surprised but delighted at Arabella's sudden whim and, as always, moved quickly to grant her whatever she wished.

Within days, the *ton* had been deprived of two of its brightest stars, but true to its fickle nature, after some initial comment, it forgot all about them and carried on as always, flirting, dancing, and gossiping.

CHAPTER 29

It would have been too much to hope that a return to the country could restore Cassie's former equanimity, but as she rose each day to peace and solitude and descended to the library after her morning chocolate, and as she took long walks in the lanes around Cresswell, smelling the sweet scent of roses in the hedgerows and responding to the "Good to see you back, Miss Cassie," from passersby, she did begin to regain a measure of serenity. Having put the possibility of meeting Ned as well as the scenes of their latest disastrous encounter at a distance, she was able to gain some objectivity.

At first she resumed her studies only for the diversion they offered, hoping that if she occupied her mind enough with these, it would not revisit the uncomfortable thoughts which had recently been torturing it. Initially the distraction she sought evaded her, but she kept at it, and as the days passed, she discovered that her studies not only took her mind off unhappy memories, they offered solace and a chance to recapture the sense of ease with herself that had been so badly upset by her discovery that she was head over heels in love with Ned Mainwaring.

He was still constantly in her thoughts, but she was freed from the powerful emotions aroused by his immediate presence, and was able to reflect more calmly and rationally on the situation. You were friends before you realized you were in love with him, Cassie Cresswell, and you can continue to be friends no matter whom he loves, she told herself. If this seemed a rather bleak future to look forward to after the intensity of the feelings she had experienced in his company recently, it was at least peaceful and one she could bear to live with. True to say, the passion with which she had reacted to his kisses, though it had exhilarated her, had also frightened her in the power it seemed to have over her. Cassie could imagine nothing more wonderful than surrendering herself to it in Ned's arms, but at the same time she was afraid of what would occur if such a situation did befall her and she did happen to give in and allow herself to be swept along by it.

You're probably well out of it, my girl, she congratulated herself. Why, given the chance, you might degenerate into a mindless hedonist devoting yourself entirely to pleasure. Ned had helped her to discover a propensity for this in herself that was nearly as alarming as the revelation that she was in love with someone who, far from wanting to indulge in these propensities with her, was more accustomed to regarding her in the light of a younger sister, a precocious younger sister, but a younger sister, nevertheless.

Sorting out and coming to terms with all these new and disturbing emotions was a slow process and there were times when Cassie despaired of ever regaining her peace of mind, but gradually she began to take pleasure in life again, helping Teddy practice his cricket, playing fetch with Wellington, punting on the pond, and galloping over the countryside in a way she was never able to do in London.

One day, nearly a fortnight after her flight from Town, she was congratulating herself on the commencement of her recovery from all this madness of love and passion when Teddy burst into the library, trailing his cricket bat and followed by his three devoted spectators. "That lady with the mean eyeth ith here, Aunt Cathie, and she'th looking for you," he announced.

"The lady with mean eyes?" Cassie was mystified.

"You know, the one in the park," he elaborated.

Cassie continued to look blank. Sighing heavily, he continued, "You know, when we were there with 'that man' and we lost the boat and Wellington rethcued it and we saw Ned and that lady with the mean eyeth."

Enlightenment dawned. "You mean Arabella? She's here?" Cassie asked incredulously, not able to fathom the idea of Arabella anywhere else but London in the middle of the Season.

Teddy nodded vigorously just as Arabella, elegant in a peach-colored walking dress, followed the footman into the library. His mission accomplished, Teddy departed with as much haste as possible. Wellington, Nelson, and Ethelred, having taken full measure of the lady with mean eyes and come to no very complimentary assessment of her character, were at his heels.

"Cassie, so delightful to see you," Arabella drawled as she stripped off her gloves and draped herself gracefully on a nearby settee. "Are you rusticating because you are as *ennuyée* and exhausted by the incessant social demands as I?" she asked, heaving a sigh and trying to look as fragile as a voluptuous figure would allow.

Cassie, never ordinarily at a loss for words, remained nonplussed while Arabella, oblivious to her surprise, rattled happily on. "Of course, keeping up one's role as an incomparable can be quite the most wearing thing. I was beginning to look positively hagridden, and Ned"—here she paused significantly before continuing—"*dear* Ned, was naturally so concerned."

"Ned," Cassie repeated stupidly.

"Well, yes. Of course he doesn't want me to tire myself out and he does worry so about my happiness, poor boy, though in the circumstances it's only natural."

"Of course," Cassie agreed, totally missing the careful emphasis her visitor had put on the word "circumstances."

Arabella was becoming quite annoyed. Really, for all her reputation as a bluestocking, Cassie was being remarkably obtuse. Her back to the wall, she was forced to dispense with subtle hints and adopt some degree of falsehood. "Certainly it's only natural, isn't it, for a man to want his intended to be in radiant health?" she inquired archly.

"His intended?" Cassie echoed. "I didn't know. I hadn't heard . . ." Her voice trailed off.

Having committed herself to a course of deception, Arabella could do nothing but brazen it out. And it wasn't such a very big lie, after all. With Cassie disposed of, Arabella felt confident of bringing such a situation to pass. She tossed her head and smiled condescendingly. "Of course it's not yet formally announced, but surely you've known this age of our understanding."

Cassie's mind was reeling. All her hard-won peace of mind evaporated in an instant. She felt dizzy and there was the oddest sensation at the pit of her stomach. Raising her hand to her brow, she said faintly, "Excuse me. I'm afraid that I haven't been the hostess I should be. That's delightful news. Now, if you'll excuse me, I have the most dreadful headache." Without a backward glance she rushed from the room.

"And that," Arabella announced with satisfaction to the empty room, "is that." She pulled on her gloves and rang for a footman, smiling at him prettily as he led her to her carriage.

With no clear idea of where she was going, Cassie ran to her room, tore open the cupboard, and pulled out her oldest, most comfortable riding habit. Struggling with the last few buttons, she raced to the stables calling to Jim to saddle Chiron.

"But Miss Cassie," he protested, "the sky's that dark. It's coming on to storm for certain."

"I don't care!" she snapped in an unusual show of temper. "Just saddle him!"

"Yes, miss," he replied, looking aggrieved. John would have his hide, but when a woman looked that upset, he knew better than to argue with her. He threw her into the saddle and she tore out of the stable yard as though the hounds of hell were after her.

Cassie still had no very clear idea of where she was headed. All she knew was that she had to get away—away from everything and everybody that was familiar. She wanted to escape to the anonymity of the open fields, where she could ride until she was too exhausted to think.

CHAPTER 30

Not long after Arabella's triumphant departure another visitor rode up the gravel drive at Cresswell, rang the bell, and requested to see Miss Cassie. It was Ned. Unable to endure another day of uncertainty, he had ridden down from London the night before. He had spent the night at Camberly, where he made the unpleasant discovery that sleeping in his old room and visiting the scenes of his childhood, so much of which had revolved around Cassie and Freddie, only made the longing to see Cassie and to beg her to marry him that much stronger. He had spent a restless night trying to sort out his thoughts and deciding on the best way to convince someone he had just insulted that he wanted nothing so much out of life as to spend the rest of it with her. Finally, giving up all hope of sleep, he had gotten up and began to pace the floor. At the first light he had thrown on his clothes and ordered Brutus to be saddled and brought 'round. Though it was still far too early to think of calling on anyone, Ned hoped that a long morning ride would clear his head, calm him down, and make the time pass more quickly until he could call on Cassie. He had ridden for hours and poor Brutus's flanks were glistening with sweat before he had the courage to present himself.

"She's not here!" he exclaimed in dismay when the footman who had answered the door returned from an unsuccessful search of all the rooms.

"Perhaps she's out in the garden, sir. If you care to take your horse to the stable, you could ask them there," he suggested apologetically.

Ned led out a sigh of exasperation and headed off to the stables.

"Miss Cassie left some time ago, sir," Jim replied when questioned as to his mistress's whereabouts.

"What?" thundered Ned. "You saw the sky and you let her go? Where are your brains, lad?" An ominous rumbling in the distance made him demand more urgently, "How long has she been gone?"

"Not long, sir. I'm that sorry, sir," the stableboy apologized. "You know Miss Cassie. When she gets something fixed in her mind there's just no stopping her." He shook his head.

"Which direction did she go?" Ned was beginning to sound frantic as another crack of thunder and a flash of lightning increased his concern for Cassie's welfare.

Jim pointed to the fields on his right. "She went that way, sir, but there weren't no stopping her," he spoke again in defense of his actions. If he had been apprehensive before about what John Coachman would say when he discovered that he had let Miss Cassie go off in such weather, he was even more worried by the dreadful expression on Ned's face. Master Ned was a gentleman who could handle anything. Why the stories he'd heard about his and Master Freddie's adventures in India would make your hair curl! But he looked proper frantic now. "I'm sorry . . ." he began again, but his words were cut off as Ned leaped on Brutus and clattered out of the yard.

The wind had picked up by now and the first large drops of rain were beginning to fall. Ned rode like a madman in the direction Jim had pointed, trying vainly to distinguish the outline of a horse and rider as the rain, falling in earnest now, streamed down his face. The motion eased his tension somewhat, and as he began to think more clearly he recalled a favorite ride Cassie often took on the ridge the other side of a small wood. He headed straight into the trees, in too much of a hurry to seek out the path he knew was there. Branches slapped in his face and tore at his clothes. He lowered his head on Brutus's neck, grimly urging him on.

The thunder was closer now and the horse whinnied in terror as there was a loud crack directly overhead.

After what seemed an interminable time he burst clear of the trees and saw before him the ridge with a horse and rider barely visible in the distance. "Cassie! Cassie!" he shouted, even though he knew full well she could never hear him above the storm, especially at that distance.

He urged his horse to greater speed, but just as he was sure he was gaining on Cassie and Chiron there was a terrific flash of lightning followed by a truly deafening clap of thunder. Frantic with fear, Chiron reared, throwing his rider, who landed with sickening speed and lay there ominously quiet.

"Cassie!" Ned was desperate now as he dug his heels into his mount.

Minutes later he was on the ground beside her, lifting her tenderly in his arms and wiping the mud off her face with his soaking handkerchief. "Cassie, my love, are you hurt?" he asked frantically.

She shook her head mutely, the rain streaming down her face.

"Cassie, my precious girl, please tell me you are all right," he pleaded anxiously.

"No," she gasped. "I am *not* all right. I don't know how I could have been so stupid to have fallen except that my mind was on something else." She shook her head defiantly, spraying drops of water in every direction.

He smiled at her tenderly stroking away the tendrils of hair sticking to her face. "That's my lovely Cassie, pluck to the backbone. But what were you thinking of?"

She was silent.

Cupping her chin in his hand, Ned tilted her face up to look at him. "What were you thinking of?" he asked again softly.

A blush crept up her neck, staining her cheeks. "Nothing," she whispered.

He thought she had never looked more adorable and he ached to pull her to him and kiss her until she was breathless, but he wasn't sure. He cared so desperately for her and he didn't want to frighten her or ruin anything now. "It can't have been nothing if it caused Lady Cassandra Cresswell to be unseated by a horse," he teased gently. "Cassie?"

Cassie looked down at her hands as she twisted them nervously.

"Cassie, look at me," he commanded.

She threw back her head defiantly, her eyes bright with unshed tears.

"Oh, my love." He caressed her cheek with his hand. "I passed Arabella's carriage on the road to Cresswell. Did she visit you?"

Cassie nodded.

Ned's face darkened. His previous experience with spoiled beauties, and this one in particular, had taught him that when one of them visited another woman, her motives were highly suspect. "What did she tell you, my love?"

Cassie shook her head.

He tilted her chin so he could look into her eyes, his heart wrung by the sadness he saw there. "Cassie, my darling girl, she means nothing to me. She never truly did. At one time I thought she did. I was infatuated with her, but it's you I love. It always has been you my best, my dearest friend."

A sob escaped her and she buried her face in his shoulder as he pulled her into his arms. "I love you so desperately, my love," he whispered against her hair. "Please tell me that I'm not wrong. Please tell me that you do care."

Cassie pulled away and looked up at him, tears clinging to the dark lashes and drowning the dark blue eyes. "I do. I do love you, only I was so scared," she whispered.

"Scared? Of what, my love?" he asked, smiling tenderly at her.

"Oh, I don't know. Of loving you so much, of wanting you so dreadfully, of losing myself. I was overwhelmed with all sorts of emotions and I wasn't sure I liked that. Oh, I can't explain it." She looked at him pleadingly.

His smile disappeared to be replaced by an expression of

great seriousness. "My beautiful love. You'll never lose yourself. We'll be as we've always been. You'll pursue your own interests and share them with me. I shall pursue mine and share them with you, and we shall continue as the best of friends and lovers." He spoke gravely, striving to reassure her as best he could. "Marry me, Cassie?" It was his turn to look pleading now.

"Yes, Ned," she replied solemnly.

His lips came down on hers and he pulled her close to him, caressing her, warming her, molding her body to fit his as the rain poured down around them.